RUINED KINGDOM

RUINED KINGDOM DUET
BOOK 1

NATASHA KNIGHT

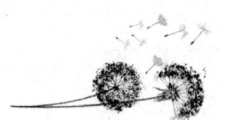

Copyright © 2022 by Natasha Knight

All rights reserved.

No part of this book may be reproduced in any form or by any electronic or mechanical means, including information storage and retrieval systems, without written permission from the author, except for the use of brief quotations in a book review.

This is a work of fiction. Names, characters, places and events are either the products of the author's imagination or are used fictitiously. Any resemblance to actual persons, living or dead, business establishments, events or locales is purely coincidental.

Cover Design by Deranged Doctor

Cover Photography by Rafa Catalana

PROLOGUE
AMADEO

15 Years Ago

Hundred-dollar bills float to the peeling linoleum floor. Five. Ten. Fifteen. Fifteen-hundred dollars. It's what a life is worth to them.

My mother can't stop sobbing. She's going to choke on her tears. My father stands defiant, his hands fisted at his sides.

Fifteen-hundred dollars lie on the old green-and-yellow floor. Does he expect us to drop and rush to collect them? Thank him for his generosity? He's going to be disappointed if that's the case.

Lucien Russo moves to his father's side, inadvertently stepping on one of the bills with his polished, expensive shoes. Or maybe it's not so inadvertent. I ignore him, though. He doesn't matter. Not now. He is not the one in control.

He whispers something to his father while I take in the cut of the older man's suit. The scent of their combined cologne permeates the air in the small room as if syphoning out the oxygen. As my father instructed me to, I keep my gaze low and memorize the ring on Geno Russo's finger. The insignia. Lucien has one too. It looks out of place on his hand, though. Like a boy wearing a man's ring. He's new to his family's business with hands like that. His father's hands are dangerous. Violent. Although I know the damage Lucien can do. Today is evidence of it.

"No hard feelings, Roland," the older Russo says.

My father clenches and unclenches his hands. I shift my gaze up, just for a moment. I want to know if Russo has seen that fisting and flexing. That barely pent-up rage.

He has.

"You won't make trouble, Roland," Russo says, and I realize he hasn't missed my glance either because his eyes meet mine.

I step forward, flanking my father's right.

"Amadeo." My father says my name like a warning. He's still looking at the older man, who smiles a cunning, terrifying smile as he lays a heavy hand on my head.

"Amadeo," Russo repeats. "Your son is brave," he says to my father, then shifts his gaze to Bastian, who peers out from behind my father's back. "Tell me, are you as brave?" he asks my younger brother.

My mother swallows back a sob.

"They are children," my father responds, and it sounds like they're having a different, parallel conversation alongside the spoken words. The undercurrent of danger is undeniable.

"Two boys. Boys who will grow into men."

No one says a word for a long minute as the unspoken threat hangs between us. My mother's crying is the only sound in the room.

"We had a sister, too," Bastian says, his voice high. He's not yet a man.

They all turn their attention to my brother, and I know this is a fatal mistake. This moment.

Just then, the door opens, and we all turn to it, surprised when a little girl comes hopping into our small, ugly kitchen. She's softly singing a Disney tune and seems oblivious to the tension as her eyes quickly scan the room and land on Geno Russo. She smiles a huge smile.

"Daddy," she says. "Look what I picked. Daffodils." They're actually dandelions. She holds her bouquet up to her father.

Her father.

A man comes running in after her, expression hurried, frazzled. "I was... She..."

Russo gives him a deadly look that lasts an instant before he bends to scoop up his little girl. "So pretty. Go pick more for me, will you?"

She nods, but she's sensed something is off. I see it in her expression. And as he carries her toward the door, she catches my eyes on her before my mother's cry steals her attention. She tilts her head in confusion. "Daddy?" she starts, a dandelion dropping from her hand. But a moment later, she's gone, and the door closed.

My father pushes me backward with a heavy hand when Russo returns his full attention to us. Dad steps between the older man and me. And I know everything has changed. We're down to the real business of his visit now. I wonder if Bastian hadn't spoken, if I hadn't defiantly met the older man's gaze, what happened next would have gone differently. Would they simply have left? Hadn't they done enough damage?

"I won't make trouble," my father says tightly. "Neither will my boys."

Russo smiles, glances at us, then at his men. He nods almost imperceptibly, and my mother screams, throwing herself at his feet.

The rest happens so quickly. Someone drags my mother away. Her screams keep coming even after a bedroom door slams shut. Two men grab my father. Another takes my brother and me by the arm. Russo and his son step backward and watch as kitchen drawers are opened and rummaged through. Bastian cries beside me, and all I hear are my father's pleas telling him we're just boys. Children.

A soldier comes out of the back of the house. He's been in my room. I know because he's carrying my baseball bat.

"Dad?" I find myself asking as one of the two men holding him snickers. It's the same time another soldier—how many did he bring into our small house—approaches my brother and me with the kitchen knife my mother uses to peel apples for pie. It's sharp. We're not allowed to touch it.

Bastian screams, and I don't know what is more terrifying, the sight of the bat being raised high then brought down on my father's knees, the sound of his scream, or my own as that razor-sharp knife carves a line into my face from my ear to the corner of my mouth. That of Bastian's as they slice him next. And blood. So much fucking blood soaking our socked feet. The money on the floor. Blood pooling around the tiny, wilting dandelion the little girl dropped. Blood dirtying expensive shoes as Russo and his son walk out, Russo adjusting his jacket, his diamond cuff link glinting as it catches the bright noon sun coming in from the open door.

And we're left lying in heaps, broken. All of us broken.

1

VITTORIA

Present Day

Incense burns like perfume. My father always loved the smell of it. When we went to Mass on Sundays, he'd always inhale deeply as it poured out of the small church before the doors were even opened.

Organ music vibrates low and constant. I feel it under my feet as we approach the cathedral entrance. People have gathered at the square. Word got out. Of course, it did. An unnatural silence falls over the space as they lay eyes on the casket. On me. The eldest daughter of Geno Russo. His only child in attendance. I escorted his body on its final journey from New York City. My brother was too much of a coward to come if you ask me. But then again, what do I know? I'm a woman in a man's world. Perhaps my father would have wanted that. For him to stay out of reach. Safe. He is my father's successor.

I lead the procession toward the open doors. Guards stand sentry around the square to keep people back, but I don't think it's necessary. They keep their distance, the women making the sign of the cross and kissing their rosaries as I pass as if I'm a vampire. Like they're warding off the bad luck I'll bring. The evil that surrounds me. My father was too young to die.

The cool darkness within the cathedral walls is a stark contrast to the brightness of the day outside. The sun shines brighter here. Dad was right. We lead the procession forward, my heels a soft click on the stone floors where the dead rot beneath. The man holding the camera turns into the center aisle.

My brother will watch from the live feed.

Someone clears their throat. A door opens behind the altar, then closes. An altar boy relights the candles that blew out when we entered.

I wear a modest black dress. Different from how I'd imagined it would be when I came here. When I would wear white lace and my father would walk me down this very aisle to my groom. He spoke of it often. That dream died, though, along with him.

No pews creak as people settle into their seats. No one will be in attendance to hear the mass. The guards will make sure of that.

I lead the pallbearers who carry the coffin containing my father's body on their shoulders.

When I reach the front pew, I step into it, and the men set the casket on its decorated dais. It is overloaded with white lilies, their smell sickening beneath the lovely one of incense.

It's my turn to watch the procession of the priest as plumes of smoke accompany the chanting. Half a dozen altar boys follow him. Some of them can't be more than ten. They all glance at me from the sides of their eyes as if they've been told not to look directly at me.

A Russo is here, back in Naples, after too long in exile.

Once the priest takes his place at the pulpit, the man behind the camera zooms in on my face. I try to ignore it. I want to punch him. He is communicating with my brother through an earpiece. It's my brother who has requested the close-up. What does he expect? Tears or strength? Neither will be good enough for him.

I wonder if he's letting Emma watch, though. I don't know if I want that. Emotion dampens my eyes at the thought, and I steel myself. She's only five. She won't understand. Although she knows her father is dead. Not that he's ever been much of a father to her. And my brother? I wouldn't be surprised if he had her locked in her room. It's maybe best for her. She's safest away from him. I'm the only one who stands between her and his wrath. The one who stood between her and my father's hate. I wanted to bring her if only to keep her with me, not my brother. She's not safe in that house.

I draw a trembling breath in as Father Paolo clears his throat, the microphone screeching momentarily before carrying his voice over the loudspeakers. I'm not sure why he's using it. It's only the pallbearers and me if you don't count the guards. The camera finally moves off me and slides over the casket.

But just as the final notes of Mozart's Requiem fade, the doors open again. Loudly. And footsteps stalk purposely toward the front of the cathedral, echoing off the vaulted ceilings.

The priest stops midsentence, his face going ashen. He makes the sign of the cross. Screams come from outside. The man behind the camera stumbles backward in an effort to run. But he doesn't get far. A soldier appears from a door behind the altar and cocks a gun at the back of his head.

It all happens in an instant. I turn to look and gasp at the sight that greets me. An army of soldiers pouring into the church, drawing the large, heavy doors closed again and blocking out the last of the bright afternoon light.

My brother sent men to ensure our safety, but I don't see them. They're gone. Vanished.

Footsteps like that of a stampede approach the altar as I watch. At their head are two men in suits, their faces half-covered with black bandanas. Two men with matching scars across their faces visible above the coverings holding shiny black Glocks at their sides.

One catches my eye as he nears. Gray eyes like the coldest, cruelest steel. And suddenly, I'm transported to that afternoon. To the garden full of bright yellow dandelions. The memory washes over me like a slip in time, a flash of another place. It makes me stagger. I grab the edge of the pew to steady myself, and as I do, the two men leading the soldiers split, the one farthest from me raising his pistol to the priest who tries to run. The other, the one with the steel eyes, grabs my arm, his grip like a vise.

This is what my brother was afraid of. This is why he did not come. We have many enemies here.

Someone fires their pistol as he tugs me from my place in the pew and toward the coffin. A body goes down on the stone stairs leading up to the altar, blood splattering the pristine white lilies.

I stumble as I'm tugged toward the coffin, and all I can think through the chaos of gunfire is please don't let my sister watch me be killed. Please don't let her see that.

More screams from outside. More bullets fired. More blood as red as the lipstick I wear to stain the sacred floors. It is the color of violence. Of death.

We reach my father's casket, and the man who has me kicks one of the legs of the pedestal. I gasp as the lilies are knocked askew, and the priest scrambles backward, falling. The other man with the scar climbs the three steps up to the altar, gun raised, not caring that it's a sacrilege, the violence of the act in this holy place.

"Up," he says, gun arm extended to the priest. "On your feet, padre."

I watch as the priest does as he's told, trembling, holding the Bible up between himself and this man as if God will save him now. That's the thing with God, though. You can serve him all your life long, but he will not meddle in our affairs. He will take our souls back once we pass, but we're on our own down here.

"Open it," the one who has me orders, pointing with his pistol to the pallbearers, the two who remain standing, alive, who look at each other, unsure what to do. Afraid. They turn to me, and so does the man who has me. He grins. "Tell them to open it, Dandelion."

Dandelion.

I stare up at him and blink to clear my head. He

gives me a shake, and I nod my head to the men. Two step forward to raise the lid and a shift in the atmosphere is palpable. I am released, thrown into the arms of a soldier who takes hold of me as I watch in horror while the two look at the body of my father. One spits into the coffin and the other curses him to eternal damnation before emptying his Glock into my father's body.

That's when I scream. That's when my screams drown out all the other noise.

Once his pistol is emptied, he kicks the pedestal hard enough to knock the casket onto the floor. Then he kicks the box again. And I glimpse my father inside it, his dead body riddled with bullets. His face unrecognizable. The two with the scars look at one another, nod, then the one who called me Dandelion turns his full attention to me and smiles. Walking swiftly toward us, he takes me back from the soldier.

"Let's go put your father in the ground," he says, drawing the face covering down as he turns away from the camera. The scar runs to the edge of his mouth. The other one laughs a strange laugh as he gives orders for the soldiers to bring the man with the camera.

I'm forced out of what should have been a sanctuary into the too-bright light. Into a waiting SUV, one of a dozen. I'm shoved into the back, the man sliding in beside me. And when I try to climb out of the other side, the other one with the matching scar on his face gives me a grin and climbs in, the two trapping me between them. The last thing I see as we drive away is the pallbearers carrying the desecrated body in the destroyed casket.

2

AMADEO

Vittoria Russo is shell-shocked. It's the only way I can think to describe her. She's pretty, even scared as she is. Grown into those big blue eyes I still remember so vividly and wearing an expensive dress, expensive shoes, and carrying an expensive bag. All designer. Money. She has plenty of it. I'd expect no less from daddy's little princess.

She immediately tries to climb out the other end of the SUV, but my brother, who had just reached to open it from the outside, climbs in beside her. He gives her a wicked grin, and she scoots farther from him only to press her thigh against mine. I close my hand over her leg.

"Relax. You're not going anywhere."

She freezes between us, somehow still clutching her bag. I take that, toss it into the front seat as we set off for the cemetery where Geno Russo will rot. It's about a twenty-minute drive along the outskirts of town.

I put a new magazine into my Glock and tuck it into its shoulder holster. Emptying my gun into Geno Russo's body was satisfying. Not half as satisfying as it would have been had he been alive, but it was something.

No one speaks, and once we arrive, the girl resists when I tell her to climb out of the vehicle, so I take her arm and slide her across the leather seat. She clutches the headrest of the chair in front, but it's little effort to get her out, and once I do, I let her drop onto her ass on the ground.

Men start arriving in the other SUVs, and the pallbearers are already carrying the casket toward the hole in the earth.

"Don't you want to see Daddy buried? Isn't that why you came all this way?" I ask her.

We look at each other. I can't quite see her face behind the net of the hat, so I reach down and tug it off.

She cries out as the pins pull her hair. I toss the hat aside. She rubs her head and meets my gaze with those blue eyes that burned themselves into my memory so many years ago. It's strange seeing her in person. I've watched over the years mostly online or in magazines. Russo was trying to go legit, to untangle himself from his ties to the mob, and his beautiful daughter was a part of that. But he never could quite clean the dirt out from under his fingernails. He was a thug through and through. Him and his son both. That's not something you can just wash away.

"Get up," I tell her, but when she doesn't move, I reach down to haul her to her feet.

She's lucky it hasn't rained here in a while, or that expensive dress would be covered in mud. Once she's up, she slips her foot back into her shoe. It must have fallen off when I let her drop.

"Where's Father Paolo?" she asks, looking around. Her first words to me ever. I still remember when she spoke that day so long ago. Holding up a bouquet of dandelions she'd picked from our garden. Weeds she'd thought were daffodils.

"Father Paolo won't make it," I tell her, walking her toward the hole.

"What did you do to him? We need a priest. The rites..."

"That priest was getting sucked off by his mistress about an hour before the burial. But don't worry, we'll say a few words." I stop at the foot of the grave.

"Fucking heavy shit," my brother complains as he and another man open the lid of the casket. Bastian reaches into the casket, and a moment later, he tosses Russo's ring with the insignia I remember so well to me.

I catch it with one hand, take a quick look at it, then tuck it into my pocket.

"Oh God," Vittoria Russo says, her hand going to cover her mouth.

"If you're going to be sick, do not get it on my shoes," I say.

She doesn't reply, and she doesn't get sick as my brother, Bastian, looks at me, and I give him a nod.

"Rot in hell, motherfucker," Bastian says.

"Like I told you, we'd say a few words," I tell her as he and two others tilt the casket and her father's bullet-riddled body tumbles out and lands with a thud facedown in the ground.

The girl cries out. It's somewhere between a, "No," and a choked sob.

I put my hand on her back to give a little push, and she spins to shove me away.

"What's the matter? Don't want to go in there with dear dead Daddy?"

"What the hell is wrong with you? I don't even know who you are!"

I lean toward her, towering over her. At five-feet-five-inches plus the heels, the top of her head almost comes to my chin. "Are you sure about that, Dandelion?"

She blinks and looks at me through thick lashes heavy with tears.

I turn from her to the grave and give Russo my own private send-off, wishing him an eternity in hell for what he did to our family. Then I face the man holding the camera. It's one of our guys—I guess theirs got a little squeamish. And now I'm addressing Lucien Russo, Geno's son. The man who set all of this in motion fifteen years ago.

"I'm coming for you next, bastard," I tell him. The camera is switched off then, and I turn to the girl. She is still staring all huge eyes and a face streaked with tears at the grave of her father's desecrated body as my men begin the task of burying it. "We're done here," I tell her and wrap an arm around her middle to take her to the waiting SUV. When she resists, I simply lift her, press her back to my side, and carry her. She's light. Lighter than I expect. But she's a fighter.

"Be still," I tell her, pausing to jerk her tighter to me when she kicks my shins. "Do not make me punish you. I promise you won't like it."

She rams her elbow into my stomach and spits but misses me and hits the ground.

I shake my head, carry her the rest of the way to the car, and thrust her up against it. Fisting my hand in her hair, I tug her head backward. She winces but stares daggers at me.

"I'll remember that when we next meet."

"Let me go."

I search her face and watch a tear slip out of the corner of one eye. Her mouth is open, lips a deep red. "Or what?"

Her hand slides across my chest, slipping under my jacket. I grin and catch her wrist just as she closes that hand over the grip of my Glock.

"Or what?" I ask again, my voice quiet, forcing her hand away from the pistol and holding the small fist she makes between us, squeezing it.

"You're going to break my fingers," she says, her tone betraying her panic even as she tries to sound angry.

"Better your fingers than your neck."

She swallows hard as I tug her head farther back. I'm hurting her. I see it.

"Let me go."

"Say please."

"Please!" she cries. It's the first of many times she'll beg.

I smile, loosening my hold on both her hair and her hand. I let her go altogether but stay close and open the door of the SUV. "Get in."

She glances at the vehicle, at the soldiers standing nearby, then back at me.

"Get in the fucking SUV."

She looks over my shoulder at the grave site, then back at me, that panic flickering in her eyes before she masks it. "Where are you taking me?"

"Be grateful I'm not leaving you here because if I were, you'd be in the ground." I gesture to the back seat of the SUV.

Her forehead furrows, she studies my face, then turns to climb into the vehicle.

Good. She'll learn to obey. She's used to giving orders, not taking them, but I'll break her of that habit. Stepping away, I gesture to two soldiers to sit beside her in the back for the ride to the villa in Ravello. I close the door as my brother walks up to me and sets an arm around my shoulders. We watch the car disappear, the windows too dark to see the girl.

"We should have dropped her in there with him," Bastian says.

"Not yet. You know what we have to do."

He doesn't look convinced.

"Patience, brother." I face Bastian. He's five years younger than me, and although his rage matches mine, he's reckless. If I'd left it to him, she probably would be in that grave too, but it's too soon for pretty Vittoria Russo to die. "When we're finished with her, she'll join her father. But she has a purpose to serve yet."

3

VITTORIA

I can still feel his hands on me, his eyes on me. His breath along my cheek. I try to level my breathing, to count it out. If I had food in my stomach, I'm sure these men would be wearing it now. Closing my eyes, I exhale, telling myself I'm all right. If they wanted to kill me, they'd have done it.

We drive out of the cemetery and away from the city.

"Where are we going?" I ask the men although I don't expect an answer. And I don't get one. But about twenty minutes later, I see we're headed toward the Amalfi Coast. It's a beautiful drive, one my father and I followed online. One I always longed to take. But there's nothing beautiful about this day.

"I need my purse. My phone," I say, leaning

forward to take it from the front seat but the two on either side of me stop me.

"No purse. No phone."

"I need to call my sister. She's only five years old. She'll be scared. Please," I plead although I'm not sure why I bother. It's like talking to a stone wall. I'm not surprised. It's how our guards are too. I've just never been on this end of things. Not that I've been very involved with the business. My father always kept me out of that side of things. My brother is the one who is heavily invested. In recent years, I've been the face of Russo Properties & Holdings, a company specializing in luxury hotels and residences along the East Coast of the United States. My father was looking into bringing the business to the Amalfi Coast. He was born in Naples, and his family had lived there for generations.

Although I've never been told outright, I know our family has always had ties to the mafia both in Italy and the States. I'm not sure how deep those ties run, but there is no denying that they're still involved in our lives. Before I was born, my grandfather got into trouble with a mafia boss in Naples. It's the reason he moved his family to the States, first to Philadelphia and eventually to New York City. I don't know the circumstances of that trouble, but it must have been bad if he had to move his entire family. My father has always talked about returning someday and showing me his birthplace. Our home.

I'm not sure if my grandfather planned on keeping out of that world once in the States, but he didn't manage to keep his nose clean. The mob was in his blood.

When Grandfather passed away a few years ago, my father began to focus on Russo Properties & Holdings. He wanted to shift the business away from the criminal world but never really could. Not with the ties our family had made. The things he'd done.

My brother, Lucien, is a different story. He likes the life and loves the power. The money. The fear his name instills. He and Dad were always at odds about this. But my father had the final say, and Lucien somehow always obeyed him.

My mind travels back to the funeral, the camera. How much did he watch? Did he allow Emma to see any of it? Please, God, make him have sent her away. She's too young to see this side of a life she was born into. The life I want to get her out of. Because generation after generation seems to get sucked back into it.

Sadness washes over me. My father is gone. My sister is alone in a house where she is unloved and unwanted. And I am trapped here with enemies. I think about their rage. The way they handled my father's body. Why? What had he done to them? I know my father's hands are in no way clean, but what could he have done that would make men do what they did today?

I take a deep breath in and lean back against the seat. I have to think. They could have killed me, but they didn't. They need me for something. And I need to remember the most important thing is that I live and get back to Emma. I'm all she has.

Almost two hours later, we turn off onto a single-lane road that will take us up to Ravello. I know the town. I know all the towns. I've studied so many maps of the area I could give directions. I've always wanted to visit the small square where Grandfather would reminisce about men gathering to drink coffee and read the paper. Where the church bells ring morning, noon, and night, and the smells of delicious cooking pour from the windows.

Along its outskirts is a five-star luxury hotel my father had his eye on. He hadn't gotten around to buying it yet, though. Dotted throughout are private, remote villas with some of the most beautiful views in the world. It's a place where deep purple bougainvillea grow like weeds, climbing along pillars and snaking around marble balconies and balustrades to provide shade for the patios below and splashes of rich magenta against the lush green and blue landscape.

The house we pull up to is no exception. Tall iron gates open as we enter, then slowly close behind us. When the house comes fully into view, it steals my breath away. It's a villa actually, not a house. It's set at the highest point of the property, centuries old white stone crafted into a majestic mansion. Two stone pillars bookend the large, ornate double front doors of Medieval style heavy wood with ironwork that I wonder the age of. Upstairs along the balcony's perimeter is more of the same stone carved into an elaborate cylindrical design, and from what I can see, it wraps all the way around to the other side.

Once the SUV comes to a stop, the men climb out. I follow, not wanting to be manhandled again. The driver carries my small purse in his giant hand, and I walk between the two tasked with guarding me as the doors open, and an older woman stands wiping her hands on a towel. She's heavy-set and maybe in her early sixties with wiry gray hair pulled into a bun and a bright yellow apron tied around her waist. She watches me approach, and when I get to about two feet from her, another woman just a few years younger than this one comes running out.

"Nora, you gave me a scare," she says. "I leave you alone for five minutes and what do you do but go wandering off." I notice she says all of this in English.

The woman turns to her and smiles. "I heard the cars and saw the pretty girl." She turns back to me. "The one with the dandelions."

I stop dead in my tracks. Dandelions. Again.

But before I can think about it, Nora's face falls. "Where is Roland?" she asks the other woman who gives me an unkind look before turning her away and walking her back inside.

"Come on, Nora. Let's go take a nap. The boys will be back before you know it."

The boys. Those men are no boys. Are they her sons? They could well be brothers.

"Move," someone says to me, giving me a shove that sends me tripping into the house. I barely have time to look around the grand room with its marble floors and twelve-foot ceilings before I am told to proceed up the stairs and to one of what must be a dozen rooms up here. A soldier opens a door and gestures for me to enter.

"I want to call my sister," I try once in Italian then again in English. I'm fluent in Italian. My brother was never interested in studying the language and his mother, who is French, made clear she wouldn't force him to once the trouble between her and my father began. It was in case we ever came home, according to my father. Whenever he said that, Grandfather rolled his eyes. I wonder sometimes if dad was afraid of him. I know Grandfather found him weak at times. I hated that for him.

The soldier's response is another shove. The door is closed and locked behind me and I find myself standing in the middle of a large bedroom. There's a king-size bed in the center with a sheet over the mattress, a single flat pillow, a thin, worn blanket on top. The dresser is empty, as are the nightstand drawers. No lamps even, only the overhead. On the bureau beneath the window is a small vase with a bunch of wilted dandelions inside it.

My stomach turns.

Looking away from it, I walk to the bathroom and close the door behind me grateful for the small push-button lock. It's beautiful, all white, gold-veined marble with a claw-footed tub against the far wall and a walk-in shower big enough for two. The house is old, but the bathroom has been refurbished, the fittings modern although designed to look like they're original. The cabinets here are bare too. Only a toothbrush and a tube of toothpaste. A used bar of soap in the dish.

I wash my hands with that soap then cup them to drink some water. I pick up a towel and straighten to take in my reflection in the ornate, antique mirror. My hair is half in, half out of its chignon with strands sticking out where he pulled my hat off. It had been pinned into place. A streak of mascara smears my cheek, and my lipstick has worn clean off. On the side of my chin is a splatter of dark red which I wet the corner of the towel to wipe off.

Blood.

I wonder whose it is.

I keep my gaze on my reflection as I pull the rest of the pins out of my hair and drop them along the marble counter, long blond hair caught in some. I think about the scene at the church. Think about where our men went during the attack. My brother had sent a dozen guards at least, but no one lifted a finger against the intruders.

It feels better to have the pins out of my hair, but the headache wasn't from the tight chignon. It's everything else that's happened. And as I finger-comb my rebellious hair, I wonder what I'll do. How I'm going to get out of this. Get back to Emma.

It's with her in mind that I return to the bedroom, where I try not to look at the dandelions. I close my eyes against the vision that comes. The same one that had my knees buckle at the church.

I try the windows, both of which are locked, along with the doors that lead out to the balcony. I'm on the backside of the house, and the view from here is something else. Blue ocean as far as the eye can see. Blue sky meeting it. Not a single cloud. I bet the stars shine bright here at night.

I walk back into the room, to the bed, and slip off my shoes to stand in stockings that have ripped in the chaos of the day. I slide my hand along my thigh beneath the dress to the small dagger strapped there. It was a birthday gift a few years ago. A pretty, small, opal-handled dagger. An antique, according to my father. Whenever I go out, I take a small pistol in my purse and strap the dagger to my thigh. In the car, when the man with the scarred face had grabbed my leg, I'd been grateful it was the one without the dagger or I'm sure he'd have taken it. I haven't ever had to use either weapon. I've always had guards around me. But a lot of good they did me today.

Taking the dagger out of its sheath, I lie down on the bed and tuck it under the pillow. I keep my hand wrapped around it, pull the ratty blanket over myself, and close my eyes while I wait for my captor to return. I'm sure he'll look through my clutch and find the pistol. He won't be expecting another weapon. I wonder if he'd think me too squeamish to use a dagger. I hope he tests me.

4

AMADEO

The sun has turned the sky a deep, fiery orange as it sets, the blue ocean swallowing it whole. It's so beautiful here. I don't know how my parents could have left it. Although beauty is a thing enjoyed by the wealthy. Men like my father wouldn't have lived where I live now, and life is very different depending on how deep your pockets are. My mother's reason for leaving is a different story.

I bought this house a few months ago. Only a handful of people know about this location. For all intents and purposes, I live in the Naples house of my family. My mother's family, that is. Nora Del Campo was once Nora Maria Caballero, eldest daughter of Humberto Caballero, the leading mafia family in Naples, Italy. My mother's secret marriage to my father, an American-born nobody who served as a foot soldier for my grandfather, caused him to disown her. Even when the trouble with Russo came about, my grandfather wouldn't have anything to do with it or her. He'd washed his hands of his daughter.

It was when my father began his final decline into an alcoholic stupor he would never recover from that I sought out my grandfather, and my brother and I swore fealty to him.

He took Bastian and me in, but we were punished for our mother's transgression. We worked as the lowest of the low within the family for years. But I was the same age as Angelo, his beloved grandson, and Angelo and I became best friends. Angelo would have done well following in his grandfather's footsteps. He was brave and fair. As good as anyone in this business can be. But he died. We were twenty-five when he and I were ambushed. I took a bullet to save him, but in the end, I didn't save him at all. I survived. He did not. I may have the scar to show for it, but that hardly matters.

Although it did for Humberto.

Humberto had two children. My mother and her younger brother, Sonny. I gathered quickly upon my return that Sonny was a disappointment. His son, Angelo, however, was not. Angelo would be the one to rule once Humberto stepped down. Angelo would displace his own father.

I'm not sure how much love there can be, truly,

in a mafia family, when fathers can disown daughters and set sons aside, but my grandfather was not an easy man.

After Angelo's death and much to Sonny Caballero's dislike, I became the beloved grandson, the golden boy who was not only born into the family but had proven himself by taking a bullet for Angelo. I took Angelo's place as Humberto's successor. I even took my grandfather's last name, adding it to my father's. It was important to be accepted by the family. I became Amadeo Del Campo Caballero. Bastian did the same.

Not to say I came with the best of intentions because I have had one goal in mind for as long as I can remember.

Vengeance.

Make the Russo family pay.

And I knew the way to do that was through my grandfather, even if it meant becoming the man my mother did not want me to be.

But Sonny had support within the family, and my brother and I were American-born usurpers. When Humberto named me his successor, Sonny was not happy. He still isn't. Although, that's his problem as far as I'm concerned.

As the driver comes to a stop at the front entrance of the villa, I see it again. The glances I sometimes get. I don't care. Let any one of them stand against me if they dare. I have made examples of people, and I will again. My hands are bloody, as are Bastian's.

I glance over to Bastian as we step out of the SUV and climb the wide stone stairs toward the 18th-century door. It was taken from a church in Pescara Del Tronto, an ancient village devastated by an earthquake. I brush my fingers over the wood, thinking about all the men and women who have passed through it over the years. All those forgotten souls.

"Where is our mother?" Bastian asks one of the soldiers as we walk into the house.

"In the kitchen, sir."

"The girl?"

"Upstairs in the room you had prepared."

"Good."

Bastian and I head toward the kitchen. "The Russo business is weaker now that Daddy is gone. It's time to bring him to his knees," Bastian says. "We don't need the girl to do what we need to do."

"We made a plan, Bastian. We're sticking to it. Why are you second-guessing it now?"

He stops, and we face each other. "She's going to make trouble. I feel it."

"I have no doubt. But it's nothing we can't handle."

He studies me. "I saw how you looked at her, Amadeo."

"Brother—"

"She's a fucking Russo. There's only one place she belongs, and that's with her father in the ground."

"Patience, Bastian. Trust me." I continue toward the kitchen.

"Fine. Gift her to the men," Bastian says casually, too casually, as we near the door. "It would go a long way to gain their favor." Since our grandfather's death, our uncle has managed to split the family in two. My brother and I need to present a united front at all times. But fuck if I'm giving anyone a gift to gain favor.

I set my hand on his shoulder. He is younger than me. His hate of the Russo family expresses differently. It blinds him. And if we are to win this the right way, he needs to see.

"Fuck their favor. They work for the family. We *are* the family."

Bastian squares his shoulders and looks at me. He's my height, my build. We could be twins but for the color of our eyes and the five-year age difference.

"Besides, how would that make us different than Lucien Russo if we were to *gift* her to anyone?" I ask him.

He glances away momentarily, then back, jaw set tighter. "Hannah," he says as if I need reminding.

"How would gifting Vittoria Russo to the men make us different than him?" I repeat tightly. In his heart, he knows what he's suggesting is wrong. I know he does. "And why would either of us care about gaining favor with the men?"

"Brother—"

"No one touches her. She belongs to us now. And we look after what is ours."

He studies me, and I can see the wheels turning, his doubt clouding his vision. He's wanted this for so long. We both have. And I understand what he's saying. She will make trouble for us, this girl.

"Are we on the same page, brother?" I press, squeezing his shoulder because I need to make this very clear now.

He doesn't answer for a long minute. I raise an eyebrow.

"Bastian, we want the same thing."

He finally nods. "We're on the same page," he says. "I smell Mom's tomato sauce. Let's go eat."

I push open the swinging door to the kitchen to find Francesca and our mother. They're busy at the stove stirring the bubbling tomato sauce Mom has been making since we were babies. It instantly puts a smile on my face.

"Boys," our mother says, beaming when she sees us. Bastian is first to go to her, hug and kiss her cheek. She looks at me, smiles, and I kiss her other cheek. "Where is Hannah?" she asks, looking over our shoulders toward the door.

It takes all I have to keep the smile on my face. I glance quickly at Francesca, who gives a small shake of her head, which means it's been one of those days.

"Is that her friend who's visiting?" my mother asks.

She must have seen Vittoria. I'm suddenly not sure bringing her here was my best idea. I could have taken her to the Naples house, but I need to keep her hidden for now.

"I told you, Nora, that wasn't Hannah's friend. She's someone else," Francesca says, turning Mom to face her. "Remember?"

"Oh. Yes. I remember." Mom looks back at us. "Are you hungry? We made your favorite sauce."

"With homemade pasta?" Bastian asks.

Francesca gives him a look. "How much time do we have in our day?" she teases him, but I know taking care of Mom is a full-time job. Her decline began the day our sister, Hannah, died along with the baby she was carrying. Hannah was only fourteen. Her body wasn't close to ready to deliver a child, even if it was premature. If we'd known about it, if we'd known she was pregnant at all, she would be alive today. But shame made her hide, retreating from her family and her life. I still can't puzzle out what she'd planned to do if she'd managed to carry the bastard full term and give birth. What then?

My throat tightens as it always does when I come back to this. It's been fifteen years. Fifteen years and still nothing changes. Still, all I have are questions and few answers.

My mind slips to the girl upstairs. Vittoria Russo. The little girl with the bunch of dandelions she thought were daffodils.

"You get started. I have to take care of something. I'll be down soon."

Bastian nods and distracts Mom as I walk out of the kitchen and down the hall to the library, where Bastian and I each have a desk. I remove my jacket, shoulder harness, and tie, then undo the cuffs and roll my sleeves up to my elbows, glancing down at the dandelions tattooed on my forearm. The time for our vengeance has come. I pour myself a whiskey and stand at the window to watch the last of the fading sunset as I drink. The stars begin to shine, the few lights of boats far in the distance visible from here. Amalfi begins to light up, as do several lone houses along the water's edge. It's beautiful here. Peaceful. The quietest, stillest place I have ever been.

Today was a good day, I tell myself as I finish my whiskey and turn to my desk where Vittoria's purse lies. It's a small velvet clutch with a rich satin interior. I recognize the designer. I dump the contents and find lipstick, her phone, and a small pistol. No tissues, I notice. Did she not expect to cry at her own father's funeral? Not that he deserved anyone's tears.

I run a hand over the lining to check for hidden pockets but don't feel anything. I pick up the pistol.

It's small, made for a woman, but just as deadly as my Glock. The bullets are intact. Not that I expected her to have used it. I empty it and lock both bullets and gun in the top drawer of my desk. I pick up her phone, but it's password protected, so I can't get into it. I tuck that into the pocket of my slacks, put her lipstick back into her purse, and head upstairs with it.

Time to properly introduce myself.

5

VITTORIA

My eyes open, and my hand instinctively curls around the handle of my small dagger. I hear the rumble of men's voices outside the door, so I sit up, leaning against the headboard. I draw my knees up, legs slightly apart. I'm tempted to confront him with the dagger in hand just to show him who he's dealing with, but I need the element of surprise. I don't exactly have a plan of attack or escape, but I won't be playing victim anytime soon, so I push the pillow to my side and tuck the knife beneath it, then face the door and watch as it opens.

Steel eyes give nothing away as the man from the church enters, and my heart thuds against my chest. I glimpse the guard outside my door before he closes it. No one bothers to lock it this time. They're not worried about me getting by, I guess.

He keeps his eyes on me as he walks around the bed, only glancing at my discarded shoes on the floor. I track him, too. He's taken off his jacket and tie. He tosses my clutch onto the bed, then tucks his hands into his pockets and watches me. His shirt-sleeves are rolled up to his elbows, and on his forearm, I see a tattoo. Dandelions that have become wishes.

I make myself look up at him, but it's harder to hold his gaze than I like, and when that strange feeling of familiarity threatens to wash over me, I look away, grabbing my clutch. I open it to find only my lipstick. Of course, he's gone through it and taken both my pistol and my phone. Kidnapping 101. Men like him learn that before they learn to walk.

I set the bag aside and turn to him, swinging my legs over the side of the bed and slipping my shoes on before I stand. He's a lot taller than me, so I need all the height I can get.

Once I'm up, I face him.

His gaze moves over my black funeral dress. I don't hide myself. He meets my eyes again and takes my phone out of his pocket.

"Password," he says. It's not a question.

I smile and spell it out for him. "F. U. C. K. Y. O. U."

"That's funny." He cocks his head, then tucks the phone away. I'm not sure it's a good thing or a bad one that he's not going to force it out of me. He looks at my ripped stockings, hands casually in his pockets again. "Found your gun. Pretty little toy you brought to a funeral."

"If you give it to me, I'll show you what kind of toy it is."

"I'm sure you would." He looks me over. "Strip."

My eyebrows shoot up. "Excuse me?"

"Your clothes. Take them off." He gestures with a nod of his head.

I try to appear unbothered. Unafraid. All while my heartbeats slow to heavy drumming against my chest.

"I don't think so. I need to call my sister."

"You're in no position to make demands. Strip so I can search you."

"She's only five. She'll be scared."

"Honestly, a phone call should be the furthest thing from your mind at the moment, given your predicament." He steps closer, and I steel myself to remain where I am. He's near enough that I pick up a hint of aftershave, the same as earlier.

He studies my face while I study his. I'm unable to meet his eyes, though, so I focus on the scar that dissects his right cheek. The deep, white line is ten, maybe fifteen years old.

"That must have hurt," I say when I'm able to meet his eyes. I remind myself he can't see the beating of my heart or hear the rush of blood in my ears.

I've never really been afraid of men. My brother, Lucien, maybe, but it's not quite fear that I feel with him. Maybe because our father always stood between us. He's actually my half brother. We have different mothers. Emma and I share the same mom. But a palpable violence radiates off this man. A rage. Lucien doesn't have that kind of passion.

This one? He scares me. But I cannot let him see that fear. If I do, he wins.

"Do you remember me?" he asks, surprising me.

I glimpse the dandelions on the table over his shoulder but shake my head.

"I don't know you."

"Hmm," he mutters. He reaches out, and I flinch, but he just rubs the pad of his thumb along the side of my face. It's calloused. He's a man who works with his hands.

A strange sensation makes my stomach flutter, and I find myself standing still. I guess I expect him to hurt me. He looks down at his thumb, and I do too. It's streaked a dark red. I must have missed it when I wiped my face earlier.

He takes hold of my jaw. It's not a tight grip, and it doesn't hurt. Yet. But he tilts my head up and searches my eyes. "Funny you don't remember me because I remember *you*, Dandelion girl," he says. "You thought they were daffodils."

A flash of a memory unsteadies me as I pull free of his grasp. I have to catch myself with a hand on the bed. I straighten, pushing the image aside. Dandelions in a field. A cozy, small house. A family inside.

I blink, look back up at him to find him standing exactly as he was, watching, watching, fucking watching.

"You were young," he says. "But I think a scene like that would have made an impression."

"What do you want with me? Why did you bring me here?" I don't ask him why he desecrated my father's body. I can't focus on that.

"Questions and demands are all I hear from you when you've been given one simple instruction."

"I'm not getting naked in front of you."

"You are. Question is more a matter of how. I can help you, of course." He scans my body. "I wouldn't mind."

"I'll fucking kill you if you touch me."

"You're welcome to try." His arm shoots out, and he takes hold of mine, spinning me around. When I feel his hand at my zipper, I reach for the hidden knife, grab the handle, and twist back around to put the tip to his throat.

The zipper is halfway down, so the dress hangs on one side, baring my shoulder, but I don't move to adjust it. I have his full attention.

"Step the fuck away from me," I tell him, pressing the flat of it against his throat.

One side of his mouth rises in a smirk. He snaps

his fingers, and the sound makes me look. The instant I do, he grabs my wrist with his other hand. It was a stupid distraction. I push the tip of the knife into his skin, breaking it, watching a drop of blood slide along the virgin blade.

He's testing me like I wanted him to. And I'm failing. Because I may have grown up in a family heavily involved with the criminal underworld, but I've never so much as slapped a man. My father kept me well out of that side of life.

"I'm warning you!" I say as his hand tightens around my wrist. He's not pulling the knife away, but he has control now. I've just handed it to him on a silver platter.

"Vittoria, let me teach you two things," he says, dragging my knife along his throat, not even flinching when he slices a shallow line while I just watch like an idiot. "This here is the jugular. It's what you want to go for to kill a man." He presses the flat of the blade against the throbbing vein, and I swallow. He pulls my hand away, and even though I resist, it doesn't seem to cost him any energy when it's taking all of mine. He twists my arm behind my back until a whimper escapes me. Then he twists just a little farther.

My eyes water, and it takes all I have not to beg him to stop.

"Second," he says calmly, his voice a low, deep timbre, vibration more than sound. "When you decide to act, act quickly. Any man here will easily overpower you." As if to prove his point, he twists again, and this time, I do cry out.

As soon as I do, he shifts his grip, taking my wrists as if he was waiting just for that. For me to cry uncle.

My arm throbs. He was too close to breaking it. When he squeezes, the dagger slips from my hand. He bends me over the bed and leans over me, crushing me. His warm breath is at my neck, my cheek, and I hate that I feel a tear slide across the bridge of my nose.

He's right, though. I could have done it if I'd moved quickly enough. If I hadn't been too afraid to.

"Because really, if you do what you just did, you're just going to piss off your opponent, and he'll be forced to punish you."

As he says it, his nails dig into the back of my thigh. He drags his fingers up, ripping my stockings as he goes, raising my skirt until he grips my ass cheek hard, then slaps it.

"That's for earlier." He raises his hand and does it again three times in quick succession as I push my face into the bed to wipe away the tears and muffle my sounds. "And that's for now."

He shifts his grip from my wrists to my hair and drags me upright. He turns me to face him, then drives me to my knees as he kicks my dagger just out of reach.

"Got all that, Dandelion?"

"My name is Vittoria."

I try to pry his hand off. He's pulling, and it fucking hurts. But he only squeezes harder.

"A dandelion is a weed. I think it fits." He leans down so we're nose to nose. "I asked you a fucking question."

"Yes, I got it, asshole!"

He chuckles, releases me, then picks the dagger up off the ground and steps back.

"Good girl. Now do as you're told and undress."

I put my hand on the bed to get to my feet, cursing him all along, knowing I'm on the fucking edge of sobbing, and I can't let him see that.

Emma. I have to focus on Emma. I need to survive and get back to her. "I need to call my sister. If I do this, you'll let me call her."

"There you go making demands again."

"Please."

"Better. We will see. After you've shown me you can take an order. Count yourself lucky that I'm giving you this opportunity. I don't like repeating myself." He checks his watch like he might have somewhere to be, the fucking asshole.

I grit my teeth and reach back to pull the zipper down the rest of the way. It catches, but I manage, pulling my arms out and letting the dress pool at my ankles. I take the strap and holster off next and stumble as I get the stockings off so I have to sit on the edge of the bed to do it. I stand when I'm in my bra and panties. His eyes are on mine. Not looking me over like I expect him to. Like I expect any man would.

"Everything."

"What could I be hiding in my underwear?"

He casually shrugs a shoulder. "I just want to get a look at you."

"You're an asshole."

"So you've said."

I slip off my bra and panties, trying not to think about it. Not to think about being naked in front of this man and so completely vulnerable.

"Satisfied?" I ask, forcing my arms to remain at my sides. I will not cower.

He lets his gaze move slowly over me. It feels like he's touching every inch of my skin. It takes all I have not to cover myself, and I feel my face grow hot with fury or shame, I'm going to tell myself it's the former when he finally meets my eyes.

"Spin."

"I don't have anything on me. There's nowhere to hide anything."

He shrugs a shoulder. "Give yourself more credit than that, Dandelion. I'm sure you can be crafty. Don't force me to do a more thorough search."

"You wouldn't."

"Try me."

I hold up my middle finger. This is to humiliate

me. To punish me. So instead of doing a quick spin, I look him in the eyes and turn, keeping my gaze over my shoulder, glaring as he takes me in.

"Seen enough to jerk off to later?"

"Why jerk off when you're standing right here? Now face me."

My heart thuds at his insinuation, and it takes all I have to face him. To keep my spine straight and look at him.

"Good girl."

"Fuck you."

He casually turns to move to the bookshelf. Earlier, I'd seen the single leather-bound volume that looked more like a photo album than anything else, but I hadn't investigated the contents. He pulls it out and sets it on the table by that vase of wilted, drooping flowers, flipping through a few pages before closing it and turning back to me.

"Not-so-light reading for you to pass the time," he says and heads toward the door. "You can get dressed now."

"Wait!" I call out as he opens it, stopping short when I see the guard's face as he pokes his head in and sees me. I flip him off, then wrap an arm over my breasts and set my hand between my legs.

He hands the dagger to the soldier and makes a point of leaving the door open when he turns back to me.

"Yes, Dandelion?"

"My call. You said I could call my sister."

"I said we'd see, and I saw and decided you won't be making any calls just yet. I mean, where is the lesson to be learned if I just let you make the call? Give you what you want when you throw a tantrum. It's how you spoil children, isn't it?"

Rage uncoils inside me. "You said—"

"I said we'd see." He checks his watch again, and this time, when he spins to leave, that rage that starts as a slow burn in my belly courses through my veins, and I find myself charging him. He turns just in time to catch me when I jump, all claws and nails. I get my fingernails into his neck, but he's too fast and, within moments, has me on my back on the bed, his full weight on me, both of us breathing heavy. He pins my wrists over my head and draws back a little, looking at me as I process what it is I'm feeling. What it is that's pressing between my legs.

"I'm going to enjoy you, Dandelion," he says with a slow thrust of his hips.

I freeze, unsure what to do. Unsure how far he's willing to go. And he holds on to me until I finally look away, being the first to break eye contact. Another victory for him.

He straightens, then adjusts the cuffs of his shirt. I remain where I am as he stands looking down at me. I know I'm beaten.

He turns to go.

"Is it money you want? Ransom?" I ask, sitting up. "My brother—"

At that, he spins angrily back, and I find myself cowering from the sudden storm in his eyes. "Look around you. Does it look like I need your money?" He looks like it's taking all he has to hold himself back from launching at me, and I wonder if I got off lucky just now when he resumes his walk toward the door.

"Tell me your name," I call out. He stops. "I don't even know your name. I don't know who you are."

He looks back at me. "Amadeo Del Campo Caballero. Now you know my name." He points at the book he left on the bureau. "In there, you'll see who I am."

He gives me a once-over, and I'm very aware of how naked I am. I draw my knees together and tuck them to myself. His eyes meet mine, and there's nothing victorious or arrogant in them. Just a deep, unending darkness like a void. And after everything that's happened now, that makes me shudder. That has me pulling the blanket close and hugging my arms around myself.

A moment later, he walks out without a word or a backward glance, and the door is once again locked.

6

AMADEO

I take the dagger from the guard. It's a small but sharp knife, both pretty and deadly like her. I go to my room and slip it into the nightstand drawer, touching the place on my neck where the cut has already closed up. The scratches from her fingernails burn. It's a good reminder that even stripped naked, she has claws. I want to take a shower before returning downstairs to clean the filth of the afternoon off me. And I need a minute.

I've known this day was coming for fifteen years. The day I would take my vengeance for what the Russo family did to us. But it's a different reality to have her here, in my home, flesh and blood.

She may be innocent of the crime that led us to this day, but I remind myself that the fact that she's oblivious to the violence brought upon my family, the thing that put Hannah in the ground, makes her as guilty. She's lived her merry little life all these years while we've dealt with the consequence of what her brother did. What her father ordered done. It is enough to push me to the edge of the void that is the deep, dark fury inside me. But I can manage that. I knew it would be like this with her. She was too young to remember. Even though she saw it, she didn't understand, that is certain, and her own memory coupled with her love for her father would have buried the reality of what happened that day in our small kitchen.

She took a risk coming to Naples. She knew it, she must have. Her brother, the coward, watched from an ocean away. But she honored her father's wish to be buried in Italian soil. She loved him and he loved her. Probably more than his other children. More than the sister for certain. I can understand why. But Vittoria is no longer a child and she must know the things he's done, the people he's hurt. Does it not make her as evil as him to love him regardless?

I switch on the shower, strip and step under the flow. I see her eyes the instant I close mine. That vivid blue so bright. I open them again and pick up the bar of soap to scrub myself clean. My reaction when she mentioned her brother is something I will need to get hold of. I can't hurt her in a rage. Not when I may need her more than I like.

The image of her naked body, her spread legs

when I stood over her, it makes me want. A voice inside my head reminds me that I can take her. Have her. She is mine. I switch the water to ice cold and suck in a deep breath, turning my face up to it.

I am not that monster. Because like I told Bastian, that would make us no better than her brother. It would erase what he did to Hannah.

I switch off the water, grab a towel and dry myself off, looking at my reflection as I wrap the towel around my hips. I pick up my comb and brush my hair back, leaning in close to see the scar Geno Russo ordered his men to carve into my face. Mine and my brother's. He thought it would frighten us. Make us tuck tail and disappear. But he was wrong. It only enraged us. Drove us to this point. My only regret is that he died before I could kill him.

Switching off the bathroom light I walk into the bedroom. I own this house, have this life, because of my grandfather, Humberto. What I have should have been Angelo's. But he didn't live. That's another wrong I will right. I have yet to punish all the men who killed my best friend. But it is coming.

Choosing a light charcoal cashmere sweater and dark jeans, I get dressed and head downstairs, pausing only momentarily at her door.

"Anything?" I ask the guard.

He shakes his head. "Not a sound."

"Francesca will bring food up. Check the tray when it goes in and when it comes out." I wouldn't put it past my little captive to steal a fork to stab me with.

"Yes, sir."

Downstairs, the kitchen door swings open, and my brother steps out, saying something that has my mother and Francesca laughing. When he sees the scratches and the cut to my neck, his expression grows serious.

"Our Dandelion has claws," he says casually.

"That she does."

He eyes the damage more closely. "Don't tell me she ambushed you."

"She had a dagger on her."

"Hm. I guess I'd be more surprised if she didn't."

"How's mom?"

"Not great. She asked when Hannah's coming down to eat."

Our mother's dementia has progressed to the point that she can't be left alone. Francesca is her nurse but also a companion to her. I guess I should be grateful she can't remember that Hannah is dead. That she's been dead for fifteen years. Maybe it's a blessing. But seeing her decline too soon is hard.

"What's she like?" He gestures upstairs.

"More ballsy than you'd expect."

"She will make trouble for us, brother. I'm telling you now."

"I'm sure she will but like I said, it's nothing we can't handle."

"I'm going to go have a shower. We still on to go to Palermo tomorrow?" Palermo is where the man who actually pulled the trigger that killed Angelo is being held. A man they call The Reaper. He's American. Brought in especially for the job apparently. Stefan Sabbioni, the man who controls Sicily, caught up with him on his property once I'd put the word out. He's been holding him for me. I want to question him before I kill him.

I nod. "I'll go alone, though. I think one of us should stay here and keep an eye on our captive."

He glances up the stairs, the idea clearly appealing to him.

"Besides, I owe The Reaper personally." Because his was also the bullet that almost killed me.

"Amadeo," mom calls out from the kitchen, interrupting us. "Are you coming? Your food's getting cold."

I give her a big smile. "Coming, mom."

7

VITTORIA

I hear a woman's voice outside my door, followed by a man's who I assume is the soldier. They speak Italian, and a moment later, the lock turns, and the door opens. I sit in the center of the bed and watch.

After Amadeo left, I got dressed and resumed my place. I haven't looked at the book he left here for me. Seeing it from the corner of my eye gives me a little anxiety, to be honest. What's in there? What will I learn that I don't want to know? It could be lies, *his* lies. But he seemed so confident. So sure.

The woman nods to me. She's the one from downstairs who came running after the other one. The soldier gives me a bored look from his place at the door.

I track her as she carries a tray of delicious-smelling food to the table, pushes the leather-bound tome aside, and sets the tray down. She glances at me briefly, then hurries back out, and the door is closed and locked again.

My stomach growls as I get to my feet. I pad barefoot over the carpeted floor to the table. On the tray are a fork and spoon, no knife, a tall glass of water, a small salad, garlic bread, and, under a lid to keep the food warm, a huge bowl of spaghetti covered in what smells like the most delicious tomato sauce I've ever had. Or it could be that I haven't eaten in I don't even know how long. Since yesterday maybe. I don't remember having breakfast this morning. I pull the chair out, pick up the fork, and twirl the pasta. It's piping hot and richly flavored. I eat fast, devouring the spaghetti, followed by the salad and the grilled garlic bread.

When I'm done, I sit back with a hand over my belly and look out the window at the beautiful night. It's quiet in here. I bet it's quiet out there, too. We live in a high-rise in the city back in New York, and although it's quiet within our penthouse, it's a different sort of silence. And the sky over the city doesn't boast even an eighth of the stars that sparkle like diamonds in black velvet here. Looking at the horizon, I can't tell where the ocean ends and the sky begins, but I see the lights of distant ships and yachts, just a few in the vast sea. It is beautiful, even if a little lonely.

I put the lid back over the dish and rub my eyes.

I'm tired and want to sleep, but I need to shower first. Need to scrub the day off me. I knew today wouldn't be happy. I knew I was taking a risk coming to Naples. And maybe it was naïve of me, but I never expected what happened to happen. I had guards to protect me, and what could anyone want with me? My brother, I could understand. But I have nothing to do with that side of the family's affairs. Had my father gotten into trouble with this family? Done something so horrible they did what they did?

Dandelions in a field blur my vision.

Getting to my feet, I push all those thoughts aside. I need to focus on what's important right now and that is getting out of here and back to Emma. And until I can get back, I need to find a way to make contact with her to make sure she's okay, make sure she knows I am too. Because one thing I know for sure is that Lucien won't be looking after her. At least she'll have Hyacinth, the nanny, with her. She was going to spend the nights with her while I was gone, but now who knows how long I'll be or if I'll return at all. What then?

But I can't think about that. I need to focus all my energy on getting out of here.

I walk into the bathroom, lock the door, and strip off my clothes to shower. No shampoo or conditioner can be found, so I use the bar of soap to scrub my hair and my body, then comb my fingers through my hair as best as I can. A glance in the mirror proves it's not very effective. My hair is a thick mass of tangled blond waves around my head and rebellious in the best of times which this is far from. Since I have no other clothes, I put my underthings and dress back on because I'm not sleeping naked. I return to the bedroom, my gaze landing on that leather-bound book once more before I climb into bed. I fall asleep almost as soon as my head hits the hard, uncomfortable pillow.

THE FOLLOWING MORNING AND AFTERNOON PASS uneventfully with the same woman bringing me food and taking the old tray for both breakfast and lunch. The soldier at the door remains watching, and she doesn't speak a word to me. Hardly looks at me. I don't know what I expect, but Amadeo doesn't return all day. I don't even know what I want. I'm afraid of him returning, but I also need him to. He's my way out. I know that.

I wonder if he was on the helicopter I saw take off late in the afternoon. I guess it's the fastest way to get places from such a remote location.

So when I hear men's voices outside my door several hours after dinner that night, I sit up at attention and watch as the door opens. But it's not Amadeo who enters. It's the other one. His brother, I'm pretty sure. They look so similar, but this one has strange amber eyes, whereas Amadeo's are that steely gray. He's also younger. He shares that same darkness I sense from Amadeo, but this one has something reckless about him, too. Something as dangerous as Amadeo but wilder. Unharnessed and unpredictable.

The man enters and closes the door. He looks around the room, his gaze halting momentarily on that damn book before he faces me.

"Get any reading done yet?" he asks.

"What?" I ask, even though I know.

He gestures to the book. "Your family history. Did you read it yet?" He makes a point of annunciating as if I'm slow.

I don't answer him, but I do hold his gaze. I already decided I'm not stripping naked for anyone again. If they want that, they're going to have to make me. Then it will be out in the open the kind of men they are.

"Get up," he says.

"No."

"Get. Up."

This time he picks up the desk chair, pulls it out a little, and slams it back onto the floor so violently it makes me flinch.

"Why? You want to get a look too? Like your brother?"

He grins, touching his thumb to the corner of his mouth the way men do when they're appraising you.

He takes a predatory step toward the bed, and I find myself leaning away.

"I thought my brother would have made it clear that you take orders. You don't question them."

"Are you the baby brother?" I ask, watching his eyes narrow infinitesimally. Button pushed.

"Are you hard of hearing? I said get up."

"So are you following big brother's orders, then?" I ask, standing now because I need to be ready. I know I'm treading on thin ice. "Because from my understanding, Amadeo is the man in charge. He didn't mention anything about my having to take orders from his baby brother."

He grins, and I know I've pushed too far. "You know what? I'd have thrown you in the grave with your father if it were up to me."

I swallow hard, not doubting for a moment he'd still do just that.

"But I'm beginning to think Amadeo was right to keep you. You're going to be fun, aren't you?" he asks, that grin disappearing behind a curtain of darkness. "That or stupid. I'm going to put my money on the latter."

"You're as big an asshole as your brother, you know that?"

"No doubt. Let me make things abundantly clear for you," he says low and menacing, and in the next instant, he takes my arm in a grip like a fucking vise and tugs me into his chest. He's just as big and as strong as Amadeo, and I know I made a mistake pushing him. He's going to make me pay.

I press my hands flat to his chest, but I won't budge him. He towers over me, like his brother, and hauls me up on tiptoe so we're nose-to-nose. He's so close I can see the stubble of a five-o'clock shadow along his steel-cut jaw.

His eyes hold mine, but I concentrate on the scar across his cheek. The one that matches his brother's.

"When I say get up, you get up. When I say sit, you sit. When I say kneel, you kneel. Are you following me?"

I shove and try to get free. "Let me go, you bastard."

He gives me a shake. "Are you fucking following me?" he asks, his voice low and hard.

"Yes!"

"Let's test it," he says, releasing me so abruptly I drop to my butt on the bed. He looks me over. "Get on your knees, dandelion girl."

I swallow hard. I'm not sure it's the command, the humiliation it will bring, or the dandelion girl reference. A memory flashes so vividly, it makes my brain rattle. Two boys in that room. One just a few years older than me.

I know it's him. He's that boy. The younger of the two. When my gaze falls to his scar, my blood runs cold.

"I said kneel."

Ruined Kingdom

I slip to my knees, the carpet rough against my bare skin. I look up at him. He was there in that small house. We were all there in that house.

"Already better." He takes a step away to clear a path for me to the desk, and I know what's coming. "Crawl."

I don't move. I can't. All I can see is the book on the desk. And the room in that small house. Their faces when my father carried me out as a dandelion fell from my hand onto the linoleum floor.

He crouches down and takes a handful of hair to tip my head back.

I grunt with the force of it, my eyes watering as I meet his searing amber gaze.

"If you prefer, I can strip you naked and use my belt to whip your ass all the way across the room if you don't start crawling, dandelion girl. I'm being kind. Don't take advantage of that kindness."

He releases me, straightens, and puts a hand on the buckle of his belt.

"Crawl," he commands, drawing the belt out of the first loop.

I don't wait because I have no doubt he will do exactly what he threatened, so I crawl across the room, feeling him at my back.

"Sit," he says as if commanding a dog. I look up to see how his jaw is set, his hand on the back of the chair.

I sit in the chair, gripping the edges of the uncomfortable wooden seat.

When he leans over me, I catch the faint scent of aftershave. Different than his brother's. I watch as he opens the book to an obituary.

Hannah Del Campo. Age 14. Beside her name is a photo of a smiling dark-haired girl.

Survived by father, Roland Del Campo, mother Nora Del Campo, and brothers Amadeo, aged 15, and Bastian, aged 10.

I glance up at him. This is Bastian. But his eyes are intent on that photo and what I see on his face, it's pain. So much so that it's almost hard to look at him. I shift my gaze back at the book and catch just a few words that I don't understand. *Nameless child to be buried separately*. He turns the page, and I find myself hugging my arms as I see a photo of a very different scene. My father and brother from about fifteen years ago. My brother looks to be eighteen there. My father's hair hasn't gone gray yet and beside him is my beautiful mother, young and alive although not quite smiling like the photo I keep of her beside my bed.

They're at a charity fundraiser. According to the headline, my father is donating a considerable sum to children's cancer research.

"They attended that party the same night we buried our sister. Just washed their hands and carried on like nothing had happened at all. Like lives weren't destroyed." His eyes meet mine. "But I guess for them, nothing had happened."

He turns the page, and there's a picture of me at a ballet recital. I remember that night. How proud I was in my pink leotard and magenta ruffled tutu.

"You had everything, didn't you?" He flips through several pages too quickly for me to do more than glimpse a photo or a headline.

In my periphery, I see the little glass jar with the bunch of dandelions stuck inside it. They're drooping over the sides.

He closes the book but remains where he's standing.

"Does your brother still like to fuck little girls?"

My gaze snaps to his, and I want to ask what the hell he's talking about, but he continues.

"How many others did Daddy pay off to keep silent? How many knees did he break?"

"My father..." I shake my head. "He wouldn't do that."

He cocks his head to the side, eyes narrowing, and suddenly, he looks like his brother. The emotion, the intense pain of moments ago gone. Now he's just frightening. He chuckles. "No, you're right. Wouldn't want to get his hands dirty."

"He wasn't like that." I stand. "He's dead. You desecrated his body. You had no right—"

"That's rich," he says. "Back on your knees, dandelion girl."

My heart pounds but I ignore the voice inside my head telling me to do as he says and stand my ground. It's dangerous, I know, but I've never been good at taking orders.

"No."

One corner of his mouth curves upward as he exhales, shakes his head, and in the next instant, his hand is in my hair. Mine wraps around his forearm, and he's pushing me down, crouching with me as my knees hit the floor. I think I should have saved my dagger for now. For this brother.

"I remember you. Hell, I can still hear the tune you were singing. Not a care in the fucking world," he says.

"You're making a mistake. I don't know you and you don't know me. Whatever happened to your sister, I'm sorry about it, but it has nothing to do with me or my family."

"But you're here now. Ours," he says as if he hasn't heard me at all. He brings his face closer and inhales like a predator might his prey. He's so close I can feel his breath on my ear and down my neck when he speaks. "Ours to punish. To level the scales."

His hand tightens in my hair, and a tear slips from the corner of my eye.

"When I say kneel, what do you do, dandelion girl?" He tugs my head backward painfully, and I make an involuntary sound as more tears come. I swear he's going to break my neck.

"What. Do. You. Do?" he asks again.

"I kneel."

He releases me and straightens. I stumble onto my hands and see the dirt on his shoes. I wonder if it's from the cemetery. God. Did all of that happen just yesterday?

"Good girl," he says condescendingly. "It'll be in your best interest to remember that." He looks around the room. "I think my brother was right to keep you."

I don't like the grin on his face.

He walks to the door, and I watch him go. "You get some reading in. There may be a pop quiz, and you won't want to fuck that up."

8

VITTORIA

I shudder, exhaling as I watch the space he just stood. A hint of aftershave lingers as the minutes pass, and I remain sitting on my heels, unable to move.

Hannah Del Campo. Fourteen years old. Dead.

Nameless child to be buried separately.

The field of rich green grass dotted with the brightest yellow flowers flashes in my mind's eye. The soldier who'd been left to watch me while my dad and brother ran an errand had gone off to piss against the wall of the tiny house. I don't know how many children that age hold on to memories, but I remember giggling at that before slipping out of the car to pick a bouquet. I thought they were daffodils.

I glance at the dandelions on the table now. The book sits like a dark thing before the limp, dying flowers. I push myself to my feet. My knees feel raw, scratched by the carpet. I sit back down in that chair, and I remember his eyes. The almost unbearable pain I saw inside them when he opened it to that page. To the girl's photo.

Does your brother still like to fuck little girls?

Nausea swells in my stomach, and the food I ate threatens to come up. I force it down and open the book to that page. I look at the girl's face. She was pretty with big brown eyes and a dimple in her right cheek as she smiled at the photographer. Although the smile doesn't quite reach her eyes. Inside them is a shadow.

I force myself to read Hannah Del Campo's obituary. She was at the top of her class at the school she attended, a large public school in a lower-middle class neighborhood of Philadelphia. We had a two-story penthouse just minutes from the neighborhood but a world apart. She loved to dance. Ballet was her favorite, but she'd recently fallen in love with modern dance. The cause of death isn't stated, but the date is the same as the unnamed child who was stillborn. Did she die in childbirth?

I look at her photo again. She looks too young to have been pregnant. Fourteen is too young. I went to an all-girls catholic school where my every movement was monitored. I know circumstances are different for most people. I know I grew up with a silver spoon in my mouth with a mother who loved me and a father who would dote on me. Who made me feel like the center of the universe. It caused trouble between Lucien and me. Lucien was jealous of our father's attention, but he was thirteen years older than me. Our father had divorced his mother to marry mine, and I know Lucien resented her and probably me as a product of that love that took his father from his mother.

Blinking, I refocus on Hanna's photo. Pregnant at fourteen?

Does your brother still like to fuck little girls?

I shake my head and turn the page to read about the fundraiser, smiling when I see my mother's photo. She's been gone for a year, and I still miss her every single day.

My mind wanders to Emma at the thought of Mom. She was with her in the car. Was trapped inside it with the dead body of her mother for almost six hours until another car drove by and saw the wreckage. One of the photos the papers had printed showed Emma's small pink suitcase beside my mother's larger one lying along the side of the road, the trunk having popped open during the collision. They were almost to Atlanta. I'd been at school most of the day and had so much work to do I'd holed myself up in my bedroom after getting home. When dinnertime came and my dad and I were the only two at the table, he said they'd gone out overnight. A little trip for mommy and daughter. I remember being surprised and a little hurt that I hadn't been invited. She hadn't even mentioned it to me.

I flip the pages of the book finding clippings from events my family attended, some with me, through the years. When I get to the one of my mother's funeral, I stop because a flood of emotion rushes through me. It was raining, the clouds heavy and dark over our heads. I'm wearing a dress similar to the one I'm wearing now and holding little Emma's hand. She's wearing black too. She didn't understand why she had to wear black. I remember how she tried to take the dress off. She'd already stopped talking by then. Hadn't said a word since they'd found her. We'd thought it was shock, but it's not.

I can't imagine what Emma felt during those hours alone in the car with our mother's body beside her. How scared she must have been out there in the dark all alone. What is she thinking now? Is she wondering where I am? Did she see them take me? See the violence those men did at her father's funeral? Does she think I'm hurt or worse?

A feeling of hopeless sadness overwhelms me. I close the book and stand to go to the window. It's a clear night. Emma would count stars with me if she were here. I leave the light in the bathroom on and the door slightly ajar so it's not full dark. I need to be alert for the next visit by one of the brothers, but I'm tired. Exhausted. So I climb onto the bed and lie down, staring up at the ceiling, wondering what happens next. Wondering if I'll walk out of this house and get back to Emma. If I'll walk out at all.

9

AMADEO

I wash my hands and take the offered towel to dry them.

"Thank you, Stefan."

Stefan Sabbioni keeps his gaze out the window on the boat speeding away from the island. It carries the body of the man who went by The Reaper. His real name was Bob Miller. Generic. Unremarkable. A hired assassin.

"Humberto was a good man. And Angelo did not deserve to die so young," he says, then turns back to me. "Come in. Have a drink with me."

"Thank you." I follow him into the beautiful house. Set in Palermo, the views are similar to my house, but he's much closer to the sea than I am. I don't know Stefan well, but he's been an ally and supported Caballero's decision to place me as the man in power of the family. "You and your wife live here alone?"

We go into the study, where he pours us each a whiskey, then sits in the armchair across from mine.

"Gabriela's brother spends about half the year here. And of course, there's Millie, who dotes on Gabriela these days. Our first child is due in a few months."

"I didn't realize your wife was pregnant." Stefan is incredibly private about her. I've only been here a handful of times, but I've never met her. Never even seen her. Gabriela is the daughter of Gabriel Marchese. Stefan had taken her as payment for a debt Marchese owed, and he ended up falling in love with her. Strange world.

My mind wanders to Vittoria locked in her bedroom.

"Men in our world will always have enemies looking for a way in. A weakness," Stefan says, interrupting my thoughts. "I realize I can't keep the birth of my son a secret forever, but I'll hold on to it as long as I can."

"I understand. Your secret is safe with me, and I am in your debt."

He shakes it off, then sips his drink. "How is Bastian?" Stefan has made no secret of his dislike for my brother. But I know he's been betrayed by his, so perhaps that's why.

"He's well. We moved our mother to the house a few months ago, so he's with her now."

"That's good." He studies me as he drinks, and I know he has more to say, so I wait. Stefan is about my age, give or take a year or two. "Family is important, but brothers can be a tricky thing."

My jaw tenses. I know what he's saying. Watch my back. Trust no one. But I have to trust Bastian. What I'm doing, it's for him too. We've come this far because we've trusted each other.

"Bastian carries guilt over what happened." I hate Vittoria Russo, but I think guilt makes him hate her more.

"Guilt? How so? He was a child when what happened to you happened."

I recall the day in our kitchen. Bastian speaking up and getting Geno Russo's attention.

"Too long a story." He nods, although he's still assessing me. "And he is young. He'll learn."

"I'm sure he will," he says after a beat, which makes me wonder if he's sure at all. He finishes his drink and checks his watch.

I finish mine. It's time I head back. We stand. "Thank you again."

We shake hands, and he walks me out to where Jarno, my trusted right-hand man, and two soldiers wait beside him. One stubs out his cigarette as we approach. His driver will take us back to the airport, where I'll take a private jet back to Naples, then the helicopter to the villa. It's the fastest way to travel. Living remotely has its advantages, especially to keep my mother safe, but it presents a challenge if you need to be anywhere fast, so I bought the chopper along with the house.

I mull over my conversation with Stefan as I travel home. Bastian's guilt over what happened that day in the kitchen. Not Hannah's death but what they did to our father, to us. If he'd stayed quiet, would they have left? Would we have appeared less of a threat?

Bastian *is* young. He's only twenty-five years old, but I know he's loyal to me. In spite of disagreements we've had in the past, we're always aligned on the bigger things. Although, I wonder if that's how he sees it.

My phone pings with a message, and I unlock the screen. It's a text from Bruno. Bruno Cocci worked for Humberto for twenty years and has sworn fealty to me. In fact, he thinks I need to do more with my uncle Sonny to quash any further dissent and finally unite the family. But Sonny is my blood, my mother's brother, and she needs him now.

Bruno: *Check the headlines.*

Several links follow both in American and Italian papers. I open the English language one, and there, across the front page, is a picture of Vittoria Russo in a ball gown posing for the camera at a

Ruined Kingdom

fundraiser for children, according to the banner behind her.

The headline reads "Luxury Hotel Heiress Kidnapped by Rogue Italian Mobsters." The rogue reference stinks of Sonny.

Scrolling through, I find photos of the chaos, although nothing that would make either Bastian or me identifiable. Not that that would be hard to do given our matching scars, but this isn't about getting the authorities involved. My brother and I are unnamed. Sonny wouldn't go that far.

The other papers are similar, using the same photos. I text Bruno.

Me: *I'm going to guess Sonny is involved.*

Bruno: *I spoke with my contact at the Italian papers, and I can confirm that. He's working with your enemy. It gives you grounds, Amadeo.*

Me: *He's my uncle.*

Bruno: *Blood and loyalty do not always go hand in hand.*

I know this.

Bruno: *One more thing. Russo sent a message asking if $1500 is about right for ransom amount.*

I burn at the casual mention of the hush money they intended to pay after he impregnated my fourteen-year-old sister and his bastard spawn killed her. I rein it all in. I must stay in control. It's close now, the destruction of Lucien Russo. The erasure of the Russo family from this earth.

Me: *Then he remembers us. Good.*

Bruno: *You don't want the authorities involved, Amadeo. Not now. They're in Sonny's pocket.*

I know that. And Sonny will make trouble. But I'm prepared.

Me: *Let them get involved. I have a plan in place. You know that.*

Bruno: *Too soon for that, isn't it?*

Me: *I'm flexible. Arrange a dinner tomorrow night. Very public. I want Sonny there. And his lovely wife.*

She's a cunt.

Bruno: *Why? You go out in public, you risk arrest.*

Me: *I'll be fine. Arrange it. And get the word out to anyone and everyone. That includes Chief Greco.*

Greco is itching to take my brother and me down. He backs Sonny and is as corrupt as they come.

Bruno: *Are you sure about this?*

Me: *Do it.*

I scroll through to find Bastian's number and text him.

Me: *You up?*

Bastian: *It's midnight. I'm not an old woman.*

I smile as I tell him to meet me in the study. I tuck the phone away and take in the grand white house as the chopper comes in to land. I climb out, keeping my head low as I make my way to the back entrance of the house.

It's a little after midnight. My mother will be in

bed. Francesca as well. Bastian meets me at the library door.

"Did he talk?" he asks.

"With some encouragement."

He grins.

"He gave Sonny up. In exchange for a bullet between his eyes."

Bastian nods. We knew Sonny was involved in Angelo's murder. As sick as it is to imagine.

"There's not a human bone in that man's body," Bastian says. "We should take him out. Now. The family will be on our side."

"They may, but the authorities will not. They won't protect him. Us killing Sonny would essentially take out two birds with one stone. We'd be behind bars before we could blink. But we will make him bend a knee."

Bastian snorts. "He's not going to do that. I can guarantee that, brother."

"If he doesn't, then we act. We have a dinner tomorrow night. With our uncle, in fact."

"What dinner?"

"I'm guessing you've seen the headlines?"

"Bruno mentioned it. Who cares? They don't know where she is. They didn't see our faces."

"We're going to head it off before it goes any further. Go public."

"You're really going to do it? Tie yourself to a Russo."

"One of us has to. If you're up for the task, I'm happy to step aside."

"You drew that straw, brother." He pats my back.

"I'll go get her."

"Will you need me to give you two a minute?" He chuckles.

"Fuck you, asshole."

I head up to Vittoria's room and nod to the guard, who unlocks the door and opens it. I find Vittoria lying on the bed on her back staring up at the ceiling, her blue eyes bright in the dim room. The only light is from the bathroom and the moonlight coming in through the window. I had all the lamps removed. Basically, had it stripped bare in preparation of her arrival. If she'd been hideous, would I have kept her?

Vittoria sits up and presses her back to the headboard. She hugs her knees to herself and watches me. Even from the little bit of light, I can see she's been crying. Good. She's still in the same dress, but the clothes she'd packed for her trip should be at the Naples house by now.

I glance at the leather-bound book on the nightstand. "Learn anything new?"

"I'm not interested in your version of history."

"But you've read it."

She raises her head in arrogant defiance. "Because your brother made me."

"Bastian can be convincing if he does lack decorum."

"He's an asshole."

I shrug a shoulder and gesture to the door. "Come with me."

"Why?"

"Because I said so, and I'm guessing if Bastian was here, you've had a lesson in obedience. He has his tastes."

Her eyes bore into mine, and I see a flush creep up her neck. I wonder how far Bastian went.

"You both know how to charm the ladies, don't you?" she asks.

"Neither of us cares to charm you."

"Well then you're doing a stellar job."

"Up. Let's go."

She gets up, slips her shoes on, and walks ahead of me into the hallway. I wrap my hand around the back of her neck. She tries to pull away, but I hold tight and guide her down the stairs and to the open library door where Bastian is waiting.

"Dandelion," Bastian says, making a show of inviting her in. "So good to see you again."

She stops short and looks from Bastian to me. I guide her past him, noticing how she tries to avoid touching him.

"Sit," I tell her as Bastian tops up his glass and pours us each a healthy serving of whiskey. She sits in the middle of the leather chesterfield that faces the two matching chairs and takes in the space. I see it anew, remembering how I'd fallen in love with the two-story library with its huge arched window overlooking the vast sea. I know she doesn't want to be impressed, but she is.

Bastian sets her glass on the coffee table, hands me mine, and takes his seat in the armchair beside the one I sit in.

"Is it poisoned?" she asks as she lifts the glass.

He grins. "If we wanted to kill you, you'd be dead."

She drinks a big swallow, and I know the tough exterior is a façade. She's scared.

I take her in properly. She's pretty. Very pretty. Even in this state, with her hair a tangled mess over her shoulders. She must have washed it and didn't have a comb. I'd only left the bare minimum. Long blond waves spill down her back. Her makeup is completely gone, and she looks younger, apart from the shadows under her eyes. Eyes that scan the room searching now. My guess is if she sees something she thinks she can use as a weapon, she'll jump to it.

"What do you want with me?" she finally asks, addressing me.

"Why did you accompany your father's body to Italy for burial? You knew the danger."

"He wanted to be buried in Italian soil."

"So why not send the body with guards? Watch from behind a video like your coward brother?"

She raises her glass to me in a mock toast and sips. "I think you just answered your own question. I'm not a coward. I'm not scared of either of you."

"I think you are, Dandelion," Bastian taunts.

"But let's shelf that," I say. "Are you scared of your brother?"

"Lucien?"

"Unless you have another we're not aware of."

She eyes me suspiciously. "No."

"Were you afraid of your father?"

"No, of course not."

"Now that he's dead and conveniently days before your twenty-first birthday, you and your brother will share Russo Properties & Holdings, is that right?"

"What does that mean?"

"It's a fifty-fifty split?"

She drinks. Nods once but looks uncertain.

"You sure about that?" Bastian asks.

"Either way, it's none of your business."

"Oh, we already made it our business. Your brother has a creative way of managing funding."

She sets her jaw, and I wonder how much she knows about how exactly Lucien Russo finances his personal debt.

"What do you want with me? Why am I here and not in my prison?"

I get up and walk behind my desk. It's an antique, and my brother's matching one sits across the room facing mine. I unlock a drawer to take out a folder and hand it to her. She takes it but looks dubious.

"More reading?" she asks.

I lean against the back of the armchair. "Financial reports going back seven years for Russo Properties & Holdings. The real ones. Not the ones your family doctors. You owe money to some dangerous men."

She sets her drink aside and opens it, glances through the sheets then closes it and sets it down.

"I don't believe you. You could have made these up yourself. It wouldn't be very hard, even for an idiot."

Bastian chuckles.

"You have some balls considering you live at our pleasure," I say.

"I live because you very clearly need me," she says, standing. She walks over to me coming closer than I expect. I'm surprised by her boldness. She cocks her head to the side and touches the collar of my shirt, then tilts big blue eyes up to mine. "You missed a spot," she says, then licks her thumb and rubs my collar to show me the smear of red. "Your type of work never ends, does it?"

"You should know. Your father dealt plenty with the mafia. His hands were never really clean."

She turns away, but I grip her wrist and tug her back to me.

"But your brother, that's where those relationships get interesting."

She tries to free herself, but I don't let her go. "What do you want? Why am I here?"

"Do you know how he intends to pay back the money he owes? Looks like he borrowed from the business but that, of course, left a hole."

"I don't believe you."

"Did Daddy know about your brother's bad habits?"

"I don't know what you're talking about."

Bastian snorts impatiently, then stands. "That's not really what we're here to discuss, is it, brother?" he asks me but keeps his gaze on Vittoria. "Dandelion here has a different purpose to serve," he says, letting his gaze move over her. "Tell us something, Dandelion. Have you ever been fucked by two men at once?"

She gasps, looking scandalized, and I can't help my chuckle. But that expression changes to anger when she turns back to me and tugs to get free. When she can't, she raises her free arm to slap me. I catch it, holding both wrists, and walk her back to the wall.

"Never do that unless you expect me to repay you in kind," I warn.

"You would, wouldn't you?"

"Don't test me."

"Let me go."

"Answer my brother's question." I stretch her arms over her head and lean close. "Have you ever been fucked by two men at once?" I ask. Brushing my jaw over her cheek, I bring my mouth to her ear. "Given the look on your face, I'm going to guess no. So maybe what we should ask is if you're turned on by the idea."

"I would never... I... you..."

"What is the expression, the lady doth protest too much?" Bastian chimes in.

I bring my face to Vittoria's and switch my grip so I hold both wrists in one hand. Her breasts lift as her breathing comes a little faster. She licks her lips. I wonder if she's aware of it as her eyes search mine. The blue is darker, the pupils dilated. Her nipples press against the silk of the dress. "You're very pretty when you're turned on, Vittoria."

"I am not turned on, Amadeo."

"No?" I brush my knuckles over one hard nipple before cupping her breast.

She sucks in a breath and tries to free herself. I pinch that nipple, twisting it, and she cries out. I smile and lean my face to hers.

"Are you willing to bet on that?" I ask.

"Get off me."

"I'll take that bet," Bastian says from a few feet away. "I'll put my money on yes. She's turned on."

"I'm not. Let me go."

"Why would we do that? Where would be the fun in letting you go, little Dandelion?" Bastian says.

"Stop calling me that."

"Back to the question at hand. Are you willing to bet that you're not turned on?" I ask.

"I tell you what, let's just see," Bastian says. "If she's not turned on, we stop now. But if she is, well, she may just need some encouragement. Maybe she's just shy," he says to me.

"Maybe," I taunt.

"I'm not shy. Let me go."

"We can discuss this for days, but there's really only one way to know for sure," I say. "I'll just have a little look, and we can put this to rest."

"What?" she asks, panicked.

I drag my free hand up along her inner thigh, under her dress, and over the crotch of her panties.

"What the hell are you doing?" she demands to know.

"Aroused or not? You want to tell me, or you want me to see for myself?"

"I get the feeling she wants you to see for yourself," Bastian says, clearly enjoying this.

I move my finger over the outside of her panties and feel how her clit has swollen. Feel her dampness.

"This can't be happening," she says.

Bastian leans against the wall. "Maybe give her some incentive to come clean."

"Good idea," I say. "You admit it, and I'll make you come. Right here, right now."

"I don't want to come!"

"Everyone wants to come, sweetheart. It's what makes the world go around." This isn't how I expected tonight to go, but like I told Bruno earlier, I'm flexible. "Just a quick look it is, then..." I trail off and slip my fingers inside the crotch of her panties only to hear her whimper as I circle her clit and watch her bright, disbelieving eyes. "Oh, little Dandelion." I cluck my tongue, rubbing her clit until her mouth falls open, her breathing coming in gasps. "Brother." I don't shift my gaze from her. "Are you seeing this?"

"Can't look away."

"You like that, Dandelion? Like my fingers on you?"

"I..." She swallows hard. "No."

"No?" I draw my fingers out and bring them to my nose. I inhale, then lick them, tasting her. "You are definitely wet. There is no denying it. But if it makes you feel better, I'm hard for you too," I tell her, pressing myself against her.

"Get the hell away from me."

I smear my fingers over her lips, then release her. Walking back to my desk, I pick up my whiskey and drink a long swallow.

"Let me ask you another question."

"I'm not answering any of your fucking questions."

"This one is about your brother." I turn back to find her still standing where I left her, still looking shell-shocked. My brother leans against the wall a few feet from her, arms folded, eyes dark on her.

"Do you love him?" he asks.

True to her word, she doesn't answer.

"More importantly, does he love you?" he probes.

She blinks, clearly confused by where this is going.

"Or your baby sister?"

"Emma?" she asks, her expression changing.

And I know my way in.

"Sit down and finish your drink. We have a proposition for you."

10

VITTORIA

I'm not sure what the hell just happened, but at the mention of Emma, I cross the room on shaky legs and sit. Honestly, I could use the drink because what the fuck was that? And how can he just walk away so unaffected? Casual and cool like this is a normal day, a normal thing.

Bastian comes to sit beside me on the sofa but keeps some distance between us.

"How old is Emma? About five?" Amadeo asks.

I nod.

"You love her. Is that right?"

"Of course, I do. Is she okay? Did something happen to her?"

He shrugs. "As far as we know, she's fine."

I exhale, swallow the rest of my whiskey, and bite my lip, but my relief is short-lived.

"For now," Bastian adds.

I feel the blood drain from my face. "You can't hurt her. She's a child."

"We wouldn't hurt a child. Ever," Amadeo says almost angrily.

"Then I don't understand."

"How safe is she in that house? How safe was she with your father?" Bastian asks.

I turn to him, confused. It's hard to keep up with their questions, and I wonder how they know so much.

"She was in the car when your mother was killed, wasn't she?"

I don't have to answer. Anyone with access to public records would know that.

"Was she supposed to survive?" Amadeo asks, no joking in his tone.

"What does that mean?" My stomach turns.

They watch me so closely I feel like a caged animal. I am that, aren't I? "Do you want her out of your brother's control or not?"

"Don't play with me. Not about this. Tell me what you want and what it has to do with my sister."

Amadeo swallows the last of his whiskey and stands. "You are very easy to read, do you know that?"

I get to my feet and throw my empty glass at him. He ducks just in time, and it crashes against the wall, crystal shards raining down to the parquet floor.

"Temper," Bastian says as Amadeo looks at the

wall. It all pisses me off. The fact that they can be so casual.

I fist my hands, and it takes all I have not to attack them. It would be stupid. There are two of them, and one of me, and I couldn't even take on the one, much less both at once. I know physically I'll lose like I did last time. Like I would every time.

"Stop playing fucking games with me!"

"This isn't a game, little Dandelion. It never was," Bastian says, tone dead serious.

"Tell me what you want and what my sister has to do with it."

"Tomorrow, we will have dinner together," Amadeo announces.

I blink, taken aback.

"You like Italian?" He pauses as if he's expecting an answer.

"You'll get to meet our uncle," Bastian adds, then turns to me. "Is his cunt wife going to be there?"

"What is this about?" I ask.

"We will arrive arm in arm, a couple in love for all the world to see, including your brother," Amadeo says as Bastian drinks his whiskey.

My mouth falls open.

"We'll announce our engagement then," Amadeo continues.

"What the fuck are you talking about?" I ask, my throat dry because I'm sure I didn't hear correctly.

"We're going to get married, Vittoria."

"Married?"

I nod.

"I'm not marrying you, Amadeo."

"You are."

"I'm... Why?"

"Because I said so."

"No. Why would you want that? You hate me."

"It's not a love match I seek, Dandelion."

"I don't understand. Why would you want this?"

"You sound like a broken record."

"Then answer my question."

"That's my business."

"But—"

"We can make you, of course, but my brother is willing to give you something in exchange for your cooperation," Bastian kindly adds, and I note that he specifies it's Amadeo who is making a trade. Not him. "That's the point of our meeting. It's why you're here now and not in your prison as you mentioned earlier. My brother is too kind."

My hands unclench, my muscles relax. "You need me," I say, finally understanding. Neither of them answers. They just watch me, barely even blinking. "And you'll use my sister to make me give you what you want. That's what this is."

Amadeo nods, not bothered by how wrong this is.

"She's five!"

"You were five, weren't you?" Bastian asks,

drawing my attention. He sounds different. An edge to his tone. "Carrying in all those dandelions. When you're born into this life, age doesn't really matter."

"It has to." I shake my head. "Why? Why give me anything at all? Like you said, you can make me."

"Because my brother is a nice guy," Bastian says.

I look between them, trying to figure out if my gut is right. They're not quite in agreement on this. If there's a rift between them, I can exploit it. Divide and conquer, right?

"How would you get her out of the penthouse anyway?" I ask, changing tack. "I'm sure Lucien has it locked down tight."

"She has a standing appointment with a shrink on Thursday afternoons, doesn't she?"

I don't like how he says shrink. "She was trapped in the car with our dead mother for six hours. Anyone would need a *shrink*, which he's not. He's—"

"You're missing my point."

My brain works furiously. Why would he want this? What does he stand to gain? I study him, and the thing is, it's all I have because I'm his prisoner. And he can make me do anything he wants. This is something at least. It's the only thing. And if he can get Emma out, I'll do it. I have to.

"How do you know about the appointments?" I ask, realizing what he said.

"Do you think we stumbled upon you at the church by sheer luck?"

No, I'm sure they didn't. My father's funeral in Italy was a secret, but word got out, as it does. It's how they found out. And if I recall the book upstairs, this plot of his, whatever their plan, it's fifteen years in the making.

Being my father's daughter, there was always some element of danger, someone unhappy with him and willing to use any weakness to get to him, and for the men he dealt with, nothing was off-limits. Not even children. This, though, it feels different. It's not about some slight or money. This is much more than that. Amadeo and Bastian have been plotting their vengeance, seeding and feeding their hate, for fifteen years. That's more than half of my life. And I understand now just how dangerous they are. And how far they're willing to go.

"I'm not fucking either of you," I negotiate, my mind wandering to what happened just moments ago. I still have to unpack my reaction to him. To them. But now isn't the time. I need to get very clear. Make an agreement now. Because they will force me to go through with this insane plan if I don't acquiesce anyway. And if he's offering a lifeline to Emma, I can't let that slip through my fingers.

Amadeo grins a devious grin, and his gaze sweeps over me. "We'll discuss fucking another time." He turns his back to me to pour himself another whiskey. He's showing me he's not afraid of me.

"No. Give me that. I'm not fucking you. Either of you," I say to Bastian too who seems to have lost interest because he's swiping through his phone. "You're not going to make me do that."

Amadeo turns to study me for what feels like an unending moment. I feel myself begin to wilt under his scrutiny as I recall that article, the unnamed child who would be buried separately of its mother.

"It's not real. It's a fake engagement. That's all," I trip over my words needing to end this strange, frightening silence.

"There's nothing fake about it, but if that makes it easier for you to get through the night, fine by me. Just be convincing."

"Will you let Emma and me go? After you get what you want." Because if Emma and I are together, we can get out together. Escape. Get away from this life once and for all.

Amadeo's expression hardens, but apart from that, he's unreadable. A glance at Bastian tells me I have his full attention again.

"We understand you're used to people doing your bidding, but those days are over. You should learn that and learn it fast," Amadeo says.

"She's an innocent child," I remind him.

"So was our sister," Bastian says, all seriousness again. No hint of the taunting, arrogant man.

The photograph of the little girl plays before my eyes, and I see her eyes see how even as her cheeks dimpled with her smile, it didn't touch the shadows inside them.

"So was my brother," he continues. "So was I. So were you. Collateral damage. We are all that, to some extent, until we take control. Because we all grow up, don't we? Your father's words. He thought sons were dangerous. I don't know if that's quite right. I think daughters can be just as dangerous as sons, depending. We've discussed that often, haven't we, brother?"

Amadeo nods. "One thing we do know is he made a mistake letting us live. Scarred and battered, irrevocably damaged, but alive. Because when you have nothing to lose, you are willing to risk everything."

Dread creeps into my veins, making me wrap my arms around myself as I understand his meaning. Getting Emma out, having her with me, will be a temporary reprieve. But what choice do I have?

"If you agree, you'll have our protection. No one will touch you or your sister."

"But that protection has an expiration date. When you're done with me, when you get what you want, that protection ends. Is that right?"

"How safe do you think either of you were or would be in your brother's house now that Daddy is in the ground?" Amadeo asks harshly. "Have you ever wondered about his sudden death, by the way? He was a healthy, fit man, as I understood it at least."

"My father had a heart attack."

"Did he?" Bastian chimes in.

I can't keep up. My brother may dislike me, hate me even, but he has no cause to hurt me. And what Amadeo is suggesting, that our father's death wasn't natural, that's not right. My brother isn't that kind of monster.

But the image of that little girl comes to mind again. Because there are worse monsters, aren't there? The ones who hurt little girls.

I drop to a seat on the couch and set my hand on my forehead.

They have an agenda, I remind myself. I am their enemy. They will sow the seed of doubt. If I give them an opening, they will exploit it like he just did with Emma. I'm easy to read. He said so himself. He will use my love for my sister to get what he wants, no matter the cost to her or me. And creating doubt about my father's illness, my brother's loyalty, is part of his game. His agenda. I can't forget that.

But I'll do the same. If I see an opening, I'll use it. And Bastian has given away his hand. He isn't fully on board with what his brother wants. This is Amadeo's plan.

"Your answer, Vittoria," Amadeo says.

I look up at him, study his eyes, watch the storms churn. There's that rage again, tightly controlled. For now. Fifteen years' worth of rage.

We may have been collateral damage once, but

they've taken control. They are no longer that. Me, though? I'm a means to an end. As is Emma.

"Vittoria. Your answer," Amadeo drags me back to reality. None of this matters. What I'm thinking, understanding, it makes no difference. My hands are tied, and we all know it. So I decide. I decide to choose for myself rather than have them choose for me. To force me. And I make a mental note to dig for the rift between them. Because that is my way out. And that is what gives me the courage to nod my consent.

11

VITTORIA

The following morning, I'm escorted downstairs by two men. They're just leading me to the front door when the kitchen door opens and a woman, the one from yesterday, comes strolling out, humming quietly. She stops when she sees me and gasps as if taken aback. I don't know her. I'm pretty sure I've never seen her before.

"Move," the guard orders in a low enough voice that she wouldn't hear him.

"Are you Hannah's friend?" the woman asks, taking a tentative step toward me but stopping when she looks up at the men on either side of me. Is she afraid of them?

"I'm Vittoria," I say with as warm a smile as I can muster. There's something wrong with her, clearly.

"You're the girl who likes dandelions." Dandelions again. She smiles, but it's a strange, wavering smile like she's unsure. "I know where they grow."

"I used to think they were daffodils," I tell her, remembering my mother and how she'd humor me, putting every bouquet of dandelions I picked in a pretty vase for me.

"They're both yellow. Did you eat breakfast yet?"

The guard's hand tightens on my arm, and I glance up at him. He's clearly been instructed not to upset this woman. "I haven't, and I'm quite hungry," I tell her. I'm not, but I am curious.

"Come and have breakfast with me then. Francesca will be here soon too. She overslept."

"I'd love that," I say.

The guard clears his throat and doesn't let go of me when I take a step toward the woman, but just as I do, another door opens, and Bastian steps into the corridor. He stops short when he takes in the scene and is quick to come to his mother's side.

She turns a bright smile to him. "You slept in too," she says to him, then hugs him. "Are you hungry? We can all have breakfast together. Won't that be nice? And when Hannah wakes up—"

"Hannah's not here, Mom, remember?" he says abruptly, eyes like stone on me. He tips his head to the front door, and the soldier tugs me toward it. Bastian turns his mother back toward the kitchen, smiling at her before glancing back at me with daggers in his eyes as I'm led out the front door and to the waiting SUV.

My guess is their mother has some sort of dementia. She doesn't seem to be much older than sixty. It's too young for the disease. She thinks Hannah is still alive. And she recalls the dandelions. I guess she was also in the kitchen that day. I don't remember her, though.

But my attention is diverted when, much like the day they brought me to this house, I'm driven to a large gated mansion overlooking the sea in the Chiaia neighborhood of Naples. Many of these old palaces have been converted into apartment buildings, but this one is a home. I take in the beautiful stone of the exterior walls beyond the lush green garden. It's familiar, and I realize I've seen it before in a luxury homes magazine. My brother had commented on it as I'd flipped through the pages. He'd known the owner's name and had made some comment about it being a mafia boss. I hadn't paid much attention, telling him he was wrong, and we'd carried on our separate ways. I guess he was right all along.

The SUV pulls to a stop, and I slip out when the soldier opens the back door. No sense in letting them manhandle me, yet one takes my arm anyway. I guess there's no getting around it with these men.

I think about what Amadeo said last night about

having their protection as I glance up to the giants on either side of me, at the gate that's already closed behind me and the men standing sentry there. They're not brandishing machine guns, but I'm sure they're packing something.

"Move," the oaf to my right says when I stumble. I shift my attention to the front of the house as the doors are opened by a woman in uniform, and we enter. I barely have a chance to look around as I'm led to the marble stairs, which are simple compared to the sweeping staircase at the Ravello villa but impressive all the same. I want to look around, take in the history of the place because although it's been modernized and has contemporary touches, they've managed to maintain the historical elements.

The entry is long and spacious, and the ceilings must be twenty feet high. And from every window, I see the sun glinting off the water of the Riviera of Chiaia.

"Move," oaf number two says when I pause to look out of the large arched window at the farthest room.

"I'm moving," I tell him and make a point of climbing the stairs as slowly as possible.

Along the upstairs hall are six doors, and I'm led to one at the far end, where oaf number one unlocks the door and gestures for me to enter.

I do and turn to him. "Where's Amadeo?" I ask as he pulls the door closed. "Hey!" I try to stop him from closing it, but I'm pretty sure he'd slam my fingers in it, so I pull back just before it shuts, and I hear myself being locked in. Again.

Fine.

I turn to survey the room. It's a large, beautifully furnished room in an Italian style with both antique and modern furnishings, the touches working beautifully together. The four-poster mahogany bed in the center has an intricately carved headboard and posts. It looks about a hundred years old. The bedding, curtains, and carpet are all dark and very masculine. For a moment, I wonder if it's Amadeo's or Bastian's bedroom, but I see no personal touches. The bookcase is empty, as is the walk-in closet. I sit on the edge of the bed to test the mattress. It's comfortable, as are the pillows, opposite my hilltop prison. If this is a guest room, I wonder about the other rooms in this house.

The best part of the room, though, is my suitcase sitting open on a luggage stand across the room.

I leap to my feet and go to it, ignoring the French doors that lead to a balcony and a view of the gardens and the sea beyond. I'm still wearing the dress I wore to the funeral, and although I'd packed light, thinking I'd only be staying a few days, I'm grateful to have my things.

Rifling through the suitcase, I'm aware someone has been through it. My bras and panties are lying on top, and I push the idea of Amadeo or one of his oafs handling my personal things out of my mind. I wasn't hiding weapons in here. I'd come to my father's funeral. And from what I can see, nothing is missing, so I take my bag of toiletries and head to the bathroom.

The bathroom is marble, as expected, and just as the bedroom is, it's beautiful. Like the Ravello villa, fixtures are modern but in keeping historical elements. I lock the door and set my things on the shelf above the pedestal sink, washing my hands. My reflection shows a mass of bedhead hair that's been through it. The waves are hard enough to manage with conditioner and a comb but using just my fingers doesn't work. It's too thick and too rebellious. It's exactly like my mom's hair, though. I look more and more like her. Emma, too, although less so than me.

The thought of my mother, of Emma, dampens the momentary reprieve seeing my things had given me, so I decide to forego the glassed-in shower and move to the deep, claw-footed soaking tub to figure out how the old-fashioned knobs work. Once I get it to the temperature I want and begin to fill it, I strip off my clothes and look through the drawers and cabinets. I find most empty, apart from guest toiletries, so I take in the view from the window until the tub is full. I switch off the water and set my bottles of shampoo, conditioner, and body wash on the shelf by the tub and step in. The water is almost too hot as I descend so deep I'm in to my neck. I rest my head back on the lip of the tub and listen to the sounds of the last drops of water falling from the copper faucet. I slide deeper, going fully under, and hold my breath. I love the sound of water when I'm fully submerged. I always have. There's a silence that belongs to it that no human sound can penetrate. That lets my mind quiet and allows me to escape for brief moments as long as I can hold my breath.

I come up for air and pick up the shampoo, glancing at the glassed-in shower stall. A shower would have probably been smarter, but I've always preferred baths, so I shampoo once, twice, the water growing sudsy as I rinse my hair before applying conditioner. I take the loofah that was already on the shelf out of the packaging and clean the dirt of the last few days off me. The funeral. Amadeo. Bastian.

My father is dead. I wasn't prepared for it. I didn't expect him to die. He'd lost weight the last few weeks and was unable to keep food down at times. I'd just thought he'd get better. But then he had a massive heart attack... I haven't processed it yet, the fact that he's really gone.

I push the thoughts out of my head. Now isn't the time to start processing. Using my wide-tooth comb, I detangle my hair with the conditioner still in it. Then I descend again and let myself float beneath the surface. The tub is deep enough. What a luxury. And as I lay there hearing the sound of water, of the drip from the faucet, I let myself forget just for a moment. Just for now. I hold my breath and just let myself be.

Until a dark shadow falls over me, that is.

I shoot up out of the water, all the peace of moments ago vanished as water splashes the pristine marble floors.

"Are you trying to drown yourself, Dandelion?" Amadeo asks with a smirk, letting his gaze slowly glide over me.

"You fucking asshole. I had locked the door!" I slap the water to splash him.

He just laughs and steps back in time to avoid most of it. "I have a key," he says, presenting it to me before closing his palm around it. "It is my house, after all."

"It's a fucking bathroom. Don't you respect anything?"

He shrugs his shoulders, then pushes his hands into the pockets of his dark jeans. He's dressed casually, the sleeves of his sweater pushed up to his elbows. My gaze moves over his forearms, dusted with dark hair, and catches on the dandelion tattoo. He checks the time on his expensive watch before stepping toward the tub and reaching in.

"What the fuck are you doing?" I ask, scooting as far away as possible.

He glances at me like I'm the one with the

problem as he pulls the plug and water begins to drain away.

"I wasn't done," I say stupidly.

He shakes the water off his arm, then reaches for a towel to dry it before unfolding it and holding it out for me. As if I would step out of the tub right here, right now in front of him fully naked, and let him wrap the goddamn towel around me.

"What the fuck?" I ask again, covering myself with my arms.

"Out, Dandelion. Come on. We have an appointment."

"What appointment?"

"We need to get your ring sized before the big night." He winks at me.

"It's a fake engagement. I don't need a ring."

"But you do. Let's go. Out."

"I don't want one."

"Christ. Don't be a fucking baby." He gestures to the towel.

"Turn around."

"I've seen you naked," he reminds me, then grins that deviant grin that I at once hate and that does something to my insides. "I've touched you. Smelled you. Tasted you. You taste good. I don't know if I mentioned that last night."

I grab the nearest thing, which is the stupid loofah, and throw it at him. He just laughs like he's really amused as it bounces off his shoulder.

"I'm going to fucking kill you in your sleep!"

"I am sure you're going to try."

I reach out far enough to grab the towel, but he tugs it just out of reach, making me slip back into the tub, so I have to catch the edge before I slam my face against it.

"Careful, sweetheart. Don't want your pretty face bruised before our big night. People will talk."

After taking a deep breath in, then forcing it out, I climb more carefully out of the tub and snatch the towel away to wrap it around myself. I'm surprised he lets it go.

"Better. I'll see you downstairs in five minutes," he says and turns to walk out.

"Fine. Asshole."

He stops at the door and turns back to me. "You know," he starts, stepping back into the bathroom, which, although not huge, didn't feel as small as it does with his hulking form in here now. It takes all I have to stand still and not back away when he reaches out to tilt my chin up, then takes my jaw more tightly. "For such a pretty girl, you have a very foul mouth."

I jerk out of his grasp. "You bring out all my best qualities."

"Daddy may not have washed your mouth out with soap and water, but I just might."

I grit my teeth and hold my tongue because I

have no doubt he would, and although I've never experienced that, I'm pretty sure it's gross.

"Better. Five minutes. And remember to be convincing. If you're not, no Emma."

Before I can say anything, he's gone.

12

AMADEO

The jeweler, something Preston, I can't remember his first name, prattles on about nonsensical things. He's nosy, looking around at everything as if taking inventory. Making a spreadsheet of my net worth. My mind is on Vittoria upstairs. Vittoria naked in the tub. She doesn't shrink away like I expected her to. She also has a smart mouth. I'll teach her to put it to better use. I do worry that I find her more than a little attractive, but I tell myself that finding a gorgeous woman attractive is human. Even if her last name is Russo.

"There she is," he says as Vittoria descends the final step into the hallway. "The beautiful bride-to-be."

She looks my way and gives me a glare. I wink as she turns the corner and shifts her attention to the jeweler.

"Ah." I wrap a hand around the back of her neck and pull her to me, planting a kiss on her mouth. Surprised, she pushes against my chest, and when I release her, she gasps for breath. "My fiancée is lovely. And so sweet." I remind her before introducing her to the jeweler. "Vittoria, this is Mr. Preston. He was kind enough to do a rush job on this."

"Well, when Mr. Caballero called to tell me of his intention, I had no choice. One must help true love along whenever possible, after all."

"I'm sure the size of the diamond I'm buying didn't hurt," I say.

Preston is flummoxed.

"Don't be gauche, darling," Vittoria says with a look on her face that makes me think she's just had a bite of bad fish. She turns to smile at Preston. "He doesn't need to be here for this part, does he?" She tries to slip out of my grasp.

I tighten my hold on her neck. "I wouldn't miss it."

"Let's get started then," Preston says, clearing his throat. He moves to his briefcase, which he'd set on the antique dining table. I'm sure he's salivating to finalize this sale.

Vittoria and I follow, and he opens it to display an array of sizers, several diamond rings of different cuts and carats with varying bands as well as a few earrings and necklaces just in case, I guess. He's carrying a fortune, but he's also accompanied by two armed guards.

"Oh, my goodness," Vittoria says, laying one elegant hand delicately on her throat. She's used to this crap. I'm sure Daddy bought her whatever her spoiled little heart desired. "Are you letting me choose, darling?" she asks me, turning wide eyes that shine like sapphires to me and blinking coquettishly.

I squeeze her neck. "I only want the best for you, my little Dandelion." I release her and kiss the tip of her tiny, upturned nose for the benefit of Mr. Preston, who will have word on the street before we can blink.

If she's surprised by the kiss, she recovers quickly.

"Well, I know a thing or two about diamonds," she says.

"I'm sure you do," I mutter.

She ignores me and turns her full attention to the briefcase while holding her left hand out to Preston as he sizes her finger.

"And I never think a diamond should be alone, do you, Mr. Preston?" she asks the man.

It takes all I have to refrain from rolling my eyes.

"I wholeheartedly agree, dear girl. This one is a princess cut with accompanying diamonds. Ladies-in-waiting, shall we say?"

The two of them giggle at his stupid joke as he slips the diamond onto her finger.

"I think the platinum band. What do you think, Ms. Russo?"

"I love platinum."

He continues to rattle off details, and I step back to watch Vittoria Russo prove just how much of a princess she is.

"My fiancé is surprising me with a gown for the evening. I don't even know the color, if you'll believe it! It's all happened so fast." She turns to me and holds out her hand. She chose the most expensive ring in the case, of course. "Darling, I'll need something to adorn my décolletage and of course my ears. I don't want Mr. Preston to think me spoiled, though." Her smile is so wide and her white teeth so bright, it's almost blinding, and I realize this may have been a mistake.

"Oh, you're not spoiled, dear girl," Mr. Preston reassures her. "You are a beautiful, young thing. You should be adorned." He turns to me for the next part, voice all business. "And this may be the time to add that our shop offers our customers the option to make a donation to a charity to promote the education of underprivileged children all over the world. In a way, it balances the scales of the haves and the have-nots."

Vittoria lays her left hand with its glaring diamond over her heart. "That is just so wonderful.

I'm sure Amadeo will want to make a generous donation. Isn't that right, darling?" she asks me with a slight edge to her tone.

"For underprivileged children, of course," I say. "I'm all for leveling the scales."

Her smile falters at that.

"Let's get your décolletage and those pretty ears of yours adorned." I tug on her earlobe. "I can't wait to see those diamonds and just the diamonds on you later," I add, leaning toward her cheek so it looks like I'm kissing her. "Really, cannot wait."

She presses a hand to my chest, and the fun she was having at my expense is gone.

My cell phone buzzes. I take it from my pocket to check the screen and swipe to answer.

"Mr. Preston, my fiancée will finalize things. Send me the bill and double the amount of the jewelry for the donation to the children's charity. I need to take this call."

"Yes, sir, thank you, Mr. Caballero. You're very generous indeed."

I walk away to take the call. Catching a glimpse of Vittoria's face just before I turn the corner, I see the expression of the woman from the night before. The worried one. The serious one. I'm pretty sure her intent was to bleed as much money from me as possible with her little game. But considering much of that money will go to a children's charity, she'll succeed, but she'll also lose.

13

VITTORIA

I'm still processing what Amadeo did. Doubling the donation. I guess I didn't expect something like that from him. I was having a little fun at his expense, but he turned the tables on me, and I'm not sure I like it. I remind myself he's not human. He's a monster. Only a monster could do to a dead body what he did to my father's corpse. Only a monster would kidnap a woman and use her affection for her little sister to bend her to his will. Only a monster would consider a child collateral damage.

The door opens just as I apply the finishing touches to my makeup. I'm expecting Amadeo, but when I turn to find Bastian standing there, I find myself unprepared. My heartbeat shoots up, and I almost drop the tube of lipstick on the pretty caramel-gold gown.

"Careful. That'll leave a stain," he says flatly, a look of disdain on his face.

He's dressed in a dark suit that barely contains him. His hair is combed back, that five-o'clock shadow along his jaw accentuating the hard angle of it, that scar not ugly somehow. I remember their question to me in the library and have to force myself to blink as heat flushes my neck and cheeks. I'm not sure what's wrong with me. Why I am remotely attracted to either of them.

His gaze moves over the diamonds at my neck, my ears. He zeroes in on the ring on my finger as I put the lid on the lipstick, and I swear he's angrier when his eyes meet mine again. That anger makes the amber of his eyes burn like there's a fire smoldering just beneath ash. Like that fire will flare up again and consume everything in its path.

The thought makes me shiver.

"Ready, Dandelion?"

"Where is Amadeo?"

"Why? Am I not good enough? Or do I make you nervous when he's not around?"

"You don't make me nervous," I say, standing. I cross the room to take the wrap that goes with the dress off its hanger, and am about to slip it over my shoulders when he's at my back. His fingers brush mine when he takes the wrap from me.

My heart skips. He's so close, I can feel the heat

of his body radiating off him. Smell his aftershave, leather and spice and unyielding man.

I glance back, remembering last night yet again. Them taunting me about fucking two men at once. Fucking them.

My throat goes dry.

He takes me in, gaze moving over my face and pausing at my mouth. He leans close, so close the stubble along his jaw brushes my cheek and every hair on the back of my neck stands on end. He inhales, and I find myself leaning backward, barely catching myself before my body touches his.

I swallow hard as he sets the wrap over my shoulders. I adjust the skirt of the dress, needing a distraction. The pretty silk reaches the floor with a plunging neckline where the heavy diamond pendant of my necklace rests in the space between my breasts. The drop earrings match the necklace. I will return them to the shop tomorrow. Mr. Preston agreed to allow me to borrow them when I suggested he take that money too and give it to the charity. He couldn't not do it, although I know it hurt him. Hurt his wallet for sure. But greed is an ugly thing, and besides, I'll be showcasing his diamonds and his shop tonight.

"Do you feel safer when Amadeo's around, Dandelion?" He brings his mouth to my ear, and it takes all I have to remain still. "Because you're not."

I shudder.

Satisfied, he steps away, and I can breathe again.

"My brother will meet us at the restaurant. He had to take care of some business." He appraises me and gestures to the diamonds. "Did he buy you those?"

"Are you jealous? Did you want big brother to buy you some jewelry?"

"Just remember that Amadeo always has an ulterior motive. It doesn't take a genius to guess what it is."

Flustered, I struggle for a response.

"Let's go. Don't want to be late when your fiancé announces your engagement. Talk about awkward."

He gestures to the door, and I move, trying to keep space between us but failing. When we reach the front doors, I see the same guards from earlier and I decide to call them Oaf One and Oaf Two. All four of us walk out to the waiting SUV, the two oafs sitting in the front, Bastian and I in the back. The ride is tense as Bastian texts throughout, and I try not to look at him

I don't need to be afraid of Bastian. Amadeo won't let him hurt me. He said they'd protect me. They. But being so close to Bastian, it's like he's sucking the air out of the space. Like there isn't enough oxygen for him, his hatred and me. I can't go to Amadeo about him. I don't want to give away the fact that Bastian scares me. Not that Amadeo doesn't, but Amadeo won't hurt me. Not yet, anyway. I get the feeling he's the more reasonable of the two.

We arrive at the elegant restaurant twenty minutes later. Bastian escorts me to the front doors, and I notice a crowd has collected—journalists, I realize, as cameras begin to flash.

"What is this about?" I ask him.

"Big show for your brother," he says with what onlookers would see as a smile, but what I know is a sneer.

"My brother?"

Every table in the restaurant is full, and every single head turns at our entrance. Conversation momentarily stops.

"I guess he misses you," Bastian says as he slips the wrap from my shoulders and sets his hand on my lower back.

I stiffen instantly, the touch of his skin hot against mine. The look he gives me tells me he feels it too.

"Let's go."

I glance up at him, and he down at me. His expression is hard. Resting asshole face.

"Ms. Russo, I'm so sorry for your loss," a man says as he stands when we pass his table.

"Thank you," I say to him, although I don't know him.

"Your father and I had some business together. I'm sure we'll—"

"Excuse us," Bastian says, not even bothering with a fake smile. We weave around the tables, all eyes on us, and at the very back, I see Amadeo.

He stands, along with the men beside him. The woman at their table remains seated. One of the men looks to be in his late fifties or early sixties, and something about him is slightly familiar. The other is younger, maybe forty. The older one takes me in as we approach, and I feel his gaze slide over me like a cold, clammy hand. I shudder, slowing my step. Bastian must feel it because he presses his hand to my back, urging me forward.

"That's our uncle Sonny. It's the effect he has on everyone," Bastian says.

I glance up at Bastian trying to get a read on him. But he sets his mouth in a line and gestures toward the table.

The man to the other side of Amadeo looks me over too, but it's different with him. He's not slimy. He smiles and nods in greeting, but I need to remember it's a façade. If he's a friend of Amadeo or Bastian, then his hands are not clean.

My mind wanders to the report Amadeo showed me, the comment about our company's finances and how my brother has used them. But no. That can't be right. My father would have known if anything was going on.

"Brother," Bastian says once we get to Amadeo. I look at them standing there together. Two dangerous men. Two dangerous men made all the more attractive for the matching scars across their faces. And I am drawn to them both no matter how much I may want to resist or deny it.

But they're both monsters. I just need to remember that.

Amadeo is wearing a suit similar to the one Bastian is wearing, black on black, dark hair combed back, a permanent five-o'clock shadow along the hard line of his jaw.

"You look lovely. Gold is your color," Amadeo says as he appraises me, gaze moving slowly over me, so slowly it makes my nipples harden and the hair on my arms stand on end. "Thank you, brother," he says. A look passes between them, some silent communication.

"I'm going to get a drink," Bastian mutters and hands me off.

We both watch him settle himself on a stool at the bar across the room. He's facing us, and even from this distance, I see his eyes bore into me.

I look away from him to scan the room. The conversation picks up, although I see curious glances. Amadeo draws me to his side and traces the line of my spine with the back of his hand, raising goose bumps in his wake.

"The diamonds suit you," he says.

"You were very generous this afternoon."

"You didn't leave me much choice." He leans

close, and to the room, it looks as though he's kissing my cheek. "And I meant what I said. I look forward to seeing just them on your naked skin."

I swallow, unsure if it's his words, his breath brushing my neck, or the fingers that play along my lower back that set butterflies loose in my stomach.

I won't fuck them. I will not fuck them. Like a mantra, I repeat the words.

"Remember our agreement," he whispers.

My face feels hot as he pulls away, eyes dark with a different kind of storm than earlier. And I see all the eyes on us. The anticipation.

Convince them.

I look up at him. He's waiting for me. Waiting to see what I'll do. I raise my left hand to his cheek, the diamond in full view. I lay it on his face. It's the scarred side.

Cameras flash, and a woman gasps as light bounces off the flawless diamond surrounded by the smaller ladies-in-waiting. I lick my lips and take a breath in as my heart thuds against my chest. And I tell myself I'm doing this to be convincing. Not because I want to. I tell myself I'm doing it because I have to as I rise up on tiptoe and, looking into his eyes, I kiss him. I set my lips against his, and I kiss him.

The flat of Amadeo's hand spans my lower back as he tugs me to him, taking that kiss to another level. One I hadn't intended on traversing. I resist, surprised, but he is unbothered. He forces my head backward, and when my mouth opens, he slips his tongue inside. All I can do is gasp, my eyes flying open to meet his momentarily before someone clears their throat, and he breaks off our kiss.

I exhale a shuddering breath, staring up at him, seeing his amusement as I reach out to hold the back of a chair to steady myself. It's then I catch Bastian's amber eyes on me. He tilts his glass, swallowing the contents, and pours another from the bottle on the bar.

"Vittoria," Amadeo says, turning me away from his brother to face those at the table. "This is my uncle, Sonny Caballero." He gestures to the creep who doesn't bother to stand but nods, and it takes all I have not to shudder as that same feeling of earlier moves through me. I don't like him. And if I had to choose between him and Amadeo or even Bastian, I wouldn't hesitate to run into the brothers' arms.

"A pleasure to meet you, Ms. Russo," he says. He sits back in his seat and picks up his drink, eyes openly moving over me. Amadeo's hand tightens around my waist, and he turns me toward the woman at Sonny's side.

"His wife, Anna."

Anna doesn't even bother with words. She just lets her lips form something that might appear like the beginnings of a smile, then drops it. She holds eye contact as if through that alone, she will communicate exactly what she thinks of me.

"And Bruno Cocci."

Bruno reaches a hand to me and bows just a little in a friendly gesture. "Very nice to meet you, Ms. Russo."

I shake his hand. "And you, Mr. Cocci."

"Bruno, please."

"Only if you'll call me Vittoria."

He nods, releases my hand, and Amadeo pulls out a chair for me to sit at his side so I'm between him and Bruno. Bastian makes his way over then, sets his whiskey down, both glass and bottle, and takes his seat on the other side of Bruno. Amadeo's eyes are on his brother, and he does not look pleased.

There's that rift.

Amadeo raises a hand, and the servers descend, one carrying a bottle of champagne and another a tray of crystal flutes.

"Vittoria and I are thrilled to have you here to share this momentous occasion with us." I feel my eyebrows disappear into my forehead. "As we announce our engagement."

A moment of stunned silence descends. Someone clears their throat.

"Rather sudden, don't you think?" Sonny asks, picking up his whiskey.

"Love at first sight. Isn't that right, Vittoria?"

I look at Amadeo. If I say anything else, if I call him out on this sham, will anyone help me? Take me back home? I glance at Bastian, whose jaw is so tight I'm afraid he will crack a tooth.

"That's right," I say.

"What's the saying? True love conquers all." Amadeo deadpans. "I don't know where the papers got the idea she was taken by force, do you, uncle?"

His uncle watches Amadeo as he drains his glass, then turns to me. "I heard your father's funeral was... eventful."

I glance at Amadeo. People know what happened, don't they? There must be rumors at least. I meet Sonny's eyes. "I don't know what you mean," I say.

"Hm."

"As I was saying, I'm here to introduce Vittoria to the family and announce our engagement. Now that the sad event of Geno Russo's passing is behind us, I hope you'll join us for a celebratory drink." He pops the cork, and I jump like I always do when a cork pops. Champagne bubbles over the top of the bottle, and he pours six glasses, then deliberately pushes them in front of each person sitting at the table.

He picks his up, as does Bruno. They turn to me and wait. I pick up my glass.

All eyes move to Bastian next, and although obviously reluctant, he picks his up as well.

"Uncle?" Amadeo says.

Sonny glares at him. He hates him. I need to understand why. Sonny glances at his wife and gestures to her glass. She picks hers up, and he does the same.

"Congratulations, nephew," he says and drinks the smallest sip before setting it down.

Amadeo nods, then turns to his brother, who drains his glass, pushes his chair back loudly, and stands. "Excuse me." A moment later, he's gone, but just then, servers come to deliver our first course, and people begin to approach the table. They all go to Amadeo first—some friendly, some not—before greeting his uncle and looking at me like I'm a new act at the circus. The latest freak at the show. There's an array of press and politicians, some of whom I recognize, and even two detectives and a police chief who slips me his card. I notice they go directly to Sonny and don't shake Amadeo's hand. So he doesn't have the cops in his pocket. That's interesting.

"Chief Greco," Amadeo says, plucking the card from me and pocketing it. "So good you could be here."

The chief draws in a long, slow breath, then walks away without saying a word. Amadeo watches him go, looking amused.

When dessert is served, I excuse myself to head to the lady's room. I'm two steps away from the table when Amadeo nods his head, and Oaf One and Oaf Two flank me. Neither lays a hand on me, though, as

I make my way toward the bathroom. When Oaf One pushes the door open and looks like he's about to enter, I stop him.

"It's a lady's room. Keyword being ladies, which neither of you are."

"I need to check it."

"For what exactly? Do you think I'll find a tiny window to crawl out of?"

Just then, Bastian appears from around a corner.

"Sir," Oaf One or Two says. I can't keep track of who's who.

Bastian eyes me. "I'll take care of this," he tells them. "Go grab a smoke."

"Thank you," one of them says, and a moment later, they're gone. Bastian turns to me.

"In."

"I don't think it's appropriate—"

He cuts me off, taking my arm and walking me into the bathroom, where a toilet flushes and a woman emerges from one of the small, private rooms. She stops when she sees us, but Bastian's glare sends her to the sink, where she quickly washes her hands and scurries out.

Once the door is closed and we're alone, Bastian turns his full attention to me. He leans an arm against the wall as his gaze moves over the diamonds on my neck, down to the large pendant that hangs between my breasts. He reaches a hand to lift it, weigh it. I wonder if he knows how much it's worth.

I raise my eyes from his hand to his dark head, and just as I do, he shifts his gaze to mine, holding it, studying me through lashes as thick as his brother's. There are those burning embers again. And there's one word that comes to mind when I look at him. One very clear word.

Danger.

Licking my lips, I open my mouth to say something. I'm not sure what. But he chooses that moment to brush the knuckles of the hand holding the pendant along the swell of my breast, and I gasp.

His expression doesn't change, and I don't move or pull away. I can't. Not as he traces the exposed skin, moves that knuckle over just enough to tickle the hardened nipple making my breath shudder.

One corner of his mouth rises into a wicked grin. "Show me."

I blink, coming out of this trance, the goose bumps that have risen across every inch of exposed skin making me tremble.

"Show me how the diamonds look on bare skin."

I don't know if it's his words or his touch that sends a jolt of electric fire to my core. What I do know is I shouldn't be feeling this. I shouldn't be standing here feeling this.

I reach up to grab his wrist. "Stop."

"I don't think so."

"Amadeo—"

"News flash, Dandelion," he says in a low,

dangerous voice. "You belong to both of us. This engagement? The marriage, if it happens, is a means to an end. Amadeo will be the first to tell you that. So I'll ask you one more time. Show. Me."

I can't think. Not when he casually circles my nipple like he is. His skin like fire against mine. I need to get away from him. Get out of here.

It takes all I have to step past him toward the door. I'm sure he'll catch me, stop me, but he doesn't. He just lets me go and watches with a cocky grin on his face. But just as I reach my hand to the doorknob, the door opens violently, slamming against the wall, and I jump backward with a little yelp.

Amadeo stands in the frame as the door vibrates from its collision against the wall. He looks at me. Then at his brother.

I stand between them, staring up at Amadeo's face alight with anger. He's slow to drag his gaze back to me, allowing it to move to where his brother had just touched me. Does he know? Can he see the ash left behind by Bastian's burning touch?

"Dandelion. There you are." His tone sounds much more casual than his face looks. He closes the door behind him and locks it. He smiles, and I glance behind me to find Bastian straighten and fold his arms across his chest.

"I was..." I stumble over my words. "I—" Bastian moves behind me, then. I am flustered as his big body presses against mine and glance back, confused. When I turn to Amadeo, he steps toward me.

"Brother, what were you two doing?" Amadeo starts, eyes on me. "She looks guilty as sin."

"Didn't mean to start without you, but I couldn't help myself." Bastian's hands circle my wrists and draw my arms behind me. "Not when I saw all the pretty diamonds. So many gifts."

Amadeo brushes my hair back from my shoulders, smiling down at me.

"Let me go," I say weakly, twisting my wrists, which Bastian keeps firmly in his grip.

"I didn't want you getting distracted by their brilliance," Bastian continues.

Amadeo's hand comes to my throat, fingertips gently tracking the plunging neckline of my gown much like his brother just did, leaving me shuddering for breath as he picks up the pendant.

"She is distracting," Amadeo says, and he may be looking at me, but the brothers are having a conversation between themselves.

I'm... well, I don't know what I am. All I know is I should be repelled. I should want to escape. But all I can do is watch as Amadeo's calloused hands move up to trace my collarbones, then slip under my hair to where the dress is tied at the back of my neck.

"As brilliant as the diamonds, even." He tugs on the silk, and the top of the dress falls open, the pieces of silk making up the halter simply slipping down over my breasts, the dress only staying on because the waist is fitted.

Amadeo steps back, takes in my exposed breasts, then lifts his gaze over my head to Bastian.

"But I haven't lost sight of the endgame, brother."

I swallow hard, dragging my gaze from where I'm glancing down at my bared breasts, at the pendant hanging between them, up to Amadeo. To the reflection of us in the mirror beyond his shoulder. Two hulking men. Me between them.

"Let me go," I say weakly.

Bastian shifts my wrists into one of his hands and uses the other to lift my hair so when he leans his face to mine, his mouth is at my ear.

"No," he breathes, then drags his nose along my neck as he inhales deeply. "Amadeo," he says.

Amadeo raises his eyebrows as Bastian snakes his hand around and cups one of my breasts. I let out a whimper, squirming. I need to get away from them. Get out of here. I need to do it now before this goes any further. I cannot feel the things I am feeling in the deepest parts of myself with my kidnappers.

Bastian plays with my nipple. He's so close I can feel his heat at my back, my neck. Smell his aftershave and the whiskey he drank.

"You know I have an eye for these things," he continues as Amadeo tilts my chin up to meet his eyes. "And I'd say our little Dandelion is aroused yet again."

"Is she? Why am I not surprised?" Amadeo asks.

I swallow hard because I know what they're doing. What comes next.

"The dress is perfect. I chose it with a purpose, did you know that?" Amadeo asks me.

I shake my head.

"Not only because I knew you'd be perfect in gold." He steps even closer, takes the flowing silk into his hands. The dress has a slit almost to the waist straight down the center. It's designed so it wouldn't open that far when walking or sitting but now, what Amadeo is doing.

"Stop," I cry out as he spreads the dress open to expose my thighs, the panties, a caramel lace slip of cloth that would barely be enough for an eye patch.

"Now that's nice," Bastian says, making a show of peering down over my shoulder. "What do you think? Am I right?" he asks Amadeo.

I close my eyes and turn my head away when I feel Amadeo's hand on my inner thigh.

"No, Dandelion. That won't do. Open your eyes."

I do.

"Good. Now look at me," he says as his fingers rest along the lace of the panties.

I swallow hard but do as he says.

"Good girl. Do you know what we want?" he asks as he slides his hand inside the panties and cups my sex.

I find myself squirming and hate myself for leaning toward him rather than away.

"We want to watch you come."

"No. I... No."

"Shh." Bastian closes his mouth over the pulse at my neck and sucks, and I'm up on tiptoe as Amadeo manipulates my clit. I hear the sound of it, of my arousal, and I smell myself. It's not long before my knees are buckling, and I'm only upright because I'm leaning against Bastian.

"That's it," Amadeo says. "Give yourself over to it. You belong to us."

"I... can't..."

He leans his face to mine, the scruff of his jaw tickling my cheek as he whispers into my ear. "You can. You will. Come for us, Dandelion."

With that, he does something with his fingers, dipping two inside me, hooking me as his thumb plays furiously with my clit. I exhale loudly, lean my forehead onto his shoulder, and close my eyes because my body is no longer under my control. It's theirs. And I'm coming. I'm coming so hard I bite my own lip and cry out between the pain of it and the pleasure of Amadeo's fingers inside me. Bastian's mouth on my neck, his fingers at my nipple. I come. And when it's done, when my orgasm subsides and I'm left trembling, humiliation sets in as the brothers look at me, watch me, eyes on fire, smiles playing along their lips.

"Kneel, Dandelion," Bastian says, lowering me down as he does.

I can't not obey because my legs have turned to mush, and I can't stand on my own.

He crouches behind me, Amadeo before me.

"You're very pretty when you come," Amadeo says. He presses his fingers to my lips smearing the crimson lipstick with a glossy sheen of my own come. "Very pretty."

They stand, and from my place, I see they, too, are aroused. I remain where I am as Bastian moves to stand beside his brother, and they both look down at me, towering over me, and there's that reflection again. Me with my breasts exposed, my face flushed, mascara smeared along my temple as I kneel before them.

They wait until I turn my gaze up to theirs, and a lone tear slides down one cheek because what have I just allowed to happen? How could I come for them? How could I have taken pleasure from their touch?

"Now thank us, Dandelion," Bastian says. "Thank us for making you come."

"I hate you," I tell them, wiping that tear and the ones that follow.

"You hate us because you came. Because you liked it," Bastian says.

"I didn't."

Amadeo brings his fingers to his nose as if that were evidence to the contrary, and I guess it is.

"Thank us all the same," Amadeo says. "And we can all go home. I don't know about you, but it's been a long night."

"Fuck you," I tell him.

They glance at each other, smiling. Amadeo walks behind me, and I'm about to stand when Bastian tsks and puts his hand on his belt.

"Stay," he says.

I do.

Amadeo gathers up my hair and twists it high on my head. I know what's coming, and I brace myself, but it still hurts when he tugs.

Bastian crouches down, leaning so close that our noses touch.

"Thank. Us."

I hear the warning. The "or else." He doesn't have to say the words.

Someone tries to open the bathroom door just then, rattling the doorknob and then knocking. "Is someone in there?" a woman asks.

"Be right out," Bastian calls, never looking away from me. He grins. "I could let her in…" He straightens and stretches an arm to the lock.

"Thank you! Thank you, you fucking assholes!"

"That's better. Not perfect, but we'll work on it," Bastian says.

"She'll be a slow study," Amadeo says as Bastian gathers the two sides that make up the top of my dress and ties them at the nape of my neck. They then help me up, surprisingly gentle as they do it. Bastian stands with a hand at my elbow, and Amadeo turns me to face the mirror, arranging my hair and wiping away the smudge of mascara before he meets my eyes. "We're going to enjoy you, Dandelion. And you're going to enjoy us and hate yourself every single time you come for us."

14

BASTIAN

Vittoria sits in the back while I drive the SUV, Amadeo in the passenger seat. She's strapped into the middle seat, and every time her eyes meet mine in the rearview mirror, she quickly narrows hers to slits and glares at me. She won't look away. She's even flipped me off once. I'm glad for all of it. She'll take some time to learn, and we will enjoy teaching her.

"How was the talk with Sonny?" I ask Amadeo. He met with our uncle prior to the dinner. Personally, I'm on Bruno's side. I think we should off the fucker and set the family straight. I doubt anyone else would stand against us once that example is made.

"As expected. He denied any contact with Lucien Russo. Had no idea how the papers got the story but of course offered his assistance with the authorities since they're in his pocket."

"I'm telling you, brother. We need to get rid of him. He won't stop until we're out and he's in."

"You know we can't do that."

He means Mom. Sonny is her brother, and of all people, she has clung to her relationship with him. We didn't know she'd reached out to him after what happened with Hannah. Not that it mattered much then since it was already too late. But he's been clever, keeping in touch with her even when Grandfather wouldn't have anything to do with her. Sending money when Dad went on his binges.

"I know." I slow the SUV as we near the entrance of the Naples house. The gates begin to open, the lights of the house warm in the distance. "Ready, Dandelion?" I ask, taunting her.

"I want to go to bed," she said, speaking to Amadeo.

"We can accommodate that," I offer.

I hand the keys off to one of the men, and Amadeo opens her door. I hear her protest, but a moment later, the three of us enter the house with the girl between us. Amadeo has hold of her.

His phone buzzes in his pocket, and he hands Vittoria to me as he checks the message. He types something back, then tucks it away. "Drink?"

We need to talk. Alone. "I'll put Dandelion to bed and meet you in the study."

He nods and turns to walk away, but Vittoria calls after him, so he stops and looks at her.

"You said I'd have to be convincing. I was."

"You were," he agrees.

"Emma. You promised."

"I gave you my word. I won't go back on it."

"When?"

"Soon. Like I said. Go to bed, Dandelion."

I tug her toward the stairs, and Amadeo resumes his walk to the study.

"How? She'll be scared. I need to talk to her. I need to be there. Amadeo!"

He stops and walks back to her. "I promised you I'd bring her to you. I will do that. Period."

"You don't understand. She—"

"Go to bed, Dandelion. My brother and I need to take care of some things."

"Let's go," I say, tugging her toward the stairs. Amadeo ignores her calls, and she struggles the whole way up to her room. "Relax, Dandelion. Take it easy."

"You don't understand," she tells me once we're inside her room and I've released her. "Emma's different. She'll be scared. Please."

"She's five. I assume she'll be scared, yes, but the result is what matters. You'll have her out of your brother's house. Isn't that what you want?"

"Yes, but—"

"Nuh-uh. No but. Go wash your face. I'll wait."

She steps toward me, her forehead furrowed with worry. "I know you hate me. I understand. Well, I don't, but she's been hurt enough."

"Haven't we all?" I rub my jaw, feeling the dip in my skin where the scar that slashes my face is. Where they sliced me open. Marked me. It's not my own scar I think about whenever I touch or see it, though. It's how they did so much worse to my sister. My father. My mother. Would they have left after dropping that money on the floor if I'd kept my mouth shut? At least left us whole physically?

"Bastian..." she starts, but I've had enough. Going to her, I take her by the arms and turn her. I untie the dress and tug it off her completely this time.

"You need to learn to listen, Dandelion."

"What are you doing?"

The fabric rips as I strip it off her. Moments later, she backs to the far corner of the room, standing before me in just the heels, the small triangle of the panties, and all those fucking diamonds. She covers her breasts with her arm and sets a hand over her crotch.

I stalk toward her, and whatever she sees on my face has her wrapping her hands around the base of the desk lamp. I'm pretty sure she won't be able to lift it since it's solid heavy brass.

"Stay away from me!"

"Then do as you're fucking told." I take another

step, and she screams, so I stop. "Go wash your face. Get ready for bed. Don't make me make you." She eyes the bathroom door and the space between us. I move back and gesture to the bathroom. A moment later, she hurries to it, half running, and closes and locks the door. The shower switches on.

I drop down into the armchair and rub my jaw. I need to be careful. Something about her has me feeling everything to the extreme. The hate. The want. Has me remembering everything about that day. I'm even having fucking nightmares again.

She's fucking with us, and I can't do a damn thing about it because we need her. I know that. I don't know why Amadeo is bringing another one here, though. A five-year-old at that. But my brother has a more tender heart than I do.

Twenty minutes pass before she emerges from the bathroom, steam bellowing behind her. From the look on her face, she expected me to be gone. She's wrapped in a towel, her hair in two long braids on either side of her face, which is free of makeup. She looks younger like this. Innocent.

I stand. Remind myself she isn't that.

She watches me wordlessly as I cross the room to the bed and draw the sheets back. I make a sweeping gesture for her to get in.

"I need my night—"

"Get in."

She grits her jaw and sighs deeply but pads over. She knows I'm not leaving until this is done.

"You want me naked? Haven't you humiliated me enough for one night?"

"If humiliation is your kink, I can give it to you in spades."

"It's not—"

"You came. That's the bottom line."

"I didn't want to!"

I snort. "Right. Take it off."

She strips off the towel, drops it, and stands naked, shoulders back, face set in stone in a show of defiance.

I step toward her and let my gaze drop to her mouth. "That's better. I owe you for earlier, don't I?"

"What do you mean?"

I hold up my middle finger to remind her and back her toward the wall. Her breath comes in gasps.

"Turn around, Dandelion. Face the wall."

She glances at the door, then back up at me.

"Do it."

She turns and faces the wall but keeps her gaze over her shoulder on me.

"Hands up above your head," I instruct, taking them and dragging them up. "There. Now spread your legs."

"Bastian," she starts, tone different. Less demanding. But I've had enough.

"Do it."

She does.

"Stay just like that no matter what, or this will be much worse. Do you understand?"

She nods, shuddering as she braces herself.

I stand back and look at her. Although of average height, she's petite with narrow shoulders and a tapered waist. She's maybe a hundred and ten pounds. I trace the line of her spine and feel her stiffen, goose bumps rising in the wake of my touch. When I reach her lower back, she whimpers.

"Quiet."

She nods.

I grip her ass cheeks, and she's up on tiptoe, her hands coming off the wall.

"What did I say?"

I can see the effort it takes her to put her hands back where I want them.

"Better." I weigh her fleshy cheeks. She has a rounder ass than you'd expect for how slender she is. I raise my right hand and smack one cheek.

She jumps, gasps, and instinctively makes to turn around.

Before she can, though, I press her to the wall with a hand between her shoulder blades. "What did I say?"

"Get off me."

"What did I say?"

"How many?"

"As many as it takes for you to feel me all night long. Now put your hands where I told you."

She does, and I slap her inner thighs.

"Spread your legs. Good. Now be still." I spank her ass before she can say a word, quick hard smacks on both cheeks until she's gasping for breath and clenching her cheeks.

"That's better," I say, taking in my handprint. "Are you ever going to flip me off again?"

"Probably."

I chuckle, then slap her ass. "Good. I'd hate for this to be your last spanking."

"Fuck you."

"We'll get to it."

"I didn't mean—"

I grip both cheeks and draw her back a little so her back arches and her ass is tilted upward. The position has her shutting up. "I don't like you, Dandelion," I tell her.

"The feeling is mutual, Bastian."

"You don't stop, do you?"

"Not normally, no."

"No?" I splay her cheeks apart and crouch down to look at her. "How about now?" She's quiet. I don't think she's breathing. I see the glistening lips of her pussy and her tight little asshole. Take in the drip of arousal on her inner thigh. I lean my face into her and inhale as she gasps, then lick her from her dripping pussy to her ass to the top of her crack before straightening.

"You're going to feel every inch of me when I take those tight little holes," I tell her, voice raw with desire as I press my erection against her.

She tries to turn, but I keep her where she is.

"Please don't—"

"You know what else I don't like, little Dandelion?"

I slip one hand around to her clit and rub.

"Please, Bastian, I—"

"I don't like wanting you. But I do. As does Amadeo. But let me make one thing very clear." I thrust slowly against her, then draw away and dig my fingernails into her ass cheeks until she yelps. I lean in close so she'll feel my breath at her ear. "Don't think you'll use that to come between us. You're going to be our little fuck toy. A perk. Do you understand that, Dandelion? Because that's all you are. A weed. Something to be trampled on without a thought and eventually plucked out of existence entirely."

She looks back at me, defiance and fear warring. "Let me go. Get away from me. I did what you wanted tonight. I did—"

"Let's be very clear. You did what my brother wanted."

"I said let me go." She tries to wriggle free.

"Do you understand?"

"I understand you're fucking bipolar!"

I chuckle. "Do you feel me, sweetheart?" I grind my hips against her, making sure she does. "It's best, for your sake, that I leave your room right now, Dandelion. Tell me you understand so I can do that."

She turns her head to look at me, searching my eyes. My face. She understands the threat is to be taken very seriously. "Yeah. I understand. You hate me. That makes us the same. Because I fucking hate you, too."

"That's my girl."

"I'm not *your* girl."

I release her, stepping backward. She turns to face me. I look her over one more time. "Now get some sleep. We'll want you well-rested for tomorrow."

She wants to ask questions. Or tell me to go to hell. I get it. But before she can do either, I walk out of the room and lock the door behind me.

15

AMADEO

Bastian walks into the study as I wrap up my call with Jarno. He's in New York making arrangements to take the little girl.

"Bastian and I will fly over in a couple of days."

Bastian rolls his eyes and pours himself a whiskey before topping mine off. He slides into the armchair across from mine.

"Yes, the nanny too. The kid's five. She'll keep her calm." We hammer out a few more details and disconnect the call. I check my watch. "Took you a while. What did you do, tuck her in?"

Bastian snorts, taking a long sip of his whiskey. "I'm not sure about this, brother. She's trouble."

"You mean she's rebellious."

"That too."

"We need her."

"So you keep telling me."

"What do you propose, Bastian? We gun Lucien Russo down on the street?"

"That's a pleasing image."

"But too good for him." He sips. I know he agrees. "She under your skin?"

He considers this as he swirls the whiskey around in his glass. "Yeah, actually."

"Nightmares back?"

"I don't care about those." But he drains his glass, telling me the opposite of what he says is true. I repour and study my younger brother. "I don't want her coming between us. I don't want you losing sight of what we want. What the point of this is."

"No chance of that. What we did with her tonight? That's the beginning. She belongs to us. *Both* of us."

"Fucking her wasn't the plan."

"Well, the plan has evolved. From what I've seen, you're not exactly nauseous at the prospect."

"That's the thing. I should be. We both should be, Amadeo. But we're not. Hannah died alone and in pain. After suffering God knows what at Lucien Russo's hands. I don't want us to lose sight of that."

Getting up, I go to him and place a hand on his shoulder. "We won't. I swear it."

He nods, but his face is in shadow. He's not convinced. I can see that much. Bastian was so much younger than me when it happened. He carries the memory of it, the pain of it, differently.

"We need to see mom before we go to New York."

"We will. We'll make sure she's okay. Make sure Francesca has everything she needs."

"And tell her the story she needs to feed Sonny."

I don't like using my mother that way. She's innocent, but Sonny takes advantage of her innocence, so I figure this is just me managing that situation. Damage control.

"Are you going to go through with it?" he asks.

"With what?"

"Marrying her."

"You know I need to in order to have access to the company. It's how their bylaws are written. No outsider can own any part of Russo Properties & Holdings. But if we're married, I'm no longer an outsider." Because bringing Lucien Russo down will happen slowly. From the inside out. We will strip him of every comfort in this life before ending it. It will leave Vittoria penniless too, but penniless is better than dead. And it's not like I haven't been upfront with her about what she is. Collateral. But I see this part bothers my brother. "It's a piece of paper, brother. That's all."

"What about the diamonds? What are those?" Fire makes his eyes shine like hot coals in ash. You could always read Bastian's anger in his eyes. That's one emotion he can't hide.

"Those were a game."

He snorts. "I guess she won that one." He gets up to go to the window. "I'm going to go for a swim."

"Use the pool."

"Where's the fun in that?" He finishes his drink and crosses the room to the door. "Go check on your fiancée, brother. I'm sure she's up to something. We should have stripped the room."

"She'll behave until the little girl is here. That's when we'll need to watch her."

"Well, maybe you should go give her a kiss good night." He stops, then considers. "No, don't. I don't think kissing her will be a good idea for you." He must have watched us do it in the restaurant.

"Brother—"

"Good night."

I watch him go. I don't like that he swims in the ocean at night. Never have. But he's a grown man. And he needs to work through his demons in his own way. So I finish my drink and leave the study to walk through the quiet house up the stairs and pause at her door before reaching up to take the key Bastian would have left on the frame and let myself in. I expect to find Vittoria asleep, but she's standing at the locked French doors. Something about how quickly she spins to face me makes me wonder what she was up to because she looks guilty as sin.

"What's going on, Dandelion?"

She slips her hands into the pockets of her pajama shorts and shrugs her shoulders. "Nothing.

Was that your brother?" She turns to point out the window to the private beach the house accesses.

I cross the room to join her at the locked doors just in time to see Bastian dive under the waves.

"That would be him, yes."

"He swims in the ocean at night? Isn't that dangerous?"

I shrug, look her over. She's wearing a matching silk tank and shorts set with small teapots on it. "Interesting pattern."

She looks down. "Emma chose it. Seriously, you're not worried about that?"

"Are you?"

"No, not at all. If he drowns tonight, that's one down, one to go."

It's the wrong thing to say, and she knows it in an instant because my hand wraps around her throat and I have her pinned to the door. She stares at me wide-eyed, both hands clawing at my forearm as I squeeze.

"Don't you ever, ever say anything like that again. Do you understand me?"

"I can't... I..."

"Do you fucking understand?"

She blinks hard and one of her arms fall away, making me realize what I'm doing. I hear my brother's words. The extremes she makes him feel. She brings out the worst in us is what he meant.

I release her throat and catch her just as her

knees buckle. She hasn't quite passed out but almost. I need to remember to take care with her. Need to remember how easily I can break her.

I lay her on the bed. Her body is wracked by coughs, and her eyes have grown wide with terror.

"You're all right," I tell her as she sits up. I rub her back.

"I'm not... Jesus. You almost killed me!" She pushes me away.

I get up and go into the bathroom to get her a glass of water. "Drink a sip."

"Get away from me!"

"Dandelion—"

She shoves my arm, spilling most of the water.

"Vittoria." She looks up at me, her eyes wet and red, the skin around them puffy. "I didn't mean to hurt you."

"Not this time?"

"No, not this time."

"Asshole." She's still coughing, but it's more controlled.

"Drink." I hold the glass to her lips, and she takes a sip to appease me.

"I drank. Go away."

I set the water on the nightstand and study her as she pulls her knees up and refuses to look at me. I sit by her feet, taking in the chipping red polish on her toenails. It tells of her life right now. The chipping away of her normal. The ugly reality setting in.

"I don't understand any of this, you know that?" She runs the back of one hand over her eyes. "You hate me. You both hate me, and I don't even know you," she says to her knees.

"You read—"

"I read what you made me read," she spits, fiery sapphire eyes burning into mine. "But that doesn't change the fact that I don't know you. I didn't hurt you or your family, and I'm so sorry that they were hurt. That you were hurt."

Her eyes move over my scar. Does she realize that's the least of them? That what's on the inside is so much worse. Scar tissue thick over my heart, making it impossible to breathe. To feel anything but pain.

"But I don't understand why I'm being made to pay. Why Emma will be made to pay."

"I explained it, Vittoria. There's no other way. Collateral—"

"Yeah, I get that. I'm collateral damage. Well, you know what?" she starts, and I can hear her amping up. "I don't accept it!" She lunges at me and manages to get her hands around my neck.

I drop back onto the bed, stifling my laughter as she straddles me, and I wonder if she really thinks she'll strangle me or subdue me somehow. She squeezes her hands around my throat. Taking hold of her forearms, I can't help but laugh, which only pisses her off and, in turn, makes me laugh harder.

"Shut up! Shut the fuck up!" I flip her onto her back and trap her between my thighs, spreading her arms out wide and taking care to keep my weight on my thighs.

"That was cute, Dandelion."

"I wasn't going for cute," she tells me, ramming her knee into my back. We flip again, and this time, she tries to headbutt me. She manages to smash her mouth into my shoulder, and she must bite her lip when she does because it's bleeding when she draws back, slightly dazed.

We go back and forth for a minute. I'm not sure she's aware exactly what this is doing to me.

"Had enough?" I ask her, flipping us again.

"Have you?" she asks before, when all else fails, spitting at me. That spit lands on my cheek, which does succeed in doing one thing she wanted. It wipes the smile off my face. But her victory is short lived when our eyes meet, and she sees what's replaced that laughter.

I wipe off the spit with the back of my hand and smear it over her cheek. I lean in close.

"Don't ever do that again."

"I'll do it a hundred times over."

"I'm warning you—"

"No, I'm warning you, Amadeo."

"You want to fight for real, sweetheart? You want me to get rough?"

She hesitates, but Vittoria Russo is not one to

back down. I'm getting that. "Yeah, Amadeo. Get rough. That's who you are, isn't it? It's what you do?"

"Not typically with women, no. But for you, I might make an exception. And whether or not you accept the fact that you are collateral doesn't really change the fact or matter for our purposes."

I get off her, flip her onto her side, and smack her ass hard.

She grunts and rolls onto her back when I release her. "Hate to break it to you, but your brother beat you to it."

I get off the bed, push a hand through my hair and count to ten because fuck if Bastian isn't right. This woman can push my buttons like no one else.

"What do you mean?"

"My ass. He already spanked it."

"Did he? Clearly neither hard nor long enough. I can remedy that if need be."

She glares at me but keeps her mouth shut. I look her over as she sits up. Her top has ridden up to expose her flat belly. All that pretty, pale skin. But that's not what catches my eye now. It's the small nail file that is sticking half out of the pocket of her shorts.

She follows my gaze and at least has the decency not to try to hide it when she meets my eyes again.

I hold out my hand.

She takes the file, but I hold up a finger. "You try

to stab me with it, and I'm taking the kid gloves off. Do you hear me?"

"Oh, were you wearing kid gloves?"

"Do you fucking hear me?"

"Yes, I fucking hear you."

She lays the metal file in the palm of my hand. Clearly, Bastian or I will have to sweep the room. The housekeeper must have left this in the bathroom. I'd gone through her suitcase, and there wasn't anything there.

"What else did my brother do?"

"Apart from humiliating me and letting me know how much he hates me, nothing."

"Don't provoke him, Vittoria."

"He's insane, Amadeo. Unhinged."

"He's processing. You just be careful around him."

"As opposed to not needing to be careful around you?"

"I can rein it in."

"Clearly." She touches her throat.

I walk to the window to watch for Bastian and see him swimming back toward shore. I can relax. He's fine. I turn back to her and take her by the arm.

"Let's go."

"Where?" she asks, resisting as I walk her toward the door.

"My room. You'll sleep with me tonight." She

resists the whole way to my room, which is a few away from hers.

"What? Why?" she asks once we're inside. I see her take it all in, though.

"Because you can't be trusted."

Her gaze falls to the dresser. I follow it and see her father's ring lying carelessly on top of it. I drop it into a drawer.

"That's not yours," she says, not sounding quite so rebellious at the sight of it. Probably remembering the moment Bastian took it from her dead father's finger.

"No, it's not."

I unbutton the top buttons of my shirt, then undo my cuffs to tug it off over my head, and she's distracted. Her mouth falls open, and her eyes go wide as she takes in my shoulders, my bare chest and arms. Her gaze pauses at the scar left by The Reaper that almost killed me. I let her see.

She clears her throat, blinks, her neck and cheeks flushing red as she shifts her gaze to the dandelion tattoo on my forearm, then up to my face.

I keep my eyes locked on her, remembering how she came earlier. How she sounded when she did. How she looked at me. I walk toward her.

"What are you doing?" she asks.

"Getting ready for bed."

"I'm not sleeping with you."

"Well, I can't have you sleeping alone until I sweep the room."

"I'm not going to do anything."

"You'll understand if I don't trust you. You seem resourceful." I unbuckle my belt and pull it out of its loops.

"Stop!"

"I need to take a shower," I tell her. "Lie back."

She looks warily at the belt, then at me. "Why?"

"So I can tie you to the bed."

"What? You don't need to tie me to the bed."

"It's either that or you join me in the shower, Dandelion."

"I will skip both options, thank you."

"It wasn't a question of whether or not you'll do either. It was a question of which one. I'm guessing you'd prefer not to be naked in tight quarters with me, but if I'm wrong…"

"Oh my God, you're serious."

"As a heart attack."

"Unbelievable. You're an asshole, you know that?" She holds out her wrists.

"So you've said." I draw her wrists over her head to the headboard, forcing her to lie down as I do. Her eyes roam over my face, returning to that scar as I bind her wrists and weave the belt through the rungs of the headboard, then straighten to look at my handiwork. It makes me smile. "I like you like this, little Dandelion."

She flips both middle fingers up at me and turns onto her side, giving me her back.

"Stay put."

"As if I could go anywhere."

I take my time in the shower, and when I get back into the bedroom, she's on her back, eyes closed. She's quiet. I think she's faking sleep, but she doesn't move, and her breathing stays level when I sit on the edge of the bed. Two long braids frame her pretty face, one of them half fallen apart during our wrestling match. I comb through the soft strands, shades of blond slipping through my fingers, then re-braid the thick locks and secure them before touching her cheek lightly. She turns her face toward my hand and mutters something, soft breath brushing my knuckles. I trace the high line of her cheekbone and jaw, then run fingers over the exposed skin of her chest and the swell of one breast. She mutters again, shifting her position a little, and with a sigh, I begin to undo the belt binding her wrists.

16

VITTORIA

I wake up to a breeze blowing in from the balcony doors. It takes me a moment to remember where I am. Dark curtains bellow softly as the night comes back to me. The dinner. The scene in that bathroom. Amadeo's hands on me. Bastian's. And me coming. Me on my knees thanking them for making me come.

Shame burns its way over my neck and face. What is wrong with me? How could I have come? I should have screamed bloody murder.

I roll onto my back and press the heels of my hands to my eyes. I remember when he'd bound me before he disappeared into the shower. I don't remember anything after that. Did I fall asleep? Stay that way as he untied me? Did he even sleep here? I glance over at the other side of the bed to find the dip in the pillow. He did. He slept beside me, and I didn't even stir.

Reaching over, I touch the place where his head was. It's still warm. But it's not that I am thinking about when I see the ring on my outstretched hand. The obscenely large engagement ring. I'd taken it off along with all the rest of the jewelry. Did he slip it back on my finger?

I remember the other ring, then. My father's. I'm about to go to the dresser to get it when the sound of someone unlocking the bedroom door stops me. I gather the blankets around myself, confirming I'm still in my teapot tank top and shorts. I'm not sure what I'd expected.

"Good morning," Amadeo says. He's fully dressed in a suit minus the jacket, hair wet from a shower. "Come."

"Where?"

"Your room."

"I don't have a room. This is not my house." Not to mention I need to get my father's ring.

"There's coffee. Are you walking, or am I carrying you?" he asks, so I sigh and go with him. "You're a heavy sleeper," he says as we enter what I guess is a guest room. The balcony door is still open, deep blue curtains billowing softly in the breeze, and a mug of coffee is sitting on the nightstand.

I feel at a disadvantage. I pick up the coffee to

have an excuse to look away. How the hell did I fall asleep and stay that way with this man beside me? He walks to the door.

"You'll stay here until I'm back."

"Back from where?"

"A meeting."

"I need to talk to you about Emma."

He checks his watch. "Later. I need to head out."

"Later when?"

"I'll be home for dinner, honey."

I almost roll my eyes. "What about me? What do I do while you're gone?"

"You can stay here. Enjoy the views."

"I'm not on vacation. I want to be there when you get Emma. She'll need me to be, or she'll be scared."

"That's not going to happen. Your brother has already increased security around her, so it'll be tough enough."

"He did?"

Amadeo nods, sipping his coffee. "Bastian will be there with me."

"That's comforting."

He chuckles.

"Can I at least call her nanny?"

"Should we just call your brother and let him know we'll pick her up after the appointment with the shrink?"

"Don't say it like that."

"You borrowed the earrings and necklace," he says, ignoring my question.

It takes me a minute to follow, and when I do, I focus on sipping my coffee again. I shrug my shoulder. "I have enough jewelry." He seems surprised by that. "What's the matter, Amadeo? Don't I fit the mold of spoiled princess you made of me before you knew a single thing about me?"

He considers. "You donated the cost to the children's charity."

"Well, technically that was you since it's your money. Really, it was a win for me anyway. I still got you to part with a chunk of cash."

He smiles as if amused, not irritated like I expect. He sips his coffee. "I don't want the diamond off your finger."

I glance at it. "It's too big."

"You chose it." He moves to the door.

"Wait. Can I leave the room at least?"

"When I'm back."

"So I just sit here and do nothing."

He opens the door. "Do some more reading." He gestures to the table across the room, and I see that awful book of the Russo family wrongdoings, according to him and his brother. Like it's their fucking gospel. "If I leave the balcony door open, are you going to do anything stupid?"

"Like jump?"

"Like jump."

"No. I wouldn't do that to my sister." Besides, it's nice to have fresh air.

"Good. Consider it a test. There are about twenty armed men on the property. You try anything, one of them will bring you back and strap you to the bed until I'm home to punish you. Clear?"

I give him the fakest smile and flip him the finger.

"Clear?" he asks again, eyebrow raised.

"Clear."

He opens the door and walks out into the hallway. "Do you think I can get some bread and water at least?" I call out.

"I'll send proper food up," he says, looking me over.

"How generous of you."

"It's purely selfish. I like my women with a little more meat on the bone."

"I'm not your woman."

"Something to hold on to," he continues as if I haven't spoken.

"Fuck off."

He does, closing the door behind him and then locking it. I'm not his woman. That wasn't part of the deal. But then the memory of their hands on me draws up a very vivid image while setting butterflies aflutter in my stomach.

With a groan, I carry my coffee to the open French door, and step outside onto the small stone balcony with its ornate balustrade. It makes me think of Romeo and Juliet, which is ridiculous since this is no romance. I may be in a beautiful villa overlooking a majestic turquoise sea, but the door is locked. I am a princess in a tower. And I have to contend with not one but two dragons.

17

VITTORIA

I give it a good hour after he's gone before I knock on my own bedroom door to get Oaf's attention. He opens it and raises his eyebrows.

"What do you want?"

"I left something in Amadeo's room last night. I need to get it."

"No." He starts to pull the door shut.

I put my foot out to stop it from closing. "Look, I don't want to be gross, but I have my period and left my tampons in his bathroom. I need to change, or I'm going to make a bloody mess here." Oaf looks as awkward as I imagined he would. "It'll take a minute. I'll just run over and grab the box."

"Fine." He opens the door and takes my arm before I step out into the hallway. "Don't try anything."

"What would I try? How could I ever get away

from someone like you? You're obviously too big and strong for me." I want to puke. "Besides, even if I somehow managed it, there are more armed men on-site. I'm not stupid. I just really don't want to bleed all over Amadeo's nice things," I say, purposely circling back to the topic. "Obviously, this room belonged to someone important once."

He walks me to Amadeo's room, opens the door, and steps in with me.

"I'll be a minute. I need to slip a tampon in. I had to take the one I was—"

"Do what you need to do," he says, holding a hand up in a gesture for me to stop talking. He steps back into the hallway, and although I'd love it if he'd close the door, he doesn't. But he's reasonably busy on his phone, so I hurry toward the dresser where I saw Amadeo drop my father's ring and open the drawer. It's just tossed in there like it's nothing. I grab it out, slip it onto my thumb, even though it's too big, and close the drawer. It jams.

"Hey. You done?" Oaf calls out.

"Yeah, thanks," I say, pushing my hand into my pocket. "Grabbed some."

"Good." He takes my arm to walk me back to my room and is about to lock me in, but I stop him.

"I won't tell Amadeo about you letting me out. I know he won't like that, and I don't want to get you in trouble."

He considers this, then nods. I assume that

means he won't mention it either, so I slip into the bedroom and let him lock me in, smiling as I draw my hand from my pocket and look at my prize.

Although my win is bittersweet. Wholly bitter, in fact. There's nothing sweet about this. My father is dead. Gone. This is the last thing of his that I have, and he should have been buried with it. Buried properly in a coffin, not dropped into a hole in the ground facedown.

I look around the room. It hasn't been used for a while but has good views. Better than Amadeo's, actually, if I think about it. I open each of the drawers in the dresser as well as the antique armoire and find it all empty except for a blank notebook and one framed photo that must have been missed in the back of a drawer. I take it out and see how the glass has cracked. It's the only personal thing in here.

A white-haired man stands proudly in the center. Beside him is the one I met last night, Sonny. He has a deep scowl on his face. Next to him and with their arms over each other's shoulders are Amadeo and another man his age. Younger than Sonny but so similar in appearance, I am sure this is Sonny's son. I wonder if this was his room once. Or Sonny's. Did they live here?

I set the photo on a shelf when a knock comes on the door. I quickly slip the ring into my pocket as Oaf opens it to let a woman in with a tray of food.

Breakfast. I thank her and settle in to eat, knowing it will be a long day.

Amadeo returns as I'm lying on the bed throwing a paper airplane, one of a dozen I've made using pages from the empty notepad, across the room. He catches it, eyebrows raised when he looks at the discarded planes all around him. He unfolds one.

"Don't worry, I didn't use any of your precious newspaper articles. Only blank sheets of paper."

"Interesting way to pass your time, Dandelion."

"It was a long day."

"Did you behave yourself?"

"Of course." I smile as fake a smile as I can muster. "Who are the men with you in the picture? I recognize the one from last night, but who are the others?"

"What picture?"

I point at where it's now displayed beside that book of Russo crimes against his family.

He walks over to it and picks up the frame. Unexpected emotions darken his features. Sadness. Loss. It makes me curious.

"Where did you get this?"

"It was in the back of a drawer. And before you ask, yes, I looked through everything. You can't seriously have expected me not to."

He's only half-listening to me because his attention is on the photograph. And I'm intrigued.

"Who are they?" I ask.

"That's my grandfather. My uncle, Sonny, you met." His tone is cold when he mentions Sonny. There's a long pause. "The one who is my age is Angelo."

He sets the frame back down but is clearly a little shaken.

"He's your cousin?"

He turns to me, hands in his pockets.

"From the resemblance, I'm thinking the man I met at the restaurant, the one who clearly doesn't like you, is his father?"

"Was."

Ah.

"Sonny, my uncle, *was* his father. Let's go downstairs for dinner."

"What happened to him?"

He opens the door, and I see Oaf outside. A look passes between us, but I'm quick to avert my gaze so Amadeo doesn't catch me. But when I turn back to Amadeo, I'm not sure he misses anything at all.

"Why are you so curious, Dandelion?" he asks after a glance at Oaf.

"Bored mostly," I lie. "I literally spent my day making paper airplanes."

"Angelo was killed a few years ago. His killer left

the scar you saw last night. That man is dead now. Enough to sate your curiosity?"

"He died, and you survived the same attack."

"Correct." He walks ahead of me for a beat.

"Was the room I'm staying in his?"

"Yes, Dandelion. Enough with the questions."

"You miss him."

That makes him stop. "We were close. He was a good friend. A good man. He would have succeeded my grandfather if he'd lived."

"Oh. Is that normal? For your grandfather to overlook his son to put his grandson in his seat? Isn't there an order to these things?"

"His father, my uncle, is a lowlife."

"Lower than you?" It comes out before I can stop it.

It takes him a minute, but he grins, then takes a step toward me that has me backing up to the banister. "Oh, sweetheart. Be careful. It's a long way down, and marble isn't very forgiving." I glance down. *Does blood seep into marble, or is it easy to wash away?* I don't want to find out.

We straighten, standing too close. I look at my hands, where they are pressed to his chest. His are clenching my hips.

He cocks his head to the side, and my heartbeat picks up.

"I'm hungry," I say, trying to scoot away.

He doesn't let me. Without a word, he reaches

into my pocket and takes out the ring. I should have hidden it in a drawer. I'm not even sure why I took it. What I'd thought I'd do with it. I know I'm not going to somehow escape this prison. I know the impossibility of it. So what was I thinking?

Amadeo studies the ring, then turns his gaze to me, those thick lashes framing cold steel eyes. Any humanity I saw moments ago has vanished.

"What's this, Dandelion? Are you a thief, too?"

18

AMADEO

The ring weighs heavy in the palm of my hand. I'm reminded of that day in the kitchen fifteen years ago when I'd first seen it. Noted the size. The insignia. The matching ring on Lucien's finger.

Bastian took it from Geno Russo's corpse before dropping his body facedown in his grave. I don't know why he took it or why I kept it.

But that doesn't matter right now. She saw me put it into my drawer last night. And she somehow got out of her room today to take it. She's clever. Manipulative.

I take her arm and walk her back toward her bedroom. The soldier tasked with guarding her is still standing, smiling at something on his phone. He's clearly startled when he sees us return.

"What's your name?" I ask him.

"Anthony, sir."

"Anthony, did you let my guest out of her room today?"

The answer is written on his face as he scans hers, then turns back to me. "She needed tampons she'd left in your bathroom."

"Oh, did she?" I turn to Vittoria, who tilts her chin up, not looking at all sorry.

"Yes, sir. I didn't think you'd want her messing up your things. I stayed with her. She just went in for a minute."

"So you didn't leave her alone at all?"

"No, sir."

"Hm." I'll deal with him later. "Go downstairs and get some dinner."

He clearly senses something is off but nods and scurries away. I open the door and lead Vittoria back inside. Once she's in, I release her. She walks backward away from me as I stalk to her.

"It's my father's ring. It's not yours."

"Spoils of war, Dandelion. Everything is mine." Once she's got her back to the wall, I set the flat of one hand to her stomach and study her while I consider the best way to manage this. "So you needed tampons?"

She clears her throat as I slide my hand down to her lower belly.

"Got your period since last night?"

"I thought you'd—"

"You thought I keep tampons in my bathroom?" She opens her mouth, but I slip my hand under her dress, and she shuts up. "Do men make fools of themselves often for you, Dandelion?"

I grip her inner thigh and force her legs apart.

"What are you doing?"

"I'm guessing yes. You're a beautiful woman. A wealthy, connected one. You're a catch."

"What the hell are you doing?" She grips my forearm with both hands.

"Me personally? Not so much." I push the crotch of her panties over and, without preamble, with no ceremony, I push two fingers inside her.

She gasps, hands like claws as she rises on her tiptoes.

"If my fingers come away bloody, then you'll have proven me wrong. I'll even take your word for it that you went hunting for tampons in my bathroom and that the ring somehow accidentally dropped into your pocket." I draw my fingers out and thrust them back in. She whines. The way I'm touching her is very different from last night. "Will I be proven wrong, Dandelion?" I thrust again, unable to resist running a thumb over her clit, which has her squeezing her eyes shut and pressing the back of her head to the wall. "But let's say they don't come out bloody," I say, circling her clit, liking how she looks when she opens her eyes to meet my gaze. Her cheeks flush pink, and there's an audible shift in her breathing. "Tell me, what do you think I should do with you?"

"I just... I..."

I watch her face, see her eyes darken as the pupils dilate, and watch her small white teeth as they close over her lower lip. That's what hooks me. Her mouth. How she tasted for our brief kiss at the restaurant.

"You what?" I ask in a whisper, my face so close to hers the warmth of her breath caresses my lips.

"I..."

She doesn't get to answer, though, because before I can think straight, I press my lips to hers and kiss her. For a moment, I think she's stunned. As stunned as I am. But then she yields. I'm not sure who's more surprised when her grip softens on my forearm, and her breath turns into a moan.

That sound reminds me that I'm kissing her lying little mouth. There's a reason she's here. A reason we're here. And I need to keep my head on straight.

It takes all I have to pull away. She leans toward me, surprised, her eyes opening. I swallow, feeling the loss of her mouth on mine and the swelling of my own lips. I draw my fingers out of her pussy. They come away wet. I raise them between us, and we both look at the glistening digits. Wet with arousal. Not blood. As we both knew they would be.

"How do we punish liars, Dandelion? How do we punish thieves."

"It was my father's ring," she says weakly.

"So you didn't take it from my room?"

"You stole it from his corpse. Why would you even want it?"

It's a good question, but I'm not here to answer to her. I shift my grip to her arm and march her into the bathroom. "In some countries, thieves have their hands cut off."

"Let me go!"

"I'm not such a barbarian." I switch on the tap and pick up the bar of soap, shifting my grip to the back of her neck and leaning her toward the sink. She holds tight to the edges of it in her resistance. "Open your mouth."

She looks at the bar of soap, realizes what I intend to do, and shakes her head, her lips sealed tight.

"Open it."

"No!"

It's all I need, that little opening, and I shift my grip to the back of her head and push the soap into her mouth.

"I told you once I'd wash out your mouth for language, so I guess we're killing two birds with one stone." She tries to pry me off as I rub the bar of soap all over her tongue, the roof of her mouth, and her teeth. Her eyes begin tearing as suds form. I'm sure it tastes disgusting. "Never lie to me again. Do you hear me?" I ask, keeping the bar lodged in her mouth. "Do you hear me?"

She nods.

"Good."

I take the bar out and release her. She spits into the sink, turning on the water to wash out the soap, coughing and spitting. I set the soap in its dish and rinse my hands under the second tap, then stand back and watch her as I dry my hands. It's a long time before she straightens, and her eyes are red, her skin blotchy. I hand her the towel, which she takes and wipes her mouth. She's quiet now. Sufficiently humbled? I doubt it.

"You may be able to make fools of most men, Vittoria, but I'm no fool. If you ever pull shit like this again, you'll be begging for just a soaping of your mouth when I punish you. Do we understand one another?"

"I hate you."

"Feeling is mutual. Do we understand one another?"

"Yes," she hisses.

"Good. Good night, Dandelion."

19

BASTIAN

I wrap up my call with Jarno and find my brother in his study swallowing the whiskey in his glass like it's water. He's looking out the window over the back garden, the swimming pool, and beyond to the vast blue sea.

"Hey," I say to let him know I'm here. He's clearly distracted.

"Hey." He turns around.

"How was the meeting?" Earlier in the day, he met with Bruno regarding a tip.

"It's vague but based on chatter, Sonny is planning an attack soon."

"What's new about that?"

His forehead is furrowed. "I'm moving things forward."

"Forward how?" I ask, sitting down.

"You'll go to New York to get the sister tonight."

"Tonight?"

He nods.

"What happened to you?" I ask. "What's going on?"

He shifts his gaze to the half-empty bottle of whiskey on his desk and pours me a glass, then replenishes his own.

"What is it?" I ask, feeling dread in my gut.

"Nothing."

"It's something. What?"

"I don't think we should both be gone."

"But you think bringing another Russo here is a good idea?"

"If her sister is here, Vittoria will be more malleable. Amenable."

He means the marriage. "Getting cold feet?" I ask.

He drinks from his glass, looking far off again.

"What the fuck happened tonight, Amadeo?"

It takes him a minute to meet my eyes. "I kissed her."

I stare at him. I know my brother. I know him well. And in the few times he's talked about women, no single name stands out, and he doesn't kiss them. Claims it's too intimate. I get it. I don't feel the same, but I get it. The night in the restaurant when he kissed Vittoria was for show. Or supposed to be. But

I'd seen something in it then, and now I know it wasn't in my head.

"It's fine. It's nothing. Just got carried away," he says. Doesn't sound like he believes it any more than I do, though.

"Doesn't sound like nothing," I say.

"Anyway, with Lucien upping security around the sister and now the chatter with Sonny, I just want to get things done sooner rather than later."

"When is the wedding taking place?"

"Tonight."

"Tonight. Fuck. You sure you want to go through with this?"

He nods. "She'll be twenty-one within days. Given that and with the old man gone, she'll inherit, and there's only one way for her brother to take majority control. She has a target on her back. Probably has for a long time, actually."

"Why are you changing the subject?"

"I'm not. What I'm saying matters."

"I don't know why we should care about the target on her back." *But he does.*

"We have to as far as it concerns us."

"Is that as far as it goes for you?"

"Don't question my commitment to our family, Bastian."

"I'm not questioning your commitment to our family. I'm asking you if that is as far as it goes."

"Yes," he says through gritted teeth.

"Will you kiss her as you consummate the marriage?"

His eyes are steady on mine. "The marriage can't be contested."

"Again, not what I asked you."

"Bastian—"

"Admit it. She's under your skin."

"She's ours. The marriage, it's paper. I told you that. She belongs to us both."

"It's going to complicate things. She's going to complicate things."

"She's complicated. More than we thought. We'll manage. As far as the little girl," he says, changing the subject yet again. This time, I let him. I'm glad for it. "If we don't bring her, her brother will use her as a pawn, and Vittoria will be harder to manage."

He's right about both of those things. "What about Sonny?"

"We'll deal with him when you're back. After the will is read. You good to go to New York?"

"I'm fine." I stand. "I talked it through with Jarno while you were upstairs kissing her."

"It's not like that—"

"It's why I came to find you. I'd better go pack." I walk to the door, but before I open it, he calls out my name.

"Bastian."

I turn.

"She belongs to both of us."

"But one of us has to keep a level head. So you go on kissing her and tell yourself it's just a kiss, and I'll keep reminding you who she is and why she's here."

20

VITTORIA

It was stupid taking the ring. What was I even going to do with it? I still taste soap and humiliation from the punishment he dealt and what happened before. For how my body responded when he touched me. How my stomach fluttered when he kissed me. At least he couldn't see that.

I spend the next few hours locked in my room, staring out at the ever-darkening sky. I'm hungry. I can smell dinner, but I guess I'm not getting any. I look at the picture again. Look at Amadeo. At Angelo. Their smiles are so genuine. I haven't seen one like that from Amadeo. I remember that scar I glimpsed. It was bad. How did it happen exactly? And how did Angelo die and he survive? Wouldn't Angelo have been protected if he was next in line to take over the family? And now that Amadeo has, what does that say? Did he have anything to do with his cousin's murder? What had he said about the man who'd killed him? He was dead. But that doesn't necessarily mean Amadeo didn't have anything to do with it.

But the way he looked at the picture, I know he didn't. As much as I hate to admit it, I feel that truth in my stomach.

My growling stomach.

I get into bed because I'm sure no dinner is coming, but I can't fall asleep. What is going to happen to me? What will the brothers do to me when they don't need me anymore? And what about Emma? Am I right to bring her here? Is she truly safer here with me? How am I ever going to get us out of this?

When I finally fall asleep, it's a restless sleep. It's always restless this time of year. It's when this particular dream comes. Like clockwork, it starts a few days before my birthday and lasts a few weeks after it.

High-pitched unnatural laughter drowns out the music, the rise and fall of the soprano's lament. Faust. It's one of my favorite operas. It was, at least. Before everything. Before I came to hate it. The room is dark, my vision obscured although not blocked completely by the blindfold, which is askew. I'm panting. Or is that him?

He opens a can of beer. Drinks it down. I hear his swallows over the music. He's thirsty. Spent. His breathing is ragged, but he's still watching me as he wipes his mouth and makes a satisfied sound. He's quenched one thirst. He crushes the can, then steps toward me.

The music carries me away to a different place. A better place. My father took me to see Faust seven times because I loved it so much. I cried every time at this very scene, but I'm not crying now. Now I'm struck mute.

A flash of memory. Dad and me in our box at the Met. Me in my newest gown. Me watching him lose himself to the music.

"What doesn't kill you makes you stronger, princess." Dad's voice. I miss it.

But the memory evaporates like smoke when a dirty hand closes over my ankle, and I'm tugged back into hell.

I know it's not real. It's not happening. Not now. He's dead. The man with the rank breath and sweat-soaked hair is dead. Yet as I kick and pound my fists, his breath is still on me. He's still inside me. It's almost over, though. I keep telling myself it's almost over. And when he turns his face to mine, I hear it. The laughter. And then the bullet that abruptly ends it.

But this is the dream. I'm not there. Because the man who looks up at me is missing half his face. Blood and bone and brain graffiti the walls.

And I scream. I scream and scream and scream until I'm jolted out of that place, ripped out of that terrible nightmare. It's the only way out.

I bolt upright. That scream that was so loud in my dream is nothing but a choked exhale of breath here. Sweat drips from my forehead, and I wipe it off my eyes. The room is dark. The stink of basement and sweat and filthy men lingers.

I remind myself that I'm not there. Not in any basement. But the dream has a dark power. It's ever present, just at the edges of my consciousness. Just out of reach. The stench of that room, of sweat and beer and breath, clings to my nostrils, and I squeeze my eyes shut to remind myself it's not real. It's not real. It was never real.

What doesn't kill you makes you stronger, princess.

My father is right. I need to remember that. I'm not dead. They are.

The words make everything suddenly stop and the dream is gone. Vanished. All that's left is the sweat coating my forehead. I open my eyes. A glance at the clock tells me it's half past ten at night.

I look at my hands. I turn them over back and front and back and front. They look the same as ever.

A movement across the room catches my eye. My heart drops to my stomach, and I nearly scream. But then a light goes on. The reading lamp beside the cushioned chair. Ice clinks against crystal as Amadeo, eyes an almost animal silver in this light, brings the tumbler to his lips.

How long has he been in here? What did he see? Hear?

I blink, look away, wipe the sweat off my face and

lick my lips. I'm thirsty. Beside me on the nightstand is a glass of water. I drink it, forcing myself to do it slowly. To breathe.

When the glass is empty, I set it down and make myself look at him again. He's quietly watching. All-seeing. All-knowing.

No, that can't be. He can't see inside my head. Can't know the void in my mind now that I'm awake. Now that I've escaped that place.

"Bad dream?" he asks casually.

I remember what happened earlier. I remember our kiss. The way he looked at me. And I remember his punishment.

His hungry gaze sweeps over me as I swing my legs over the side of the bed. I wonder if he's thinking about what happened earlier too. If he's remembering the kiss.

What doesn't kill you makes you stronger, princess.

My life has been torn from me. The stability of it. The solidity of my father's protection. The routine. It kept me together in a way. Now, all of this, it's unraveling me.

"How long have you been here?" I ask.

"Long enough."

I glance away. The room is dark, so maybe he can't see my face. My eyes.

"What was it?" he asks. He stands, glass in hand, and I'm reminded how tall he is as he crosses the room toward me. How big and powerful. So much stronger than me.

There's a sickness inside me. A darkness. It's always been there. Flashes of it return when I least expect them. Like the dream. A thing hidden deep within. And that twisted thing, that sickness, he stirs it up, awakens it, because no matter what I may want or what I may tell myself, I'm attracted to this man. To both of the brothers.

"I don't know what you're talking about," I tell him, standing too. I try to slip past him into the bathroom, but he catches my arm to stop me. He sets his drink on the nightstand, takes my other arm as well and studies me. Even in this dim light, I think his steely eyes can see right inside me. Through to all those dark, hidden places.

To the blood staining my hands. The death marking my soul.

I shake my head, unsure where that thought came from.

"Tell me the dream, Dandelion."

"Why do you care?"

"Tell me."

I push against him. "Let me go."

"No."

"I need to use the bathroom."

He grins and makes a show of releasing me. It's too easy, though. I don't trust him. I study him for a long moment but can read nothing in his eyes, so I walk to the bathroom. He follows, standing in the doorway when I try to close it.

"Go on. Use the bathroom," he tells me. "Or do you suddenly have your period and need a tampon?"

"What do you want with me?" He gestures into the room, and I set my jaw, narrow my eyes. Fine. "Will you get some sick joy out of watching me pee?"

"Tell me the dream."

"I don't remember it. Do you often remember your nightmares?"

"Yes, actually. There's just the one when your brother and father invade our home, our lives, and destroy what's left of our family."

I walked into that one. But he won't get a response from me. I turn and go to the toilet. Facing him, I sit down, and although it takes all I have to hold his gaze, I do it, feeling my cheeks grow hot as he watches me pee. When I'm finished, I clean myself, flush, then wash my hands and my face. I look drawn and tired, my hair dried into tangles. I swear I still taste soap when I pick up the toothbrush and brush my teeth all while he watches. All while I'm hyper aware of how close he is. How much space he takes up.

Hyper aware of the heat coming off him. That live wire of electricity.

But I remind myself his every move is calculated. He has the upper hand, and he'll rub it in my face.

So I do what I can and stand tall to face him. What does it matter?

I force it all down and walk past him and into my borrowed closet to change into a pair of leggings and a top. Someone unpacked my suitcase. I'm running out of clothes, though.

When I return to the bedroom, he's reading a text on his phone. He types something out, then tucks the phone into his pocket and turns his full attention to me.

"Hungry?"

My stomach growls in answer before I can, and he smiles. He opens the door and gestures for me to go ahead.

I don't move.

"Come, Dandelion. I will feed you." I fold my arms across my chest and look at him through narrowed eyes. He chuckles. "Not soap. I promise."

"Asshole." I step out into the hallway. Although it's late, lamps cast a soft glow as we make our way down the stairs and through the house to the kitchen. A place is set on the table for one, a plate of food covered.

"Sit down," he tells me, taking the dish and putting it into the microwave as I sit. He leans against the counter, watching me as the minutes tick by.

"Aren't you eating?" I ask.

"I already ate."

Of course. I pick a pepper out of the salad and bite into it. When the microwave dings, he takes the dish out and carries it over to me. It's a steaming, generous piece of lasagna and the smell makes my mouth water.

I pick up my knife and fork and cut into it. He watches as I inhale deeply and put the first bite into my mouth. It's so hot it burns my tongue, but I don't care. I'm so hungry. I swallow, cut out a larger second bite and eat.

"Wine?" he asks as he pours me a glass.

I pick it up and drink, loving the depth of the red, knowing it will bring with it the softening of my limbs. The easing along the jagged edges of my strange life.

Amadeo takes the seat across from mine and watches me devour the huge slice of lasagna before I push the plate aside and start on a salad drenched in olive oil, lemon, and salt. Exactly how I like it.

When I'm finished with the food, I sit back and drink my wine as he sets the dishes in the sink, then places another plate in front of me. This makes me sit up, anxiety creeping in. I glance at him, then back down to the generous serving of panna cotta with a single candle set in the middle of it. He lights it with a match from one of the drawers and looks at me.

"What is this?" I ask, remembering how his every move is calculated. Everything he does is for a purpose. What did he want when he kissed me?

That wasn't calculated. I don't think so, at least. That was raw impulse. Want. Need.

"Happy Birthday, Dandelion. A few days early."

I'm confused. Why does he care about my birthday?

"I couldn't fit twenty-one candles," he says, and I'm trying to figure out what he's doing. "Make a wish and blow it out."

Reading him is impossible so I make a silent wish. That this game he's playing—and he is playing a game—won't cost me too much. I blow out the candle, and although I've lost my appetite, I pick up the small spoon and scoop up the custard, inhaling the soft scent of vanilla and letting it melt on my tongue. I put my spoon down.

"Don't you like it?" he asks?

"It's fine. Good, actually. I'm just not hungry anymore."

"It's my mom's recipe."

I look up at him and see a softening in the steel of his eyes, an edge of sadness. I'm surprised at his mentioning her. "Your mom is here? I thought she was at the other house."

His face darkens, eyes harden. "She is. She's safest there. Our cook makes her recipes."

"Isn't she safest here? Protected by her big, strong sons?" I make a point of looking around the room. "Where is your brother anyway?"

"To answer your first question, her life needs as

little complication and disruption as possible. The Ravello house is secluded and best for that."

I study him. It's one of the rare occasions he's giving me something. Sharing something of his life.

"She thinks your sister is still alive," I say.

"And my father."

I don't know how I should feel about this. Happy that my enemy is suffering? I don't feel happy. I feel the opposite. "I'm sorry. That has to be hard."

His forehead is furrowed, that line between his brows deepening. But he doesn't acknowledge my comment. Instead, when he shifts his gaze back to mine, it's intent. Focused like a laser. "A year of your life is missing, Dandelion."

My heart thuds against my chest at this sudden change of topic. I'm taken aback, and from the look on his face, it shows.

"When you were just shy of fifteen. You disappeared from school. Disappeared from the world. No charity events. No family photos. Nothing. Then you reappeared a little over a year later, slipping back into your life as if nothing had happened at all."

I'm not sure how to react. What to say or not say. Why it matters.

"Where were you?"

I touch my forehead. I feel a headache coming on. But then I think of something. "What day is it?" I ask, suddenly not sure how long I've slept. If it was for hours or days.

"Thursday."

"We're supposed to get Emma." I'm doing the math. It's almost ten o'clock here, which means it's four in the afternoon there. Did he change his mind? Is this another trick?

"Tell me about that year, Vittoria," he asks calmly.

I push my chair back.

"Stay," he says.

I stop. "You said we'd fly to New York."

"It's being handled."

"Handled?"

"Tell me about the year, and I'll tell you about Emma."

At that, my gaze jumps to his, and he must see my panic because before I can say anything, he speaks.

"Relax." He pours more wine, but I don't touch it. Does he really think I'll sit here and drink wine now? "Nothing bad has happened."

"You said—"

He gestures to the wine as he corks the bottle and sets it aside. "Drink."

I drink a loud gulp, the food I ate feeling too heavy in my stomach.

"Tell me about the missing year, Vittoria, and I'll tell you about Emma," he repeats.

"You will use a little girl to get what you want."

"I will." He says it without any shame or emotion at all. I think this is the most frightening thing about this man. The ability to switch off his emotions so completely.

"I wasn't well," I say, but I'm not sure why. The words sound almost robotic even to me. I try to think. "It was around the time my mom got pregnant with Emma. My dad... He took me to a specialist. That's all. Please tell me about Emma. Please, Amadeo. I am begging."

"Which specialist?"

"I don't remember his name." I rack my brain, but that year is truly a blur for me. I don't remember much of it at all. "Tilbury. Dr. Tilbury." It comes from nowhere, and I'm not even sure it's right.

"What's Dr. Tilbury's first name?" I shake my head, shrug my shoulders. "Man, woman? Location of the clinic because I'm assuming it was a private clinic?"

"Why does it matter?"

"Call me curious."

"Dr. Tilbury was a man. And somewhere in Upstate New York. That's all I can remember, I swear. And there's nothing more to it. I just... I don't know. I wasn't well."

He studies me as if he's trying to see if I'm lying or leaving anything out. I'm not.

"Are you going back on your word to bring her?"

I ask, my heart falling because he can. He can do anything he wants.

He shakes his head. "You asked where Bastian was. He's in New York. Left yesterday."

"Bastian is going to get Emma alone? He can't! He's out of control!"

"Only when it comes to you, Dandelion."

"But—"

"You'll talk to Emma as soon as he has her secured on the plane back."

"Secured. Kidnapped, you mean. She's going to be terrified."

"She'll get over it, and she'll be with you. Endgame, Vittoria. Remember it."

"What's your endgame, Amadeo?" I don't know why I ask because I don't want to know. His eyes hold mine captive, and I feel the inequity between us again. That imbalance of power. He has it all.

"Does he have her already?"

"Not yet. It'll happen in a few hours, though. At her appointment."

"How?"

"It's handled. Nothing to discuss."

While I'm not thrilled about this because she will be terrified, he's right about the result. I have to remember that. She will be safer here with me. That is a fact. And this is the price she and I will both pay.

"I'll need to FaceTime her. Not just a call. She'll need to see my face, and I need to see hers."

"Why?"

"Emma was traumatized. It's like you don't get it. At all." I pick up my wineglass, stand, and walk to the counter. I tilt the glass into the sink to empty it, then fill it with water from the faucet. It turns pink from the little bit of wine left inside. I take a sip, then set it down. Keeping my back to him, I push the heels of my hands into my eyes to stop the warm flush of tears. I hear him push his chair back, and moments later, he's behind me, hands on my shoulders to turn me. He takes my wrists and pulls my hands from my face. I look up at him, tears flowing freely now.

It's too much. All of it is too much, and I can't stop the tears from coming. I can't stand upright and challenge him, and I don't think I'm strong enough to somehow save Emma and myself.

Amadeo watches me for a long, long time, then he cups my face. There's that softening of his eyes again. A reprieve from everything, a moment when hate and vengeance are set aside. When I inhale, I smell his clean scent. Soap and aftershave. Leather and spice and strength. I breathe it in.

"She'll be safe here," he tells me, tone softer than it's been. He touches his thumbs to the soft skin beneath my eyes to wipe away the tears, and a part of me wants to melt into his touch. His warmth. The solidity of him. A part of me that needs the relief of it.

"It's too much," I mutter.

"You're tired, Dandelion."

I am. I'm so tired. I lean my face into his hand and look into his dark eyes. I remember that kiss we shared when he was so angry after finding out I'd taken my father's ring. I remember the intensity of his eyes. Remember how I felt when he broke that kiss. And I find my lips parting as his gaze drops to them. As he dips his head and touches his mouth to mine in so tender a kiss that I hear myself whimper.

But everything changes the instant he hears that. He breaks off the kiss and pulls me into him, burying my face against his shirt as the hand cradling my head turns into a fist in my hair. I hear the rumble inside his chest, the low growl, and I feel his hardness against my stomach. He feels whatever this is, too. I know he does. But he's stopping it. Cutting himself off. Like it's too much for him, too.

"What doesn't kill you makes you stronger, princess," he says, drawing back to look down at me.

I blink. The words make my heart stop beating, my blood turning to ice.

Looking up at him, I make myself see him, the real him. Not the face of the man whose warm hands held me so gently, whose lips kissed mine so tenderly, but the true man beneath. And I don't know if it's what he sees in my eyes that has his grow darker, colder or if he's just discarding the mask he'd slipped on for my benefit as his eyes burn into mine.

Princess. My dad's name for me. Not Amadeo's. To him, I'm Dandelion. A weed to be crushed out. I feel the blood drain from my head, and my knees wobble. I clutch at his shoulders to remain upright, and he shifts his grip to my arms.

How much did he witness while I lay trapped in that nightmare? What did I say? What does he know that I can't ever remember after?

Footsteps coming toward the kitchen distract me. He's unsurprised, clearly expecting whoever it is because he keeps his gaze locked on me. A soldier clears his throat in the entryway.

"Car's ready, sir," he says. "Everyone's in place."

I watch Amadeo nod to the man. "We'll be right out."

The man walks away. I listen to his retreating footsteps. "Ready for what?" I ask, my heart sinking. Who is everyone? In place for what?

"You and I are taking a drive to the cathedral."

The cathedral. He must mean San Domenico. The one where my father's funeral Mass was to be said. The one they raided, interrupting the service and desecrating his body.

"Why?" A cold sweat beads on my forehead and collects under my arms.

"For a happier occasion than the last time." He takes my ring hand. "It's time."

My legs tremble beneath me. I'm not sure if I'm

standing on my own or if he's holding me up. "Time for what?"

"We're getting married, Dandelion."

My brain rattles inside my skull. "What? You said... You said it was just an engagement. Just to show..." But the events of the last days are too much. The funeral, the brother's kidnapping me, that nightmare back again, keeping to its schedule. What I did then. The thing that made my father say those words. Half memories flash in my mind's eye. Faces, laughter, and blood. Always blood coating the walls, caking them with the gore of human life. "You said it wasn't real. A fake engagement."

"You have a very selective memory. You said that. Not me. I told you to believe what you needed to get through that night." I look down, trying to process. He brings one hand to my chin and tilts my head up. "I'm giving you what you want. What I promised. I'm giving you Emma. Remember that."

There's a long space of silence as if he's letting me absorb his words, then process them. Be grateful for them?

"You're not going to let us go, though, are you?" I ask, understanding. Or maybe I understood all along, and this is accepting. I steel myself in his grip and force my knees to lock, my legs to carry me. I push his arms off and lean away.

"I never said I was, princess."

"I'm not your princess. Don't ever call me that again."

"Daddy's nickname for you?"

I grit my jaw and shove at his chest. I need space. Need to be away from him because everything is confused when he's so close. But it's like trying to move a fucking brick wall.

"I'm happy to stick with Dandelion. It'll help me remember. Either way, you will do as you're told tonight. You will walk into that church on my arm. You will answer I do when asked. And you will sign the papers set before you. And after—"

"And after, you'll let me see Emma."

He nods with a tilt of his head and a smile that could fool anyone into thinking him a gentleman.

"I'm glad you understand," he says.

"I understand perfectly, Amadeo. I understand perfectly what you are. The lengths you'll go to get your precious revenge." I stand taller and move closer, close enough that my chest presses against his because fuck space. I can't be afraid of this man. This beast. But the touching of our bodies carries a sensation I don't want. One I can't process. And I have to tamp down the emotions I'm feeling, the confusion. "Now you understand this. I see you for what you are. I. See. You. And if you think you're somehow better than my brother or my father, you're not. You're the same as them. And in me, you will have an enemy in your home."

A heavy moment hangs between us, his eyes dark, the storm clouds collecting. Any hint of that fraudulent gentle smile has vanished. He brings the knuckles of one hand to my cheek. I don't know if he's brushing away a tear or what, but when he leans in close enough that the stubble along his jaw brushes my cheek and his breath tickles my ear, it raises every hair on the back of my neck, and I shudder.

"An enemy in my bed," he says in a low, deep rumbling of his chest before he inhales as if memorizing my scent. He takes the lobe of my ear between his teeth.

I draw a shuddering breath and press my hands to his chest when one of his comes to my breast, cupping it, kneading the taut nipple.

"I wonder who you will hate more, me or yourself, when you lie beneath me. When you beg for release."

"I will never beg you."

He draws back, bringing his forehead to mine, our eyes locked.

"Won't you?" Keeping me trapped with my back against the counter, he slides his hand over my stomach and into my leggings. I gasp as his fingers slip into my panties and curl around my sex.

My exhale is a trembling of breath, and I swallow audibly.

He grins. A small victory for him as they circle my clit.

"Won't you, Dandelion?"

"I hate you," I say as I stare stupidly up at him while he expertly moves his fingers until I'm on tiptoe, leaning into him, hands pressed against his chest as my traitorous body chooses a side. His.

"I'm sure you do. But you hate yourself more," he says, drawing his hand out and checking the time on his watch. He smiles, showing me all his teeth. He turns me toward the exit and wraps a big hand around the back of my neck. "Let's get married, Dandelion."

21

BASTIAN

It would be better to do this if my head wasn't back in Italy. On the woman there. What I know is happening there while I am here. I accused my brother of forgetting the endgame, but where the fuck is my head? I'm fucking jealous.

I close my eyes and tell myself to focus.

We should do this under cover of night, but Lucien Russo's penthouse is impenetrable, especially since we took Vittoria.

I wonder if he has secured it so completely only for fear of us or his other enemies. I know for a fact he's made many. He and his father both.

I have a photo of the little girl. Emma Russo. She's a tiny thing with a shock of curly blond hair like her sister's and big brown eyes. I sit in the SUV with Jarno as we watch her walk out of the small private school, which I guess is more of a daycare at her age. Her nanny, Hyacinth Brown, waits outside. Theirs is the only black sedan with tinted windows and a driver who looks like a fucking wrestler. The wrestler is currently dragging on the last of his cigarette as the little girl slips her hand into her nanny's, showing her a picture she must have drawn.

Through the binoculars, I zoom in on the girl's face. There's a strangeness about her. They're all fucked up, though, the Russos. Dark. I guess it's a family trait. Or Karma for what their family has done. Although that's not quite fair.

My mind wanders to Vittoria, and I force it back to the task at hand. I cannot afford distraction.

The kids around Emma are running, playing, and hugging parents. This one, though, walks with her nanny directly to the waiting sedan from which a second soldier emerges out of the passenger seat and opens the back door for them.

The nanny gives him a wary nod as she hustles the little girl into the back of the car. Jarno sends a text to the second car to let them know the sedan is on the move. They will meet us a few blocks from our destination.

"Let's get our men into the office," I tell Jarno as I start the SUV. Our men are already at the site of the girl's appointment, where we'll be waiting inside for her and the nanny to be dropped off.

Jarno nods and gets on the phone to coordinate.

Leaving two cars between us, we follow the

sedan through the city and out, crossing state lines into Hoboken, New Jersey, because I guess there aren't enough shrinks in New York City. The streets are different here. They hold memories. I grew up not too far from this neighborhood.

It would have been easier to do this in the city. Fewer memories there. Not to mention, it would be a hell of a lot easier to get lost once we had the girl. But I've never shied away from a challenge. And everything is arranged. The shrink runs his practice from his home. His receptionist called in sick today, and one of our people is in her place, provided by a temp agency, of course. The nanny and the little girl will be the only two apart from the shrink in the office. If the doctor's smart, he'll stay alive. If not, well, I just need to get the girl. The nanny is extra. I don't give a fuck about the doctor.

Jarno and I take a different direction to our destination as one of our other vehicles, an older model Ford, takes our place tailing the sedan. We arrive in time to watch one of the men walk the nanny and the little girl inside as the driver once again lights up a cigarette, walking into the woods across the street to take a piss while they wait.

I circle the SUV around to the street behind this one, and we park the vehicle at the end of a long, narrow throughway between two streets. Lucky break.

"They're in," Jarno says as I open my door and

tuck my pistol into my shoulder holster. I don't want to use it. Russo or not, she is a kid. I don't want to scare her more than she'll already be scared, but I'm also not taking any chances.

I take a look at Jarno and think about how we must stand out here in the middle of a hot day while most people are inside with the air-conditioning blasting or splashing around in their backyard pools.

Once we reach the fence of the doctor's house, his home office, the gate is opened by one of our men. Without a word, I stride up to the back door. I can see the bald spot on the doctor's head from the window. He's seated at his desk, and the little girl is on the couch beside her nanny. She catches my movement beyond the doctor's shoulder. I expect her to give me away, which could turn this kidnapping bloody, but I'm surprised when she simply stares, watching me.

An ashtray overflowing with cigarette butts sits on the small table outside the office. Beside it is a mug with remnants of coffee. You'd think a doctor would know how bad cigarettes are for you. I turn the doorknob and push the door open, and all three heads turn to face me. The little girl's mouth is still in that O, but the nanny's eyes grow huge as they settle on my face and the scar that runs across it. She's too stunned to act or make a sound. The doctor begins to stand, to open his mouth and ask the meaning of this.

Jarno cocks his gun at the back of the man's head.

"Sit down and shut up," he says casually.

The doctor sinks back into his seat as I put my finger to my lips and approach the girl and her nanny, who looks to be in her mid-fifties. She shrinks backward. But as I get closer, she opens her mouth.

"Not a sound, and no one gets hurt," I tell her.

She glances at Jarno, at his gun, then beyond me, out the door where another man waits. She hugs the little girl close.

I crouch down and meet the girl's eyes, taking her in as hers wander along the scar on my face. I see the still-angry-looking gash across her cheek from the accident that killed her mother. That almost killed her.

"You want to see your sister?" I ask quietly.

The girl's expression changes as she meets my eyes, cautious but curious. I raise an eyebrow, and she slowly nods.

I stand and hold out a hand.

"Vittoria is waiting for you."

She looks at her nanny, then back at me, at my hand.

"We need to move," Jarno says.

"Let's go," I tell her and am surprised when she reaches out her hand. I scoop her up, expecting her to yell or scream and alert the guard waiting in the other room, but she does neither. She's quiet as a mouse, only holding her hand out to her nanny as I carry her across the room.

Before the guard has to grab the nanny, she's on her feet, rushing to take Emma's little hand, and we're out of the house. It says something about Lucien that the little girl is so willing to leave with me in the hopes of seeing her sister. I don't hear a gunshot after I'm out—even silenced, you know the sound—so when Jarno joins me in the SUV as I load the girl and the nanny in and we pull away, I raise my eyebrows.

"Doc should wake up by the time their appointment is over but apart from having a headache, he'll be fine. We want Russo to get his money's worth, and shrinks are expensive."

I chuckle, then glance at the girl beside me who is staring up at me. She's still not spoken a word, sitting with her back pressed into the nanny's side.

"Her brother," the nanny starts, voice trembling, forcing me to look at her. "He'll pay the ransom. Please don't hurt her."

I snort. "This isn't about ransom." I take my phone out, snap a selfie with the girl, and send it to Amadeo. He sees it but doesn't respond. I know why. He'll be at the church by now or well on his way. And showing Vittoria the photo of the little girl will give her that nudge she needs to do as she's told and move us forward to the next step of this plan.

22

VITTORIA

Being back here is strange, especially at this time of night. It must be around eleven by now, and the square is empty, the town quiet. Amadeo's soldiers in their SUVs are the only ones making any sound at all as he climbs out of ours and walks ahead of me toward the large double doors. I follow him, a soldier on either side of me and one at my back. They're not taking any chances I'll run. As if I'd have anywhere to go. As if they couldn't catch me.

My steps are quiet on the stairs today. No heels. Just a pair of espadrilles. I'm not dressed for church. A soldier pulls the heavy, creaking door open when we reach it, and I'm comforted by the lingering scent of incense. It's my only comfort as I shudder with a chill on this warm night. The heat must never fully penetrate this place. The stone walls are too thick.

I listen to the sound of Amadeo's shoes as I follow him up the aisle. The pews are empty except for two at the front. Similar to the last time I was here. The day I was to bury my father. I hug my arms to myself, glad when I near the front to see that the blood has been cleaned off the stone floor. Although this close to the altar, I swear I can smell the perfume of the lilies from that day. A cloying suffocating stench. I hate lilies. They are the flowers of funerals.

In the front pew, I recognize the man who stands. Bruno Cocci. I met him at the restaurant. A woman beside him also stands. She's wearing a cream-colored suit and holding rosary beads in her hands. She smiles at me. I wonder if she's his wife.

Bruno steps into the aisle to greet Amadeo. They discuss something, their voices too low for me to follow. Amadeo slips him a piece of paper, which Bruno tucks into his pocket before turning to me.

"Vittoria, it's nice to see you again," he says warmly as if this were a friendly visit. As if I weren't under duress. Because he knows I am. He knows all of it. I'm being blackmailed into marrying my enemy. My sister is his hostage until I do. And even then, after, what's to stop him from going back on his word? From demanding more? Had I thought this man friendly or kind even when I'd first met him? I am an idiot.

Those last moments in the kitchen replay in my

mind, and I swear when Amadeo turns to look at me, I can feel his hands on me, his fingers inside my panties. Teasing me. Showing me just how much he owns me. Because he does. There is no question about that. I am his. I may want to deny it, at least sexually, but I live because he grants me life. He needs me. I don't know why just yet. I don't know how he'll use me, and this strange marriage is confusing. Why does he demand it? I could understand the fake engagement. He needed to get the authorities and the press off his back. My brother could make trouble for him even from the safety of the penthouse in New York City. I'm the daughter of a wealthy man. An heiress to a fortune. I'd be considered important. Whoever said money can't buy everything never had enough of it.

Amadeo approaches me, and the soldiers step away, giving us some privacy. Bruno and the woman at his side sit down and turn to the altar. I unconsciously take a step back and have to stop myself from taking another. I can't show fear. Men like him thrive on it. They eat it for breakfast.

My stomach flutters again, and I find Amadeo is right. I am attracted to him. His deep, low voice, the sense of control that emanates from him when he speaks, when he simply stands in a room, his eyes on me, his scent around me, his hands on me, I want it. I want his attention. His touch. And I do hate myself for it. Perhaps more than I hate him.

"Dandelion," he says with a smile as false as any as he takes hold of my arms. "Don't make me chase you. Not here."

"I'm not running. I'm not a coward."

"No, you're not that." Is he flattering me? The bastard. Before I can tell him to shove his compliment, he squeezes his hands around my arms. "You understand what you need to do?"

"Yes. Pretend I want to marry you. Pretend it's my choice to tie myself to a monster."

He grins. "Exactly," he says, irritatingly smug. That smugness, too, does not repel me. It's that sickness inside me. Maybe it's self-hate to want to be wanted by a monster. Or maybe I see something of myself in him.

He steps closer so there's no risk of anyone else hearing him. "If you're good, I'll finish what I started in the kitchen."

I shove at his arms, but he only tightens his grip as he searches my face. "Is this remotely funny to you?"

He sobers. "Hardly."

"Why do you want this?" I ask. "Why marry me? I'm already your prisoner."

"Prisoner is a harsh word."

"It's the one that fits."

"Believe it or not, I am protecting you from a greater danger than I."

I snort.

"As well as protecting Emma from your brother."

"He wouldn't hurt her."

"Are you so sure about that?"

I don't answer.

"And what about you? Would he hurt you?" He pauses, and I wonder if it's just for effect or if he knows something I don't. But no, he's messing with me. It's another game. "You're twenty-one in just a few days."

I feel my forehead furrow as I try to follow. "What does that have to do with anything."

"Your father is dead. Now that he's gone, your brother's hold over your family's company could grow, or it could not."

I study him, confused momentarily. "Are you talking about our shares?" I hadn't thought about this or even cared about it. I still don't. I know I come into my share of the company on my twenty-first birthday. I guess Emma has something similar in place when she is of age. Our father would have held the majority of the shares, but now that he's gone, I'm not sure how that's divided. It hadn't occurred to me what would happen to my dad's holdings when he passed. His passing wasn't something I ever thought about.

My conversation with Amadeo from days ago plays in my mind.

"How safe do you think either of you were or would be in your brother's house now that Daddy is in the

ground? Have you ever wondered about his sudden death, by the way? He was a healthy, fit man, as I understood it at least."

My father had a heart attack. In some way, I understand Amadeo's doubt, though. And perhaps it's seeped into my own mind over the days. Another small, subtle victory for Amadeo. He has sown the doubt he intended to sow. I never thought about my father dying because he was so vital. So alive. And then, in the blink of an eye, he was gone.

"I didn't think this was about money. You told me you don't need our money," I say.

"Oh, I don't. It's not about that at all. It's about bringing your brother to his knees before I put a bullet between his eyes."

I flinch at the violence of his words. At their casual delivery.

"Your father's will is to be read in a few days. I suppose we'll all know more then."

"How do you know about my father's will?"

"I have made it my business to know everything I can about anything having to do with the Russo family. Are you ready?"

"You won't hurt Emma if I do this."

"I won't hurt a child."

"Or me. You won't hurt me."

"I would have no reason to. Come." He turns me toward the altar, but I pull back.

"Let us go," I say. He faces me. Watches me. I'm

begging after I swore I wouldn't. It's beneath me, but I am desperate. "After. After you get what it is you want. Let us go."

A long silence settles between us, the air heavy and so very still.

"Come, Vittoria."

I pull on his arm, remembering the way he'd looked at me when he'd kissed me. Remembering the kiss. It has to have meant something. "Please, Amadeo. I will do what you say, and I will only ask for this one thing."

He studies me, his face unreadable, but there's something in his eyes. That intensity of earlier. A flicker of it. And it gives me hope. Because without that flicker, I would be sure there is no human soul beneath the surface. There is only beast.

A door opens loudly, breaking into the moment. Disrupting it wholly. I glance over Amadeo's shoulder to see Father Paolo being escorted out into the church, looking disheveled. Like he dressed in a hurry.

Amadeo follows my gaze, then turns back to take my hand in his, his fingers closing around mine, swallowing mine up. And when I meet his eyes again, the moment is gone. My heart falls when he turns me toward the altar, and we take the final steps toward our doomed destiny.

23

AMADEO

I can't get the fucking kiss out of my fucking head. There's an intimacy to a kiss. It's more than sex. Or maybe that's her. Kissing her is like having my breath stolen. I don't know what the fuck it is, but I can't resist, and I do know better. Because when I kiss her, I do forget. I let myself forget. Bastian is right. And like an omen, a foretelling of our future as we stand here on the edge of destiny, that kiss sparked a fire, and I'm not sure it will leave anything but ash in its path.

There is no music for our wedding. No organist to start the ceremony. I don't wait for my bride at the altar, anticipating the first glimpse of her. No guests to stand when the cathedral doors are opened, and she appears veiled in white on the threshold. The disheveled priest adjusts his collar as he takes his place at the altar, the soldier at his back his companion. Bruno and his wife, Donatella, stand as our witnesses. They turn to watch me march Vittoria down the aisle. Her father will never have the honor.

Vittoria steps are heavy. The nape of her neck feels small in my hand. Delicate. Vulnerable. She's wearing dark leggings and a simple top. Her long, wavy hair is uncombed, her face free of makeup. She's stunning all the same, although I must admit, this isn't the wedding I ever thought I'd have. Not that I'd ever planned one. But like I told her days ago, it's not a love match I seek.

When we get to the kneelers, I urge Vittoria down to hers and settle into the one beside her. Out of habit, she puts her hands together in prayer. I do the same and turn my gaze up to Father Paolo, who clears his throat.

I don't like this man. This foolish coward. A few hundred euros and he'll willingly marry a woman who very clearly is not here of her own free will. Although, to be honest, if he'd put up a fight, he'd have been easily replaced. And this was going to happen. He, like everyone else, knows it. So why not line his own pockets?

The priest opens his book. A page marker falls out of it, and he looks down over his robes, unsure what to do.

"Leave it. Let's go," I tell him.

He grants Vittoria one quick glance before beginning, keeping his eyes on his Bible as he reads words I'm sure he's said a thousand times. When he starts a prayer, I clear my throat and shake my head.

"The vows," I say.

"We need—"

"The vows."

"Of course."

He closes the book and holds it to his chest with both hands. He's sweating. I guess he remembers the last time we were here. He mutters a few words to God before his eyes settle on Vittoria. I look at her profile. Watch her throat work as she swallows. Her gaze is impassive. She's a perfect stone statue at my side.

"Repeat after me," he instructs. "I, Vittoria Russo..." He pauses, and she repeats. "Take Amadeo Del Campo Caballero..." It's a mouthful. She repeats. "For my lawful husband. I will obey and serve him..." He pauses for her.

She clenches her jaw. When a long minute passes, the priest turns to me.

"My bride is shy," I say and lean close to Vittoria, who hasn't moved. Her fingers are intertwined, her knuckles white from the pressure. "Remember what's at stake, Dandelion."

She turns to me, her blue eyes as cold as glaciers, freezing me out. "I will obey and serve him."

"In sickness and in health forsaking all others so long as I shall live."

I modified the vows. Added what I needed and removed what I didn't.

Vittoria repeats the words robotically, and it's my turn. I don't wait for the priest.

"I, Amadeo Del Campo Caballero, take thee, Vittoria Russo, for my lawful wife to have and to hold until death do us part."

Vittoria watches me as I say my part. Whose death, I wonder. She's wondering the same thing.

"Rings," I say, turning back to the priest.

Father Paolo nods, and I reach into my pocket to produce two rings.

"With this ring, I thee wed," I say as I take her hand and slip hers onto her finger. It matches the band on the diamond engagement ring she chose. She doesn't even glance at it. I hold out the ring she will place on my finger. She takes it and roughly slides it on.

"With this ring, I thee wed," she says flatly, turning away as she does.

The priest begins to go into some reading, and I interrupt him again. "Pronounce us husband and wife."

I know he wants us gone, so he doesn't hesitate, lifting his hand to make the sign of the cross as he speaks the words.

"I now pronounce you husband and wife. What God has—"

"God has nothing to do with this union, Father,"

Vittoria says with more respect toward him than he deserves. She's right about God, though. He abandoned my family years ago if he'd ever cared about us at all.

Father Paolo looks at me for instruction. "My bride is right." I stand. "Thank you, Father." I hold my hand out to help Vittoria up, but she ignores it, rising on her own instead. "Your office?"

"I need time to prepare the forms."

"I have the paperwork," Bruno helpfully offers, stepping forward with his briefcase in hand.

Father Paolo nods and turns, and we follow him through the door at the back of the altar. Bruno and Donatella accompany us along with two soldiers. His office is at the end of a narrow corridor which is lit dimly. Once inside it, Father Paolo stands behind his desk, and Bruno opens his briefcase, setting several pages in front of him.

"Everything is in order," he says. "Just need your signature here." He points and even hands him a pen.

Father Paolo takes it and makes little effort to read it before quickly signing his name. Bruno turns to the next page, and he signs that as well. Once that's finished, Bruno nods to me.

"Thank you, Father. Make sure he's paid his due," I tell the soldier who ushers the priest out. Vittoria turns to follow him, but I capture her arm. "Just a few more things."

She glances at Bruno, at Donatella, then me.

"Donatella." I smile at her, and she steps forward to sign the papers where Bruno instructs. He's next, then me. And finally, I hand the pen to Vittoria. "Marriage certificate."

She nods, taking the pen. There's nothing for her to do but sign. We are legally married. And she does. It's the next document Bruno takes out of his briefcase after setting the marriage certificate inside it with a promise to file it the following day.

"It's ready for your signature, Vittoria," Bruno says with a gentle smile. I wonder about him some days. He comes across as kind. And he is. But he is loyal first. And truth be told, no man in my business is ever truly kind. They'd be eaten alive.

"What is it?" she asks him with a worried glance at me.

"This document will give your husband power of attorney over your finances."

She's confused or surprised or both. "What?"

"Amadeo will handle your finances. Of course, you see here an allowance has been set aside for you." He turns the pages searching for the clause.

"An allowance of my own money?"

"I was generous. Don't worry," I tell her.

She shakes her head. "I'm not signing that. No. It's too far."

I smile, take out my phone, and pull up the

photo Bastian sent. I turn the phone to her. "Emma's on her way."

I see the blood drain from her face as she processes the fact that she has no choice. This will be done.

She turns wet eyes up to mine, and when I look at them, I watch the single tear spill over and down her cheek. When I see that vulnerability bared, something shifts inside me. Like it did when I heard her cry out in terror as she slept, locked in a nightmare. And in that kiss we shared. A kinship of some sort. That brokenness inside her touching the brokenness inside me.

When she asked me earlier this evening to let her go when it was over, that, too, stirred my humanity, a thing I thought dead for too long. I understand her. But that's as far as this can go.

"You're going to take everything from us," she says.

I clench my jaw. If my brother were here, he'd tell me to get my head out of my ass. To remember the endgame. Would he be moved by her?

"What you asked for earlier," I start, pausing. Processing my own words. "I will give you that. I will set you free. You and Emma." I hear the heavy thudding of my own heart and wonder what the fuck I'm thinking. Saying. Doing. Because I know I won't break my promise to her. To anyone.

A crease forms between her brows. She's trying to puzzle out whether or not I'm lying.

"You have my word," I add.

She blinks, then looks down at the contract, at Bruno's outstretched hand with the pen. She turns once more to me, still trying to gauge the truth before taking the pen and signing her name.

24

VITTORIA

He will let us go. I have to hold on to that. It's a scrap, but I'll take it. The glimpse of Emma's face beside Bastian's was startling. He'd caught her just as she'd turned her shadowed eyes to the camera, awe and fear making them wide. Making the shadows that she's too young to bear darker.

I stand just inside Amadeo's bedroom in the Ravello house. After the ceremony and the signing away of my life, a helicopter came to carry Amadeo and me here. He instructed Oaf to take me to his bedroom and disappeared into another part of the house to deal with a call.

Emma is on her way. I have to focus on that. She's on a flight now with Hyacinth. They got her without having to hurt anyone. Although Amadeo was vague about that part.

I'm so grateful Hyacinth is with her. She'll be able to soothe her at least. Although the poor woman must be terrified herself. She is the live-in nanny my father hired to look after Emma once Mom died. She's in her early fifties and like a young grandmother to Emma.

I look around, then go into the bathroom to wash my face. His room is luxurious. A master suite bigger and more opulent than I've ever seen. The bedroom is decorated tastefully with antique furnishings and modern comforts, and an unbelievable view into the horizon that is disturbed only by the magenta of bougainvillea that clings to the banister on the balcony.

The bathroom is all marble and glass, twice the size of any at our penthouse. I splash water on my face now and pat it dry as I take myself in on this, my wedding day. I don't make a beautiful bride with my uncombed hair, the waves unbound and wild down my back, shadows beneath my eyes, and my skin drawn and paler than is natural. I've lost a few pounds since the funeral. Since before it. And it shows on my face.

But it doesn't matter. Emma will be with me in a matter of hours.

I hear the bedroom door open and Amadeo's voice as he relieves Oaf of the duty of guarding me. When the bedroom door clicks closed, I open the one to the bathroom and stand in the frame. I look at my husband.

He's wearing slacks and a button-down shirt with the top few buttons undone and the sleeves rolled up to his forearms. I see that tattoo. Dandelions. He has remembered that small detail for all these years. A significant enough detail for him to tattoo it into his skin. I was their mark when I was only five years old. They always meant to take me, use me to make my family pay. He finishes what he was doing on his phone and tucks it into his pocket. My heartbeat picks up when his eyes meet mine.

"How long until they're here?" I ask, avoiding what this night is. What has to happen.

"Not long."

"You said I could FaceTime with her."

"She's asleep." He takes out his phone, walks toward me, and shows me the screen. I read the exchange between him and his brother. Amadeo asking how it's going. Bastian saying fine, that she's been quiet, which I knew she would be, and that Emma has finally fallen asleep.

I'm disappointed, but I have to accept it. It's just a few more hours.

"Will they come here? Or will we go to the Naples house?"

"Here."

I nod, thinking about the promise he made at the

church. It surprised me that he made it at all. I don't know what I expected. But then his vow rings in my ears. *Until death do us part.* My death? He could have easily lied about letting Emma and I go to get me to sign the papers. He could have forced my signature. Since I signed those papers, all he really needs is to keep me alive until I turn twenty-one. Just a few more days. He'll need to show proof of life, but after, it won't matter. It's not like anyone will speak out to help me then.

But I have to believe he will keep his word. I have no choice. It's the only way to remain sane.

He steps toward the table set near one of the windows where a bottle of champagne sits in a silver bucket filled with ice, along with a half-full bottle of whiskey beside it. The champagne has been freshly placed. He pops the cork, and I watch the liquid bubble over the side as he pours two glasses. Does he really think we're doing this? Celebrating this?

He carries both glasses toward me and holds one out.

"To my beautiful bride." Is that mockery in his voice? Anything I saw in his eyes earlier is gone. I watch as he swallows the contents of one glass.

I snort. "You mean your forced bride." We're firmly back on our separate sides of this boxing ring. I wonder if he needs to do this to be able to continue. If he needs to see me as an enemy, an enemy and a pawn, to do what he is going to do. What needs to happen.

"You are beautiful," he says as he looks at me closely. I feel myself flush. He must see it because he smiles. "Drink it."

"No, thank you. I'm tired."

"Already," he says. "That does not bode well for a long marriage, considering it's our wedding night." I watch him down the contents of the second glass before setting both aside and looking me over, one corner of his mouth lifting. "Get undressed."

"Déjà vu."

He steps toward me, amusement brightening his eyes. "Nah. Last time was to search you. Tonight is to fuck you." Heat flushes through me at his crude words. I should be offended, but when he lifts the hair off my shoulders, letting it fall between his fingers almost fondly and sets it back, it's not offense I feel. My lips swell with an ache to be bruised by his, and my body remembers the touch of his hands on me. The promise he made to finish what he started.

"If you want to get off, you're going to have to use your hand tonight. I'm not sleeping with you." I say it with more force than I feel and move to step away, but he captures my arm and tugs me back.

"You want it as much as I do, Dandelion. Don't lie to yourself. Never lie to yourself. That's another life lesson from me. You're welcome."

"You're an asshole, you know that?" I tug, but he doesn't let go.

He grins, but a moment later, that amusement is gone. "Our marriage will be consummated."

I falter momentarily but catch myself. I can't give him everything. I need to control some part of this. "I have a better idea. How about if we don't fuck and say we did?"

"You don't back down. I like that about you, Dandelion. It may be my favorite part."

"Should I be flattered?"

"Rules are rules. You can blame the church. Get undressed."

"You know what? I think I'll have that drink after all. It'll help tamp down the nausea."

He releases me and walks to the table to pour me a glass. "I don't recall you feeling nauseous when I touched you before." He pauses, and I think he's finished, but he continues. "Or when I kissed you."

His tone is different during that last part. The kiss. I'm surprised he brings it up and glad he has his back to me so he can't see my face. But I wonder, given how he sounded, how he's not looking at me, either, if it impacted him like it did me.

It's my turn to look away when he carries the glass to me. I try the door, knowing it's locked, and if it isn't, I'm not going anywhere anyway. He holds the champagne out for me when I face him again. I take it, swallowing it all down then immediately coughing because the bubbles are too much.

He grins. "Take it easy, Dandelion. We have all

night. No need to rush things." He takes the glass and sets it aside.

"That's not what I was doing."

He sets one big hand over my stomach. My back is to the door, and he's as close as he can be without our bodies touching. His face grows serious. "This has to happen. You can fight it and make it hard for yourself, or you can enjoy it and make it easy. Either way, I'll be sure to make you come. Ladies first and all."

"How romantic you are. I don't want to come."

"We've talked about this. Everyone wants to come."

"I don't want to come with you."

"Is there someone else? My brother, perhaps? He'll have his turn."

"This isn't a joke," I say only after a long pause to process the last of what he said.

"No, it's not a joke, Dandelion," he says seriously. "But it does need to happen, and it will happen." He studies me, dark eyes searching my face. "I won't hurt you. You don't have to be afraid."

I blink at his words. And when I understand his meaning, I have to laugh. It's a strange, unhinged sort of sound, and it clearly throws him off.

He is expecting me to be a virgin. Should I tell him? Prepare him for disappointment?

Amadeo eyes me, but I keep my face expressionless. I will give him nothing. The woman he glimpsed in my eyes when he kissed me, I won't give him that. Not when he will take what he plans to take from me.

He shifts his gaze to my top and begins to unbutton it. I watch his fingers work. They sear my skin at every touch, and I remain perfectly still when he pulls the shirt open and displays my bra.

I drag my gaze up to his.

"Very beautiful." He leans toward me, kisses me. It's a stolen kiss that doesn't last long enough for me to have to respond. To decide if I'm fighting him or kissing him back. I'm grateful for that.

His focus moves back to my body, my bra. I watch his big, calloused hands as he tucks the lace cup of each beneath my breasts, exposing them. The small, round mounds stand high, the nipples turned upward and taut as if already submitting to him. He dips his head, making me gasp when he licks one, then takes it into his mouth and sucks.

My hands come to his shoulders, fingers weaving into his hair, and when he sucks on that nipple, I feel sensation move straight through the center of my body and explode at my core. I can't help the low, deep moan that comes from inside my chest.

He straightens with a grin. He is victorious. "No nausea then?"

I swallow hard, trying to remind my body how it should feel at his touch. But when he draws his shirt over his head and tosses it onto the bed, I can't help how my eyes move over his shoulders, his arms, that dandelion tattoo, his muscular, scarred chest. It takes all I have to drag my gaze back up to his.

"Will you make me?" I ask.

"It has to happen."

"I'm asking if you will make me."

He holds my gaze as he slips my shirt off my shoulders and lets it slide to the floor. The bra is next. Unhooked and discarded. And all the while, I stand still as if trapped, locked in place.

"Dandelion," he says, sliding his hand into my leggings, my panties, making my breath catch when his fingers find their target. "I won't have to make you." My legs tremble as his fingers do their work. I wrap my hands around his shoulders to stay upright as a whimper escapes my throat. With a grin, he pinches my clit and forces a cry. I'm not sure if it's of pain or pleasure. He draws his hand from my leggings and brings his mouth to my ear. "You'll beg me for it."

I swallow hard, hearing the clear mockery in his voice and shake my head to dissipate this fog. My hands turn into claws in his hair. I hold him tight to me and bite down hard on his earlobe.

He mutters a curse, drawing back, one hand circling my throat in a very different grip than a moment ago. He presses me to the door as the other hand moves to his ear to gauge the damage. His fingers come away bloody.

"I will never beg you for anything, Amadeo. Never."

"That was a mistake." He shifts his grip to my wrists, twisting my arms behind my back as he marches me toward the bed.

"You play with me. You fucking mock me. What do you expect me to do? Not fight? What sick pleasure does it give you?" I ask. He deposits me onto the bed facedown and rips my leggings and panties from me. Then he flips me onto my back and straddles me, capturing my wrists again as I struggle against him, needing to fight him.

I glance at his ear. It's bleeding but not bad enough. I should have torn it off.

"Do you need me to make you? Is that what this is?" he asks, tone low but angry, any playfulness gone.

"You would, wouldn't you? To get what you want."

"Will it make you hate yourself a little less if I did that, Dandelion?"

"Stop fucking calling me that! My name is Vittoria."

"Answer my question, *Vittoria*." He leans in close, his voice a warning. "Will it make you hate yourself a little less for wanting me if I make you?"

I renew my battle against him because he's got it exactly right. He has read me like a book. If I surrender, I will hate myself. If I fight, if he makes me, I can hate him. I just need to push him a little farther even though I know I'm treading on thin ice. I'm powerless against him physically. He will always win when the fight is physical. But I have one weapon that can wound him deeply.

"You accuse my brother of having raped your sister. If you do this to me, how are you any different?"

25

AMADEO

The world goes sideways as my brain rattles inside my head. I look down at her. She's trapped beneath me, no match for me physically.

I know what this is. The logical, sensible side of my brain understands. If she gives herself to me, she will not be able to blame me. If she angers me, she believes she will force my hand. And, in turn, she believes I will force her submission. It would be easier to swallow if she can blame me. Hate me.

And this. What I'm doing. Given the sheer difference between us in size and strength, it's exactly what she wants.

I let go of her wrists and climb off the bed. I cross the room to where the bottle of champagne sits in melting ice but choose the whiskey instead. I pour myself a healthy serving and swallow it down, then pour another. I glance out the window at the vast, night sky, the stars. At this time of night, it's hard to see where the ocean ends and the sky begins.

When I turn back to her, she's sitting on the edge of the bed. She's oblivious of her nakedness, and in her eyes, I see her waiting, watching me, trying to anticipate my next move. Does she expect anger? Was that accusation to anger me into action? Or was it to stop me?

"I am nothing like your brother. Never say that to me again." I barely recognize my own voice.

She stares wide-eyed, and I swear I see the glimmer of guilt in her eyes.

"I am your husband."

"By force. Not by my choice."

"Your protector."

"My protector! That's rich. You took everything from me."

"I've promised to give you what you asked for. Your sister. And in time, your freedom."

"And I'm just supposed to believe you. You desecrated my father's body. You kidnapped me. You say I am in danger from my brother, but what about you? What dangers lurk for me in your house? In your bed?"

My chest feels tight. She's right in a way. If I force her, how am I any different? Me being her protector, it's true on one hand. But on the other, who will protect her from me? From my brother?

I swallow the contents of my glass, feeling the alcohol burn its way down.

What kind of beast does she think me? That I'd do that to her? Even if she is a Russo, I wouldn't want that for her. For any woman. My mind wanders to Hannah, but I don't allow it to linger there. "No danger will touch you in my home, Vittoria."

"Really? Everything that's happened has happened *to* me. You've done what you've done *to* me. You've stolen my life. You tell me not to lie to myself. Then don't lie to yourself either, Amadeo."

"Are we talking about honesty, then? Okay, let's do that." I feel myself losing my patience. "What was your life exactly before?" I stalk toward her. "What are you hiding? What happened in that lost year?"

She wavers, forehead furrowing. Eyes searching for answers I don't have. The thing is, I don't think she has them either.

"Or don't you know?" I ask.

She draws the blanket onto her lap, looking away uncertainly. "I don't know what you're talking about."

"What am I going to find out about Dr. Tilbury? Because I know a little already. A clue about his *treatments*." I put air quotes around that last word. It was why I didn't come up here right away once the chopper landed. Bruno was already able to find out a few things about this Dr. James Tilbury and his *therapy*. "Do you know his specialty?"

"Stop." She gets up, picks up my discarded shirt, which is the nearest thing to her, and slips it on. It's strange to see her do that. Is she shielding herself from me, or is she taking comfort from something of mine? If it's the latter, it's subconscious. But what does it mean? And why does seeing her in it do something to me? When she tries to walk around me, I don't allow it. Because if we're talking about honesty, she's going to face some shit too.

"He wipes memories, Vittoria."

She stares up at me, no fury in her eyes now. Uncertainty has replaced anger. Fear even.

"He treats a very exclusive clientele with unique needs."

"What?"

"Not that it matters for you. The past is the past. There's no going back. No changing it. But I do want to know something. What memories was your father wiping away? Because he paid Tilbury a hefty sum."

She won't look at me. "I don't want to talk about this." She turns to walk away but I capture her arm to halt her.

I take her chin in my hand and tilt her face up to mine. "What's the matter? Too much truth for you?"

She squeezes her eyes shut and jerks her head away. She presses the heels of her hands into her eyes. I keep hold of one arm.

"Although I guess if Tilbury was good at what he claimed he could do, you won't remember. So let's move on about me stealing your life away. Your father stood between you and your brother. He shielded you from some ugly shit, but he's dead now." She shakes her head, opens her mouth, but I continue. "Do you know the man your brother is? Because as bad as Geno Russo was, Lucien is the real demon. Your father's mistake was that he allowed it to happen again and again and just kept on cleaning up after his boy."

"Let me go." She struggles, twisting, not answering my question. "Please."

"I thought you weren't going to beg me." She grits her jaw. I hold tight, leaning my face to hers. "Tell me something. What does it say about me, about Bastian, about your brother that you're so afraid for your sister that you're willing to bring her here? Into the enemy's lair? What does that tell you, Dandelion?"

"She's safe with me," she says weakly.

"I told you I'd give you your freedom. I gave you my word."

"You wouldn't have to give it to me if you hadn't taken my freedom in the first place. You wanted to marry me so you could steal my inheritance when you say this isn't about money."

"Oh, it's not, and you know it."

"I don't know any such thing. You'll own a piece of a company you hate and partner with my brother, a man you claim raped your sister!"

Gritting my teeth, I cross the room to refill my glass again. Drink it. Pour myself more, but I find I can't swallow that one.

Those words spoken aloud. The image they conjure. Hannah. Sweet, young Hannah, whose innocence was stolen. Whose life was snatched. I could have protected her. I should have known. Paid attention. For Vittoria to compare what I'm doing with her to that, it's an insult. Worse.

"We wouldn't be partnering. I would never partner with an animal like him. What I plan is the absolute annihilation of the Russo name from this earth."

"I'm a Russo too, remember?"

"Not anymore. Now you're my wife. Caballero."

"My father's blood runs in my veins. In my sister's veins. You can't change that."

I almost say something then. Almost. But I keep my mouth shut. The truth is, I don't want to hurt her, and that knowledge will hurt her.

"What about that, Amadeo? Did you think about that when you promised to let me go?"

"You don't know anything, Vittoria."

"Or were you lying just to get me to sign those papers?"

"Enough!" I hurl my glass against the wall, smashing it.

Vittoria jumps. I look at her standing there in my shirt, which is too big on her, and all that hair like a tangled crown around her head. Her beauty is distracting. Her damage more so. I need to focus. Do what I need to do.

As I wipe my mouth with the back of my hand and stalk toward her, I remind myself what this night is about.

Her eyes grow huge. I wonder what she sees in me. She takes a step backward but stops herself. I remember the nightmare and how she woke from it. What I see in her eyes now is the consequence of damage. Damage makes survivors of us. And she's strong.

I see the moment she makes the decision and steels herself. Standing tall, she faces me, ready for me.

I wrap one arm around her waist, tug my shirt off her in one fell swoop, and grip a handful of hair. I tug her head backward and look down at her. I don't mean to kiss her. It is not my intention to kiss her because that is dangerous territory for me. Kissing her does something to me.

Her eyes turn into the iciest sapphires, and I don't have to think about it because it's she who kisses me. She presses her mouth to mine. I'm stunned for one fleeting moment before I kiss her back, devouring her, wanting to feel what I felt when I kissed her before. Needing that thread of connection. Needing to see the same in her. Feel it from her. And fuck, how I hate myself for that need.

Maybe we're more alike than I want to admit.

It will be easier for her if I take what I need tonight. It will be easier for me if she makes me do just that. Then we can hate each other like we should. But when she gives herself to me like this, wrapping her arms around me and drawing me down onto the bed, I feel the tables turning again. Feel her maneuvering, somehow gaining power when she should have none.

I pull back, hands on either side of her, and look into her dark eyes, thin rings of blue around the blacks of her pupils. She pants, reaching up to wrap clawed hands around my biceps, dragging me toward her.

"Do it," she says, one hand moving to unbuckle my belt.

I dip my head to kiss her again. She tastes sweet when she should taste bitter. And when she slides her hand into my briefs and fists my cock, squeezing it, I groan and draw back.

"Do it. Fuck me."

I suck air into my lungs and look her over.

"I want you to do it."

I drag the fingernails of one hand over her chest, pinching one nipple before slapping the breast only to hear her cry out, to watch her eyes, those fucking eyes, grow soft with tears. Pain I cause.

I turn away. I can't look at her. Can't kiss her. I should take what I need to take and fucking walk away, but she is kissing me again, and I can't resist her when her fist tightens around my cock.

"Do it, Amadeo. Fuck me like you want to fuck me. Fuck me and show me how much you hate me."

It's too much, all of this. What should have happened. How it was meant to be. How I was supposed to feel. The nothingness that should be between us. We are both broken, and that damage has bound us in a way it shouldn't. A way it was never meant to.

She kisses me deeply yet again, and here comes that inferno, a blaze of scorching flames that will leave only ash and smoke in its wake.

I break the kiss. I can't look at her.

Knowing I should be gentle tonight of all nights for her first time, I flip her onto her stomach and draw her hips up, holding her, opening her, and thrusting into her hard enough to make her cry out.

This is what I want. Her cry. It's all I should ever want.

But something isn't right.

I draw out, look down, and thrust again. The resistance I expect isn't there. She's tight, so fucking tight, but there's no blood. She's not a virgin.

But when she arches her back and moans beneath me, all thought vanishes, and I'm focused on her, wholly on her.

After I slide the fingers of one hand to her clit, she begins to meet my thrusts, burying her face in the blankets as she takes her pleasure from me. When I feel her walls pulse around my cock and see her fist the sheets and hear her moan my name, I come undone. I look down at her. I watch her lay the side of her face on my bed, sweat beading her forehead and making her hair stick to her face. Those pale strands catch in thick, dark lashes, obscuring her eyes as she watches me. The look inside them makes me thrust once more and seat myself deep inside her as I come hard. Filling her as she pants for breath, giving herself to me. Does she do it to save herself? To make some sort of strange cease-fire. A faulty truce. I don't know. All I know at this moment as my mind swims is that I cannot look away from those eyes that I should hate.

26

BASTIAN

The kid is strange. She hasn't uttered a word or even made a sound. Not to me, not that I expected that, but not to her nanny either. Nothing. I guess it's shock? She did stare at me for a long time. But if we were having a staring contest, then the kid won. I looked away first. Had to. I wonder if the scar on my cheek has captivated her. It matches hers in a way. She got that in the crash that killed her mom. Glass sliced through her face. I think about her brutal father and wonder if she was lucky. I'm pretty sure his intention wasn't to scar her.

Once we reach the villa, before I'm even fully out of the SUV, the front doors fly open. I climb the stairs leading up to them. An anxious Vittoria comes rushing out, followed by my brother, who has his hands in his pockets. Vittoria stops dead when she sees me. Or maybe it's when she sees her sister.

Because the little girl is asleep in my arms, her head warm on my shoulder. Vittoria takes this in and is clearly surprised. I guess she thought her sister would run screaming from the ogre she believes me to be.

I let her take it in, my gaze moving to her left hand, the gleaming diamond and the shiny new wedding band. My brother comes toward us, reaching to brush the mass of curly blond hair from the girl's face so he can see her. What I see when he does it is the matching platinum band on his finger.

Why does it fucking bother me? I knew what would happen when I left.

But there's something else, too. They both have wet hair. Fresh from a shower, I guess. He was determined to consummate the marriage. I understand that. But I expected more animosity between them than anything else after. She should hate him. But it's not hate I feel coming off either of them. There's something new between them. A thing that leaves me very firmly on the outside.

Vittoria hugs, then whispers to the nanny, who is close behind me. She takes the little stuffed pig that had finally slipped from Emma's fingers when she fell asleep along with her pink backpack and touches the little girl's head once again.

"I'll take her to her bed," I say, and walk into the house between my brother and his wife, less ready to see them, to converse with them or confront them, than I thought I would be.

It's early morning, orange light just breaking the horizon. The house is situated so you can see the sun rise from one side and the sun set from the other. Inside, it's still quiet. Everyone's still asleep.

Jostling her as little as possible, I carry the sleeping girl up to the room prepared for her and the nanny. I'm surprised she doesn't wake. Surprised she can sleep so deeply considering. But maybe that's kids.

Amadeo opens the bedroom door. Vittoria is on my heels as I enter. Two beds stand at opposite sides of the room, one for the kid and one for the nanny. The walls are still white, but the bedding is pink, and there's a pink carpet on the floor as well as a giant dollhouse, also pink, with dolls inside, a slew of toys and books, and clothes in the closet.

Vittoria looks surprised by what she sees but hurries to pull the covers back on one of the beds, and I lay the little girl down. Her curly blond hair settles like a halo around her little face, her nose an upturned button, her mouth open. Her eyes remain closed as Vittoria covers her, then sits on the edge of the bed, caressing that mass of hair. My brother stands beside me as we take it in. See Vittoria with this tiny girl. See how she wipes a tear from her eyes and looks at her like she can't believe she's here.

Love. This is the physical manifestation of

unconditional love, and it's hard to watch. Harder to look away.

Amadeo pats my back. We should go. Leave Vittoria to her reunion. He and I walk quietly out of the room and down the stairs to the kitchen, leaving the women with the sleeping girl.

I make myself a double espresso while he watches when what I want is whiskey. I wonder what he sees on my face. My brother knows me.

"Congratulations," I say, the grinder loud. I tamp the coffee down, slide the portafilter into the espresso machine, and flip the lever to watch the black liquid turn creamy. I switch it off and take the cup, holding it up to him in a mock toast. The action is too animated. Too unlike me.

"It's a piece of paper," he reminds me, hands in his pockets again as he leans against the counter. He looks refreshed. Almost relaxed. But fucking does that to you. Takes the edge off. I feel the opposite.

I drink the burning hot espresso before talking. "The girl didn't utter one word."

"I'm sure that'll change when she wakes up."

"No, it was strange. Something is off."

Just then, Vittoria pushes the door of the kitchen open and enters. I'm used to seeing her escorted by a guard or by my brother or myself. This is new. What happened between them that she's allowed to roam free?

"Thank you," she says to me, and she looks like

she's about to hug me but stops short. "Thank you for bringing her to me." The relief is clear in her tone.

I shrug. "It was more for us than you, Dandelion." She winces at my cold delivery. I've hit my mark. Put her back in her corner where she belongs. Because I like the look of my brother and our enemy standing side by side less and less.

Amadeo studies me as Vittoria fumbles for words.

"What's wrong with her?" I ask, putting my empty espresso cup in the sink and tucking my hands into my pockets.

"Nothing is wrong with her," she says defensively.

"She doesn't talk. Not a peep. That's not normal."

"I meant medically. There's nothing wrong with her. The therapist calls it selective mutism."

My brother and I exchange a glance.

"She hasn't spoken a word since our mother died," Vittoria finishes.

Amadeo's eyes meet mine. It's clear he knows as much about this as I do.

"Was she scared of you?" Vittoria asks.

I shrug a shoulder. "Maybe. I don't know. I told her I was bringing her to you so maybe not." I was surprised the girl didn't startle when I showed up at the therapist's office. Surprised when she set her hand in mine so easily.

"She's afraid of men. Our father... she was terrified of him. And Lucien."

"She's a smart kid, then."

Amadeo wraps a hand around the back of her neck possessively. He turns her to face him. Her cheeks flush when she meets his eyes, and something ugly gnaws inside me to see them like this. To be on the outside.

"Go to bed, Vittoria. She'll wake up soon enough, and you need to get some rest."

She makes a point of looking around the room. "No oaf to escort me?"

"Oaf?" Amadeo asks.

"A soldier. I'm guessing you don't want me wandering around your big house."

"You won't do anything that would put your sister and her nanny in jeopardy." A very subtle warning. Maybe it was smart to bring the little girl. "Go to bed. You'll see her when she wakes up."

She nods, and when he drops his hand from her neck, she looks up at me. Something passes between us. Not gratitude but something else. Then she's gone, and my brother and I are alone.

"You should probably get some sleep too. Doesn't look like you've had much," I tell him.

He sits down at the table instead and looks at me expectantly. I take the seat opposite his.

"I'm glad you're home safe, brother."

I nod because he is genuine. I know that.

"Everything is signed. I have control. Once the will is read and her inheritance transferred to her name, we'll own half of Russo Properties & Holdings."

"Marriage is consummated?" I hear myself ask it and hate myself for it.

He nods once, watching my reaction. I get up and grab the whiskey from the cupboard, along with two water glasses. Nothing fancy in here. I pour us both some.

"She's ours," he says when I sit back down.

"You did what you needed to do. I get that. I don't need to hear about it."

"That missing year, she was at some clinic. Told me the name of the doctor, and Bruno already—"

"I don't care." I swallow my drink and shove back from the table to stand.

He stands, too, and blocks my path to the door. "Bastian."

"What?"

"We knew what needed to happen going in."

"Yeah, well, it's different when it happens in front of your fucking eyes, I guess. You two cozy now?"

"It's not like that."

"I saw how you looked at her. How you held her." I take a breath. "It's fine, brother. I get it. Spoils of war go to the king." I shove past him, but he slaps a hand on my chest. "What? I'm fucking tired."

"I did what I had to do. You know that."

"Hardship though it was. You say she's ours. Let me ask you this. If I were to go up there and take what is ours to my bed, how would you feel about it?" He sets his jaw, and I snort. "Thought so."

"It's not like that."

"It doesn't matter. You just make sure you don't lose your head. She may warm your bed, but she'll stab you in the back the minute she gets the chance to run."

"Something happened to her, Bastian."

I take a deep breath in and wait for him to continue.

"That doctor wipes memories. Some sort of hypnosis or some shit. She's missing a year. She was locked away in that place for a fucking year."

I don't want to care about that. I fold my arms across my chest.

"She wasn't a virgin," he adds.

I tense at his words. I. Do. Not. Care. I cannot care. "That doesn't mean anything."

"Do you think she had a boyfriend under her father's watchful eye?"

I shrug a shoulder, trying to feign nonchalance. "Maybe she fucked a soldier or two or a dozen. What do we know? Maybe she's a sl—"

"Don't call her that."

"Got your hackles up?"

"She's not that. You know it."

I shrug a shoulder. "All I'm saying is why do we

care? About any of it? We're not supposed to care, remember?"

"But we do."

I don't answer. I'm not going to lie.

"Something happened to her, and that quack wiped it away."

I push my hand through my hair and take a deep breath in. "I'm tired. I need to get some sleep."

He sighs.

"We'll talk. I can't fucking think straight right now. I've been up for almost twenty-four hours."

"I know. Thanks for getting the kid."

"Someone had to. Good night, brother."

27

VITTORIA

While the brothers are in the kitchen and I'm allowed upstairs unguarded, I slip back into Amadeo's room, although I have no intention of sleeping there. During my exploration of the room while he showered, I found something that belonged to me. The small dagger he confiscated from me the night he brought me here was tucked into a nightstand drawer and forgotten.

I hurry to retrieve it, then walk into the closet to change into a pair of sleeping shorts and a silk tank top, one of the vast selection of clothes for me hanging here, tags still attached. I guess Amadeo figured out a suitcase with a week's worth of clothes, most of which have been ruined wasn't going to last and, considering the number of things he bought, I wonder how long he plans to keep us.

Taking a pillow from the bed, I tuck the dagger into the case. In case I run into one of the brothers or another soldier, I will be prepared. The bed is still rumpled from where we made love. No, not made love. Why would I even think those words? We fucked. And I don't want to think about how I told him to do it. How I did not fight him. How I came.

The space between my legs aches as I make myself turn from the bed and walk toward the door. I can't unpack what happened just yet. Things between us should be cut and dry. He is my captor. I am his hostage. We negotiated a deal. Period, the end. But it's gotten complicated. Even seeing Bastian tonight with Emma asleep in his arms has thrown me off.

I give my head a shake. It's late. I'm tired. That's all this is.

Crossing the hallway, I quietly step into Emma's room, grateful not to run into anyone on my way. Neither Emma nor Hyacinth stir as I slip the dagger from the pillowcase and look around for where to hide it. The room is stocked with toys, dolls, books, and clothes bursting from drawers in the closet. I choose a shoebox, take the sandals out and set them on the floor, then set the dagger at the bottom and stuff two sweaters on top. I place it on the highest rack where there's no danger of my sister finding it. Then I return to the bedroom.

Hyacinth stirs, smiles when she sees me, and

falls back asleep. She's been with us since Mom died. And she loves Emma as much as I do.

Picking up the pillow I brought in, I slip into the bed next to Emma, wrap an arm around her warm little body, and smell the familiar scent of her shampoo as I close my eyes. But that's not all I smell. The pillow I grabbed must be Amadeo's. I pick up his scent as I turn my face into it. Something flutters in my stomach. He could have taken what he wanted to take from me and cast me aside. Locked me back in my room. Or worse. He could have denied me Emma and left my sister in my brother's house. He didn't do any of those things. And while I know he can use Emma to force my hand, he could have forced me anyway. He didn't need to bring her.

And then there's Bastian. The way his eyes look at me like they will see right into me. The fervor inside them that he doesn't hide as easily as his brother. The way Emma slept so peacefully, her head on his shoulder. The gentle way he carried her.

He's different than Amadeo. He is perhaps more comfortable with his hate of me. But there's more, and I'm curious to know what is behind it all, which makes this harder. Which is why I need to keep one thing in mind. I need to get Emma and Hyacinth out of here. I need for Amadeo to keep his word, and if I have the opportunity to escape him, escape them, I will take it. So as much as I am aware of how deeply

I'm inhaling the lingering scent of Amadeo's aftershave on the pillow, I need to keep my goal in sight.

Survive.

Get us out.

Once we're safely away from the brothers, I'll figure out the rest.

With those thoughts, I hug the tiny body beside me, and I let myself drift to sleep.

I WAKE TO A SQUEEZE OF SMALL ARMS AROUND MY neck that instantly bring a smile to my face. I open my eyes to find Emma's locked on me in disbelief.

"Oh, sweetheart," I say, hugging her tight to me, nuzzling my face in her soft curls and just breathing a silent prayer of gratitude that she is here, she is truly here in my arms and safe.

Safe from one evil, at least.

I draw back to look at her, masking anything but joy on my face. She sits up, rubs her eyes with her stuffed pig, Rosie, and looks around the room, big brown eyes huge, little mouth open. I sit up too and see Hyacinth is slowly waking.

Emma puts her hand on my cheek, and I turn to her. She makes a questioning motion with her hands, her shoulders hunching up. What I told Bastian and Amadeo was about the extent of it. My little sister hasn't spoken a word since our mother's death. Trauma. She can hear me. And she is capable of speech. But the death of our mother, and most likely being trapped in the car with her body for hours, literally left her speechless.

The therapy I insisted we send her to hasn't helped at all. And the only people she has felt at ease with in the last year have been Hyacinth and me. Even at the daycare she attends for a few hours a week purely to get her around other children, she doesn't speak. Hasn't made a single friend.

There is hope, though. The condition can reverse itself.

"This is your new room while we stay with the brothers," I tell her, not really sure how to explain it. "Isn't it nice? And look at all the toys and books. I bet they have some of your favorites in there."

She looks at the bookshelf, then scoots off the bed and goes to it. Hyacinth and I exchange a quiet glance as we watch her choose a book and, smiling, carry it back to me, climbing back up onto the bed after handing it to me.

The Gruffalo. It's one of her favorites. Mine too.

She sits with her legs crossed and points at the book, then must see the rings on my finger. She cocks her head to the side and rubs the diamond, then looks up at me.

"Should we read it?" I ask, unsure how to explain that I am married, but she doesn't seem to grasp their significance and nods, focusing on the book. I read it to her while Hyacinth goes into the bathroom to run her a bath.

"Lots of toys in here, too, Emma," she says. "Even a pink toothbrush for you."

Emma smiles, sets the book on her pillow, and climbs off the bed, then reaches for my hand.

I stand and let her lead me into the bathroom, where she brushes her teeth at the sink. Hyacinth switches off the water, and I can see the questions in her eyes.

"Into the bath with you, little Emma," she says, helping her with her clothes, the same things I guess she was wearing to the daycare. I recognize them.

Hyacinth and I settle on the edge of the bath, and I begin to tell her what's going on. Who Bastian is, for starters. I ask Emma if he was nice to her. She shrugs a shoulder and nods. When I ask her if she was scared, she puts her fingers together to show me that she was a little scared.

"He was very gentle with her," Hyacinth says when Emma has her back to us. She's playing with a toy while I shampoo her hair. "Asked her if she wanted to come see you. She slipped her hand right into his, which surprised me. All those men, it was pretty terrifying," she whispers so only I can hear. "What's going on? Are you all right?" She looks at the rings on my hand.

I nod. "I don't know how much you or Emma saw of the funeral."

"I took her away when…"

"Thank you."

She puts a hand on my shoulder and gives it a squeeze.

"Are you…?" She trails off and is interrupted by Emma turning to show us one of the toys.

"Who's hungry for breakfast? I know I am," I say, needing time to figure out how to explain things to Hyacinth. Emma, I can distract for now.

Emma rubs her belly and nods.

"Hyacinth, if you can help Emma get dressed, I'll just go put something on. We'll get you some fresh clothes too." I think she should be Francesca's size.

But when I turn to go, Emma's face gets serious, and she grabs me, shaking her head frantically.

"It's okay. I'll be right back. My clothes are down the hall. I promise. I'll be right back. Maybe we can both wear pink dresses today. What do you think?"

That seems to appease her although her eyebrows are still furrowed. I'm able to slip away to Amadeo's room, where I notice the bed has been made, and I wonder if he slept here at all. I don't see any soldiers but do hear them downstairs, and I hurry to dress, putting on the first pink sundress I come across, simple and pretty and not too revealing. I find a pair of flat sandals and just take a quick glance in the mirror to comb through my hair, working it into a ponytail as I hurry back to Emma's room.

She's pulling on her shoes, the same ones she always wears. She loves them. They're a pair of sparkly multicolored tennis shoes Mom gave her for her last birthday. Luckily, they'd been too big for her then because since Mom's passing, she wears them almost exclusively, and it shows.

I take her hand, and we head to the kitchen. Hyacinth follows us, and I'm watchful for the brothers. I'm grateful when Amadeo walks out of his study when we get down the stairs.

"Vittoria," he says, looking me over before his gaze moves to Hyacinth. He nods to her. "Good morning. I'm Amadeo."

"Morning," she says cautiously. "Hyacinth."

"This must be little Emma," he says, crouching down in front of her. Surprising me completely.

Emma leans away a little and glances up at me, then she looks at him, studying his face as he does hers. He smiles and holds out his hand.

"It's very nice to meet you," he says.

She glances at me again, and I nod, so she puts her tiny hand in his giant one. He gives it a gentle shake, then lets it go.

"You must be hungry." He stands.

"We are," I say.

"Well, I hope you like pancakes because there are about a hundred stacks in the kitchen."

Emma's eyes grow huge, and her mouth falls open. I smile. She's so literal at her age.

"Come on, I'll take you in and introduce you to Francesca and my mom. They're the cooks, meaning they're the most important people in this house, especially regarding things like cookies." He winks at her, and although she doesn't quite smile, she's curious. He's speaking almost exclusively to her, which is surprising to me. As surprising as his gentle tone, which he has used with me very rarely and mostly to get what he wants.

"Amadeo," I say, touching his arm. "Hyacinth needs some clothes. I wonder if maybe Francesca would lend her something?"

He looks at her. "Of course. I'll get it taken care of."

We follow him into the kitchen, where Francesca and Amadeo's mom turn to greet us from where they're standing at the stove flipping pancakes. Although there aren't a hundred stacks, there are quite a few.

Amadeo introduces Emma. His mom's face beams with a smile and she hurries to the little girl, crouching to take her cheeks into her hands and caressing her hair before pulling her into a hug.

"Aren't you the prettiest thing," she says to her, and I'm surprised when Emma slips her hand from mine and pats the older woman's back. "Oh, goodness," Nora continues, drawing back a little and wiping a tear away. "I remember when Hannah was your age," she says, smiling and straightening. "Would you like some pancakes, Emma?"

Emma nods, and Nora takes Emma's hand to lead her to the table while I stand watching in amazement. Emma sets Rosie on the table and pulls an empty plate closer for her while Nora takes the seat to one side and starts to load Emma's plate with pancakes.

"She can't eat that much—"

Amadeo puts his hand on my shoulder to stop me from going forward to help. "It doesn't matter." He watches his mother with as much awe as I am watching Emma as she picks up her fork and puts a dripping bite of pancake into her mouth. Nora wipes her chin with a smile, and Emma pretend-feeds Rosie, then looks up at me and points at the chair beside hers.

I sit down as Amadeo arranges for Francesca to take Hyacinth and lend her some fresh clothes. He then makes coffee and joins us at the table, setting the mug in front of me.

"You're a quiet little girl, aren't you? Well, nothing wrong with that," Nora carries on. "I hope you like the toys and books. And we have a swimming pool."

"She can't swim yet," I say, getting Nora's attention. She smiles at me, but her gaze is drawn right back to Emma. "Emma, you can't go into the pool without me, okay? It's a rule," I say.

"Bastian loves to swim. He can teach her. His father taught him." She says this last part more to herself.

"I have to take care of some business. I thought you'd just like to explore the house with Emma," Amadeo says.

"Where's your brother?" Bastian unsettles me. Seeing him carry Emma in so gently last night was at odds with the man I'm trying to create in my mind, so until I figure out how to handle him, my plan is simple. Avoid him.

"He hasn't come downstairs yet. We'll talk this afternoon once Emma's settled."

I nod as he stands. "Thank you."

"Swim, maybe. It's going to be hot, and she'll like that, I think. Do you like to swim, Emma?"

She looks up at him, her face not as relaxed as with Nora, but not like it used to be around dad the few times he was around her after the accident. I wondered if it was too hard for him to see her, to see the scar on her face and be reminded of what happened, what he lost.

Emma surprises me again when she nods, communicating with him.

"Good." He shifts his attention to me for a moment, then he's gone. I'm baffled. I'm not sure what I expected to happen today, but this isn't quite it. This is much better.

After breakfast, Emma spends time exploring

the toys and books in her room. Nora joins us for a while, and late morning, we put on our swimsuits and head to the pool.

The pretty, oval-shaped pool at this house is bigger than the one in Naples. I have a feeling the inflatable toys bobbing in one corner were bought just for Emma, and I appreciate how much Amadeo has done but am also surprised by it. I don't trust it.

Hyacinth joins us and helps me put the floats around Emma's arms. Emma can barely contain herself as we inflate them and jumps into the pool before I do as Hyacinth sits in the shade of an umbrella. We play in the water until Emma begins to tire. Nora walks out, wiping her hands on a towel as Hyacinth dries Emma.

"Are you ready for lunch?" she asks Emma, who nods.

"Then a nap, I think, for both of us," Hyacinth says. "I'll take her in," she tells me.

"Thanks. I'll just get the toys cleaned up and join you then."

I watch them go, and when the door closes behind them, I take a moment alone. With my back to the house, I hold on to the edge of the pool and take in the view. It is a hot day, the sun high in the clear blue sky that matches the sea below. It's beautiful here. Breathtaking.

I'm just enjoying the calm and quiet when a huge splash disrupts the peace, water sloshing over the edge. I turn to find Bastian beneath the surface, gliding smoothly across the length of the pool, coming up for air, then swimming back. I watch as he approaches shark-like and emerges, shaking the water off his head, splashing me again as he sets his hands on either side of me trapping me.

"Enjoying a little downtime, Dandelion?"

"What the fuck is your problem?" I push at one arm, but he just closes in, naked chest pressing my almost naked chest, pinning me to the spot.

"I don't have a problem. Outside of you."

I search his eyes, that amber glow like fire. Water slicks his dark hair back, and I see the same steel cut of his jaw like his brother's. See the same powerful shoulders. My gaze wanders lower to the tattoo over his heart. A scale carrying a skull in one dish and a human heart in the other with dandelions littering the scene. I read the text, and it makes me shudder.

I will carry out great vengeance on them and punish them in my wrath.

When I look up I find his eyes still on me. I swallow and lick my lips when his gaze moves over my face, pausing at my lips before he meets my eyes again.

"How is sis?"

"Good. Excuse me," I say and try to slip under his arm.

He doesn't let me, though.

I spread my arms on either side of me to hold

myself up. It's too deep for me to stand, but Bastian's taller, so he doesn't have the same problem. It's either that or hold his shoulders, and I don't want to do that, so to anyone watching, we look like we're having a friendly conversation. Or a more intimate one. But his words from the first time I met him return to me.

"You're here now. Ours. Ours to punish. To level the scales."

"What do you want?" I ask, hearing the slight waver in my voice, wondering if he hears it.

He shrugs a shoulder. "Just killing time."

"Well, kill it on your own. I have things to do." Again, I try to slip away, but again, he doesn't allow it. This time, he closes his hands over my arms, pressing me against the wall.

"That's no way to behave with your brother-in-law."

"Where is my husband?" I make a point of using those words because even though I know I shouldn't push him, I see how it bothers Bastian.

"Do you need him to save you from me?"

I search his eyes, trying to figure out what he's doing, what he wants. Trying not to think about my proximity to him, especially with the scraps of clothes we're wearing.

"He won't like you so close to me," I say, but the word "ours" keeps replaying. They've both used it. Does Amadeo intend to share me? But that isn't the most troubling part of it. It's that the thought doesn't revolt me. The opposite.

"Won't he? I think he'd love it, actually. He does keep going on about how you belong to us."

I swallow.

"Don't worry, Dandelion. I'm not here to fuck you. I just want to be sure you know where you stand. He fucked you because he had to. The marriage can't be contested now. No chance of annulment. Nothing."

I don't know why his words hurt me. I know Bastian hates me.

"Don't think to come between us," he adds, and I realize why he's doing this. He's afraid.

I let my eyes narrow as one corner of my mouth curves upward. "What's the matter, Bastian? Are you scared I've already done just that?"

Bastian doesn't get a chance to answer, though, because Amadeo's low, deep voice interrupts. "What's going on out here?"

I gasp, my eyes flicking to Amadeo's. I didn't see or hear him approach and am startled, feeling caught. Guilty. Bastian only grins as if he knew all along. He doesn't even look back.

"Your brother is trying to put me in my place," I tell Amadeo, who surprises me by taking a seat on the edge of one of the lounge chairs, legs wide, hands on elbows, and watches us.

"Is he?"

I meet Bastian's eyes, confused. His grin widens.

"Tell him to let me go," I tell Amadeo, keeping my eyes on Bastian's.

"You're not keeping her against her will, are you, brother?" Amadeo asks, and it's like that night at the restaurant when they cornered me in the bathroom. The two of them talking as if I'm not there but both watching me.

"I'd never do that, brother."

Amadeo smiles. "Help her out."

This is not a victory for me. I know it and am further unsettled by Bastian's growing grin.

"With pleasure," Bastian says, and before I can think, he has his hands around me and is lifting me effortlessly out of the pool. He sets me on the edge of it, the lower part of my legs still dangling in the water, and puts his hands on my thighs, trapping me there.

I glance at Amadeo, who is watching us.

"The bikini looks nice," Amadeo says, and I begin to realize that I made a mistake if I thought Amadeo would choose me over his brother. I didn't want that. It was not what I expected at all. I just wanted his protection, like he promised. He gets to his feet and walks around the pool toward us. I watch him, unable to look at Bastian. He comes to stand behind me. "Emma's having lunch on the other side of the house," he tells me.

I look up at him. "I want to go to her."

"When we're finished here," he says. "First," he starts, reaching down to lift my wet hair and set it down my back. "It's time to understand something." He kneels behind me, trapping me between powerful thighs. His fingers trace the slight swell of my breasts before he takes the triangular cups of the bikini top and pushes each one over to expose my breasts.

I gasp and cover myself with my hands.

Amadeo closes his hands over mine and brings his mouth to my ear. "You belong to us both, Dandelion. I need you to know that. Know it in your bones," he says loud enough for Bastian to hear.

"I—"

"I want you to show us that you understand that." He takes my hands and pulls them behind my back, holding both wrists in one of his, then tilts my head so he can look at my face. "Don't worry, I know you want to."

"But—"

"Look at Bastian."

I swallow.

"Look at him, Dandelion," he repeats, releasing me, so I turn to meet Bastian's eyes. They burn like lava, but there's something else there too. His hatred. Whether it's for himself or me, I'm not sure.

Bastian drags his gaze to my breasts, then back to his brother. There's a silent exchange I don't understand.

"Now show him your pussy," Amadeo tells me, releasing my wrists.

I glance nervously up at him.

"Do it. Move your suit over so he can see your pussy."

I swallow hard, a plethora of feelings warring inside me. Arousal and humiliation and confusion. Do I want this? Does it matter? Yes, it does. Amadeo won't force me. I know that.

I lick my lips, face Bastian, and with my stomach fluttering as if with a thousand butterflies, I draw the fabric between my legs over and watch as he lowers his gaze to look at me. And I find I want him to look. I want them both to look. In fact, it's all I want right now. Their eyes on me.

I spread my legs a little wider, feeling the heat of arousal.

Bastian cocks his head and studies my naked sex. I keep it shaved bare, and I feel myself growing wet beneath his gaze.

"She's wet, and it's not the pool," Bastian says.

"I'm not surprised. I think she likes having us look at her. Touch her," Amadeo says so close to my ear that his words make the hair on the back of my neck stand on end. "You should taste her."

Amadeo takes my arms again. I twist a little, but he holds firm. It's not that I don't want it. I'm very turned on. But this is wrong. To be with both of them. To want them both. Isn't it?

Bastian draws me closer to the edge of the pool and spreads my thighs wider. He glances up at me, eyes black as coals, a burning amber glowing beneath. He keeps his gaze locked on mine as he slides two fingers over the crease of my thigh, slipping them beneath the suit. My breath is a shudder as he exposes more of me to his gaze.

The stubble of his jaw tickles my inner thigh. He turns his head, opening his mouth to kiss it, to lick a line all the way to my core as Amadeo leans me backward just a little, giving Bastian that much more of me but making me watch at the same time as Bastian's dark head moves between my legs. I feel the first flick of his hot tongue over my clit before he closes his lips around it and sucks. I let out a small cry, not sure if I want my arms free to pull him to me or want them free to push him off.

"Spread your legs wider, Dandelion," Amadeo says, mouth at my ear, teeth at my neck. "Give it to him. Offer him a taste of your pretty little pussy."

I do as he says, and Amadeo kisses my mouth. It's a deep, full kiss, devouring and wholly erotic, wet, as wet as Bastian's tongue on my sex. And it isn't long before I'm panting into Amadeo's mouth. He draws back to watch me come, to watch as Bastian's teeth graze my clit, drawing a cry from me before he closes his mouth over it and sucks. His fingers slide inside me, curling a little, just enough to make my vision go dark around the edges as my world tilts on its axis.

It's over too soon, and I'm left panting as Amadeo straightens me to sit up, and Bastian draws back, fingers of one hand digging into my thigh as he turns almost black, angry eyes to me. He wipes the back of his hand over his mouth before he swims away. I watch as he gets to the opposite edge and lifts himself up, muscles flexing in powerful arms and shoulders, water glistening off tanned olive skin. He doesn't turn to look at his brother or me but grabs the towel he must have dropped on a chair and keeps walking, his back to us, until he disappears into the house.

28

BASTIAN

This isn't what I want. *She* isn't what I want. What I should want, at least.

I stand in the shower, the water cold but not cold enough to do anything about my erection. I grip myself and give a punishing tug.

She is my enemy.

Her heart is the heart on the tattoo on my chest. I will crush it. It's what I know, what I have known for fifteen long years.

But as I stand here jerking my dick, all I can think about is how she looked at me because I am her enemy too. Or I should be. But I see again how she opened for me. How sweet she tasted. How she sounded when she came on my tongue.

The slit of her shaved pussy swims before my closed eyes, and I set one hand on the shower wall.

My dick grows harder in my fist, and when I come, it's her eyes I see. Her gasps I hear.

"Fuck!"

I switch the water to ice cold and make myself stand under it. It's not enough. Jerking myself off doesn't sate me. And the cold doesn't touch my brain. Doesn't do anything to wash the image of her away. I turn off the shower and step out, snatching a towel to dry off as I head to the walk-in closet.

I don't want this. I never wanted it. When her father died so unexpectedly and we learned of her plan to come to Naples with the body, we knew we'd take her. It was our opportunity. But she wasn't flesh and blood and human then. She was a Russo. The embodiment of our hate. We needed her to bring down her brother, and if she'd be destroyed in the process, so be it. But having her here, it's all different.

Maybe I should take my own advice. Fuck her. Get her out of my system. But if I'm honest with myself, what I'm afraid of is that fucking her will have the opposite effect like it has on my brother.

Christ. I'm going around in fucking circles.

I get dressed and comb through my hair, not bothering to shave. Hell, maybe I'll grow a full beard. I don't recognize myself these days, anyway. I walk out of my bedroom and down the stairs to the library, where Amadeo is waiting for me.

"You okay?" he asks after looking me over.

I sigh, close the door, and drop onto the couch. "I don't know. Are you? Are we?"

He gets up and pours us each a whiskey. He hands me one and leans against his desk, watching me.

"Where is she?" I ask when he doesn't answer.

"Putting Emma down for a nap." He sips. "Don't fight it, Bastian."

I look at him.

"She's ours. And she wants to be ours. You saw her face. Saw how—"

"She's a Russo."

"Get over it."

"What the fuck does that even mean? How do you *get over it*? You know what her brother did to Hannah. What her father did to us."

"That was her brother. Her father. Not her."

"Do you hear yourself? She's got your head all turned around." I swallow my drink and get to my feet. "Exactly what I knew would happen."

"Bastian—"

"I thought fucking her would relieve you of whatever it is that's going on in your head, but it's done the opposite. You're forming a fucking bond with the enemy, brother. How do you not see it?"

"Is that what you're afraid of?"

I step right up to him. "I won't lose sight of our goal, even if you will."

Amadeo sets his drink down and straightens so

we're eye-to-eye. "I have lost sight of nothing. We will get the revenge our family is owed. But she is not the enemy."

I snort. "Look at us. She's already dividing us."

"*You're* dividing us. You refuse to see."

I grab his collar with both hands. I want to fight him. Hell, I just want to fight.

"Go on," he says. "You want to punch me?"

"Yeah, maybe I do. Maybe I need to knock some sense into you."

He grips one of my wrists but doesn't quite pull it free. "Maybe it's you who needs to see sense. Logic. Brother, we want the same thing."

I snort.

"Fine," he says, dropping his arm, keeping both at his sides. "Do it. Beat me with your fists if it will make you feel better. I won't even fight back."

The breath I draw in is tight, the air around us thin. It takes me a long minute, but I drop my arms too and walk away from him, running a hand through my hair.

"Do you ever wonder if I'd just shut my mouth if they'd have walked away?" I ask. It's a question I've asked before. One that haunts me.

"What are you talking about?"

"That day in the kitchen. Do you think they'd have left if I hadn't said what I said?"

"Bastian, you're not at fault," Amadeo starts.

I put a hand up to stop him. I'm not done. "I

think about that all the time. Hannah was dead. It's not like anything was going to bring her back. But if I'd just shut the fuck up like Dad told us both to do and kept my head down, do you think they'd have left us alone? Left Dad whole. Left Mom and us."

Amadeo puts a hand on my shoulder. "No, brother, I don't." I meet his eyes, and I know he's thought long and hard about this. Maybe as long and as hard as me. "I think Russo planned what he was going to do all along, thinking to force us to bend the knee. I think he was just fucking with us all that time. But he failed. That's what I think about. And Vittoria? She's not like them. Whatever happened to her, I blame her father and her brother. They damaged her as much as they did us."

I look at him and tilt my head to see him from a different angle. Because am I really fucking hearing this? "Do you have fucking feelings for her? Is that what this is about? That fucking—"

He takes me by the collar and slams my back against the wall.

"Oh my fucking God!" I laugh a strange laugh. But before I can go on, the door opens, and Vittoria comes into view. Amadeo turns to see her, and from the look on her face, I know she's been right outside all this time. Listening. Eavesdropping.

"Hear enough, Dandelion?" I ask, freeing myself of my brother. I adjust my shirt, taking her in. Her hair is damp, her face fresh and dewy, cheeks a little pink. She got some color today.

"I knocked—"

"It's fine. Come in," Amadeo says.

"Yeah, you come in," I say as I walk toward the door. "You two discuss your plans, and let me get on with my life."

I walk out of the study and straight out the front door. Across the long drive is a five-car garage built to house our not-so-small fascination with sports cars. The faster, the better. I open the door and see them all lined up in a shiny row. I push the button to send the garage door climbing and get into the shiny new Ferrari, my current favorite. The keys are in the ignition, and I start the engine, my head on my conversation with my brother. Vittoria's face swimming in the background. The look on it. I set my foot on the pedal, the tires screeching as I pull out too fast and take the tight turn of the driveway. I don't know where I'm going. That's one thing about living so remotely. It's good if you want to be alone, but when you want to get away, lose yourself in a bottle of whiskey or some anonymous person in some anonymous dive, it's fucking impossible. And I know I should slow down around the curves, the sharp hairpin turns. But fuck it. What does it fucking matter anyway?

29

AMADEO

I watch my brother stalk out.

"Fuck."

Vittoria is watching me, and I wonder how much she heard. How much of it is fucking true. Do I have feelings for this woman?

I push a hand into my hair. "Emma asleep?" I ask. It comes out a bark.

She nods. "Hyacinth too. They're exhausted."

"Hm." My mind isn't on the little girl or her nanny. It's on my brother. He just needs to cool down, I tell myself. Bruno is expecting me at the Naples office in less than an hour. I'm sure he'll be back by the time I am, and we can talk it through then.

I look at Vittoria, who will not like what I have to tell her. Bastian should be here for it, but he knows what needs to happen, given his supposed commitment to our goal and my lack thereof which is bullshit. "Why don't you go take a nap too. I need to be in Naples."

She doesn't move. She is as obstinate as my brother. Maybe that's what they have in common.

What I see when I look at her is the woman from this afternoon. Sitting on the side of the pool, breasts displayed, bikini pulled aside to expose her pussy to my brother, to offer it to him. A thing he took with greed.

"Why did you share me with him?"

"Like I have always told you, Dandelion, you belong to us both. And I don't think you minded. Considering how you came, that is."

"He hates me."

"He carries guilt. He thinks he's betraying our family by wanting you. And I can assure you, he does want you. But I can't talk about this now. I need to think. Go upstairs and pack."

"Pack?"

"We're going to New York."

"But Emma just got here."

"Emma won't be joining us. Your father's will is going to be read in two days. You and I need to be present."

"I'm sure we can use Zoom or something."

"That's not going to work. Look, I can't talk about this right now. Just go pack, Vittoria. It'll be a short trip. A few nights at most. Emma will be looked after."

"I'm not going to New York, Amadeo. I'm not leaving her. I just got her back."

"You are. Go upstairs. Now. If I have to take you up, I will lock you in your room until it's time to leave."

She folds her arms across her chest and tilts her chin up in stubborn defiance.

If she thinks I'm joking, she's got another thing coming. "Fucking go."

"No."

"For fuck's sake!"

She must see I'm done because she spins on her heel to go, but I'm faster. She yelps when I grab her arm and walk her out of the library, through the living room, and up the stairs to her bedroom. I call for her guard, and he follows.

"I'll pack! Let me go."

"Too late." I sit her on the still-bare bed, but maybe she'll learn a lesson because she is still hostile, I remind myself. Wife or not. Truce or not.

"Amadeo, please!" she calls out as I walk to the door.

I turn to face her. "Please, what? I ask you to do one thing, but you can't fucking do it," I tell her. "So now you deal with the consequence."

"What, I'm grounded? What am I, twelve?"

I open my mouth but close it and shake my head. "Don't push me. Not now." I open the bedroom door.

"It's because of Bastian. Of what he said."

I pause mid-step. How much did she hear?

"Sir?" the soldier asks.

"Don't let her out until the little girl wakes up. Then you keep an eye on her."

I glance at Vittoria. She stares daggers at me.

"Or if she gives you any trouble, leave her locked in. Maybe then she'll learn to do as she's told."

I walk away, my mind on what Bastian said. He's jealous. I sensed it already but thought what happened at the pool would at least be a start to smooth things over, pave the road as this thing with Vittoria develops. But I think Bastian's struggle is as much with himself as me. Because, like me, things are different where she's concerned. And he doesn't like it.

AFTER MY MEETING WITH BRUNO, I HAVE THE paperwork I need for the trip to New York, all forms signed and certified. Once the will is read, the real game begins. As I'm on my way back to the Ravello house, Jarno texts me that they're headed back too along with a very drunk and very aggressive Bastian who did not want to give up the keys to his car. I'll deal with my brother. Talk to him. He hasn't answered my texts or calls, which pisses me off. Maybe he's right, though. She is coming between us. But he can't fucking blame me for this one.

The house is quiet when I get back. It's around ten at night. The soldier standing guard at Vittoria's door is now standing outside Emma's bedroom. He straightens when he sees me and tucks his phone into his pocket.

I glance at Vittoria's bedroom door, which is open, and raise my eyebrows.

"She's in here."

"Is she?"

"I didn't know what to do, and she insisted." Of course she did.

"It's fine. I'll deal with her. Did she give you any trouble?"

"No, sir. She had dinner with the little girl and your mother, and they watched a movie, then she went to bed with the child."

"All right. I'll take it from here."

He walks away, and I open the bedroom door to find the carousel of animals floating over the walls and ceiling as a soft melody plays. Emma is asleep as is Hyacinth. But as soon as Vittoria sees me, she sits up and folds her arms across her chest. Still pissed.

I gesture for her to come with me.

She slips her legs over the side of the bed. She's wearing an oversized T-shirt and is barefoot. She pads across the room, and I notice the pink on her toenails along with some stickers. I guess Emma did that for her.

We don't speak as I lead her downstairs to the library.

"Aren't you locking me in my bedroom?" she asks on the threshold.

"Get in."

I see her little grin of victory, but I let it slide, choosing not to fight this battle.

"Where is your brother?" she asks.

"On his way back."

"Oh, goody."

"Drink?" I ask her.

"No."

"No, thank you," I correct her, to which she rolls her eyes. Then I pour myself a whiskey and turn to study her.

"Who would watch Emma while we're gone?"

"I assume Hyacinth."

"Soldiers. I need to be sure she'll be protected."

"She will be protected. I'm glad you've had a change of heart."

"I don't think I had a choice."

"No, you didn't."

Commotion has us both turn to the door. Before either of us speaks, the door slams open, and a very angry, obviously drunk Bastian comes into view. He glances at me, but it's Vittoria he has in his sights as he stalks in and drops the keys onto the table beside the sofa.

Jarno appears behind him. "Boss?"

I look at my brother watching Vittoria and at Vittoria watching him. "I got this. It's fine. Good night, Jarno."

He closes the door.

Bastian advances toward Vittoria, and she backs away, their steps almost coordinated. He only stops when she's cornered.

"Get the fuck away from me," she says to him.

He grins, gaze moving over her. "I don't think so." He turns to me and eyes the whiskey at my side. "Pour me one."

"I think you've had enough."

"Do you?" he asks and glances at Vittoria. "Stay. Don't fucking move." She doesn't move as he walks to me, takes the glass from my hand, and swallows the contents down. "There. I'll say when I've had enough." He shoves the glass into my chest, and I take it.

"I was worried about you, brother," I say.

He narrows his eyes at me, and I wonder if his anger isn't burning away the alcohol as we speak.

"You were so fucking worried about me that you came to get me? Oh no, wait, that was Jarno. You sent a fucking soldier."

"He said you would have driven. Is that true? Because I don't think you're in any state to drive, do you?" He snorts and turns back to Vittoria. "You could have killed yourself if you'd driven."

"Wouldn't that be the best outcome for the two of you?" he asks, giving me his full attention again. "Me out of the fucking way?"

I step right up to him and slam him against the wall. "Don't you ever fucking say that. Don't you dare. I'm not losing you, too. God. Haven't we lost enough?"

He looks at me, his lip curled. "Tell me something. If you had to choose, who would it be? If you could save one of us, who the fuck would it be? Because a few weeks ago, I'd laugh that off. Now, though..." He glances at Vittoria. "Now I'm not so sure, brother."

"You're fucking drunk. Go sleep it off."

"Answer my question. Unless you can't, which is an answer itself. Get off me." He shoves my arms off. "It's not you I'm here to see."

He turns to Vittoria, who looks back at him in defiance, refusing to move away when he stalks to her, stopping just short of her.

"You think you've won? Got your baby sister here, and you think you'll walk away unscathed? Because I have news for you. You're not. No one walks away from something like this unscathed."

"Do you think I don't know that?" Vittoria asks, slamming her hands against his chest to shove him away. He doesn't budge. "Trust me, Bastian, I know.

You hate me because my father loved me. That's it. Right there. You hate me because my father loved me. Let me ask you a question. Do you think you're the only one hurting? You think you're the only one being eaten up by guilt? My father loved me. He loved *only me*. My brother has always hated me for it. Punished me for it. My sister? My sweet little baby sister? All he had for her was scorn."

He snorts, opening his mouth. "There's a reason for that—"

"Bastian!" I interrupt.

He glares at me, and I shake my head. It all happens so quickly I'm not sure Vittoria notices because she continues as if uninterrupted.

"You think I don't know what kind of man he was? I knew. But he wasn't that to me. That wasn't the face I saw. How can I hate someone who only ever showed me love? So if you need to hate me for that, go ahead. But there's more to it than that, isn't there? There's another side to you, Bastian. I've seen it. Saw it last night."

"You think you see me?" he asks, more sober than he was moments ago.

"Yeah, I think I do. I think you want to hate me, but you can't. You want to hate us, but you can't. And I think it makes you more human than you like." She finishes with much less vehemence in her voice. Enough to defuse some of the tension.

He grits his jaw and releases her. There is truth

in what she says, and none of us can deny it. Bastian walks backward, drops to a seat on the edge of the couch, and shoves a hand through his hair.

She walks to him. "And you see me, too. And that's eating you up because it's not as easy to hurt someone you see as human."

"You're deluded, Dandelion."

"You're angry, Bastian." She pauses and glances at me. She's measuring her words. She turns back to my brother. "So take it out on me."

They watch one another for a long, long moment.

"Do it. Like you wanted to this afternoon before your brother offered me to you." She pulls her shirt off and stands before him wearing just her panties.

Bastian's eyes move over her, and there's a palpable shift in the energy in the room. A charge to it.

"Take it out on me," she repeats, slipping her panties off, letting them drop to the floor.

I move to lock the library door.

Bastian stands. "You don't know what you're asking for, Dandelion. I told you once it would be better for you if I walk away."

"I'm not scared of you."

"No?" He steps closer, looming over her. He cocks his head to the side, and I see her spine stiffen as he picks up a lock of soft blond hair and lets it slip through his fingers. In a way, that hair, it's the manifestation of her vulnerability and her strength. Delicate to look at but strong when forced. He meets her eyes again and twists that lock and more around his fist then tugs her head backward. His gaze moves over her throat to her breasts, and she cries out when he pinches a nipple. Satisfied, my brother smiles, and when he looks at her again, his eyes are black coals, dots of amber fire burning beneath. "You sure about that, Dandelion?"

She doesn't answer. Doesn't have time to. He spins her around and pushes her to her knees. Her hands wrap around his instinctively, her head at a painful angle when she meets my eyes.

She whimpers, and I know he's hurting her as he kneels behind her, so much bigger than her.

He leans close so his mouth is at her ear. "You sure you're not scared of me?" Her body shudders as he closes his mouth over the pulse at her neck. She swallows hard, eyes locked on me. "Tell me again how you're not scared of me."

"I'm not." Defiant as ever, our Dandelion.

He pushes her forward, so she has to slap her hands onto the carpet before he shoves her face into it. But he doesn't want that. Doesn't want her face obscured. He wants me to watch her and her to watch me.

"Not scared of this?" he asks, tugging his shirt over his head with his free hand, then gripping her ass cheek. "Because it's not your pussy I'm going to take."

She doesn't speak, but I see her hesitation at his proclamation.

"And Amadeo won't help you. He won't stop me. Isn't that right, brother?" he asks me.

From inside the desk drawer, I take out a tube of hand cream and toss it to him in answer. He catches it in one hand. I take a seat in the armchair so I can see her face. Look her straight in the eye.

"That's right," I say.

"You heard him," he tells her. "So if you're scared, little Dandelion, now is the time to speak up. I'll stop now if you tell me you're scared. I'll walk away. But if you don't, if you are hell-bent on proving you're not afraid of me, know that once I start, I won't stop."

I'm not sure if it's her turning her head or he's forcing it, but she looks over her shoulder at him.

"I'm not scared of you," she says, voice unshaking.

Bastian's grin widens. "I was hoping you'd say that." He releases her hair with a jerk, then shifts his grip to her ass, opening her, taking in the sight of her. Vittoria shudders.

"Eyes on me, Dandelion," I tell her when he empties half the tube of moisturizer onto the cleft of her ass, then tosses the tube back to me. I catch it, undo the buckle of my belt and open it, then undo the button and zipper of my slacks. I take myself out, smear what's left in the tube onto my palm and wrap it around my dick. "I want to see you take him."

Vittoria licks her lips, and I know the moment he pushes a finger into her, fucking her with the single digit, then adds a second. She grits her teeth, her breathing tight. And I know from her face when he pulls his fingers out and is ready to take her because her eyes grow huge.

"This may hurt a little," he says. She glances at him, panicked. He leans over her. "But don't worry, Dandelion. I'll make sure you come too. It'll make you hate yourself that much more because your pussy is fucking dripping, and I'm just getting started."

I lean forward a little, intent on her. Bastian wraps one hand around her front to take her clit between his fingers.

"Too much," she cries out, squeezing her eyes shut as he tries to enter her.

"Relax, Dandelion," he tells her. "Take it. You asked for it, remember? You'll take my cock in your ass. Take my come in your ass."

Her breath is a hiss, her hands fisting as he settles inside her.

"Fuck. She's tight."

"I'm sure," I say.

I pump my cock in my fist and watch as Bastian fucks her. He doesn't go easy on her, and she takes it. Her whimpers turn to moans, her eyes glazing over as pain turns to pleasure, her breathing picks up, and finally, that tensing of muscle as she comes. It's the most beautiful sight, her face like this. Her moans the most beautiful sound. And when Bastian stills inside her, his eyes closing as he empties inside her, I get to my feet and draw her up a little, just enough so she can take me in her mouth. So she will have a piece of us both inside her.

30

BASTIAN

It's late. I swim in the light of the moon hours after Vittoria and my brother go to bed. Hours after I should have followed them. I can't sleep, though, not after what happened tonight.

What she said is true. I hate her—or want to hate her—because her father loved her. Because she loved that monster. And I also see her. It's what I've accused my brother of, but I'm just as guilty. I see her. And she's not what I expected. Not the villain I'd made her out to be for all those years as I planned her punishment.

Movement catches my eye when I come up for air, so I stop and turn toward it. There, standing a few feet from the pool, is the last person I'd expect to see. The little girl.

She's wearing a pink nightie with a princess on the front of it, carrying her weird pig. Her hair is a tangled mess around her tiny face as she rubs her tired eyes.

"What are you doing out here?" I ask, climbing out of the pool and drying myself with my towel before wrapping it around my hips and pulling a T-shirt on.

She doesn't answer. Just stares up at me.

"Why aren't you in bed?"

Again, no answer. I wonder how they communicate if she's got this issue.

"How did you get out here?"

She turns and points at the open door. Duh.

"Where's Vittoria or your nanny?" I look into the house but see no one.

She points upstairs.

Okay. So she came down here by herself? It's pitch black in the house. Wasn't she scared? She's got her ratty shoes on. They're on the wrong feet and unlaced. It makes me smile.

"Come on, I'll take you back up to bed."

She shakes her head.

"Do you want some water or something? Are you hungry?" What am I supposed to do with a five-year-old?

She points at the water glass which was actually filled with whiskey just a little while ago. I'm going to have the mother of hangovers come morning.

"All right," I say with a sigh. Isn't she supposed to be afraid of me? I walk toward her and I'm surprised when she holds up her arms to be picked up. I stop, confused, then bend to lift her and carry her into the house. "You know you're not allowed to go near the swimming pool alone, right?" I ask her as I close the patio door. I don't care, but I'm not a fucking monster, either. She's a kid. Don't want her drowning in our pool.

She tilts her head to the side and points at me.

"I don't count," I tell her.

She shrugs a shoulder, and I push the door open to the kitchen. I set her on the counter, take a water glass and fill it then hand it to her. She takes it with two hands, takes exactly one sip and holds the glass back out to me.

"That's it? I thought you were thirsty."

She pushes the glass at me, so I take it and set it aside. She watches me with eyes much older than that of a five-year-old. I think about what Vittoria said. How her father only looked at Emma with scorn. I guess seeing her only reminded him of what his wife had very clearly done. I'm surprised Vittoria doesn't realize it, but I don't think she does. I almost gave it away in the library earlier tonight. Amadeo would have stopped me if I hadn't caught myself. But the science doesn't lie. Two blue-eyed parents cannot have a brown-eyed child.

I lift her from the counter and look away first, which is pathetic. She's five. But then she does something unexpected. She lays one tiny hand on my cheek, right over my scar. She traces it with a finger, then sets it flat again and does the same with her other hand to the scar on her own cheek. And it does something to me. This little thing. This point of connection.

I sit down on one of the kitchen chairs and take her hand from her scar to trace it. It's still pretty red, but it will fade. And it's not as deep as mine or my brother's. It will always be visible, though. Her father did that to her. Maybe not intentionally, but it's on him all the same. What I believe he intended, though, was much worse.

"You'll grow into it. Don't worry," I tell her.

She does look worried, though. Then she lays her head on my chest and closes her eyes. And moments later, she drops off to sleep in that way kids have. It's a little disturbing.

A sound comes from the kitchen door, and I turn to find Vittoria standing there. I wonder how much she heard. She looks at Emma asleep in my arms. Without a word, I stand to carry the little girl upstairs. Vittoria follows, and when I deposit her into her bed, I expect Vittoria to stay in the room with her sister, but before I can close the bedroom door behind me, she catches it and follows me out.

We stand there for a long minute, and I'm not sure what she wants. What happened in the library was to put her in her place. But it hasn't done that. And it hasn't got her out of my system either.

"Go to bed, Vittoria," I say, and turn to head downstairs and into the library, where I don't expect her to follow. But, as usual with her, I am wrong. She walks inside and looks at the place we were. I watch her. She's wearing a tank top and shorts. Her hair, much like her sister's, is tangled from sleep. But still, she's fucking beautiful. And more. I can't fucking drag my eyes away.

"Thank you," she says when she finally meets my gaze, a flush to her neck and cheeks. I guess she's remembering what happened in here earlier too. "Again. For Emma. I didn't notice when she slipped out of the bed."

"Were you sleeping in there with her?"

"Of course. I don't want her to be afraid."

"Maybe we're not the monsters you make us out to be, Dandelion." I walk to where the whiskey bottle is and pour myself one although I don't drink it. My head already throbs.

"I heard what you said to her," she says, walking to me but stopping a short distance away. "About growing into it. You were talking about her scar, weren't you?"

I nod.

"She got it during the accident. Glass cut her face."

"She's lucky. I'm guessing the intention wasn't only to scar her."

She stops. "What are you talking about?"

I sigh. "Nothing. I'm going to bed."

"Tell me."

"Mommy or Daddy have brown eyes, Dandelion?"

"What?"

I snort. "Nothing. Never mind." I take a few steps away.

"Why?" she asks, stopping me.

"Why what?"

"Why were you talking about her scar?"

"She brought it up."

"Brought it up how?"

"Comparing hers to mine. She touched mine, then hers. I assumed that's what she was doing."

"I didn't even realize she thought about it. It's not like she's looking at herself in the mirror or something." She sits down on the couch, thoughtful, a furrow forming between her eyebrows. She's worried about her sister. I get it.

"She'll be fine," I tell her. "She may not talk, but I get the feeling she sees a whole lot more than you could know."

"That's what worries me," she says, looking up at me as if looking for an answer. It's one I'm not equipped to give.

"She'll be fine. People survive shit. Go to bed, Vittoria."

"Vittoria? Not Dandelion?"

"Don't start. I'm fucking tired."

"I guess you would be, considering the activities of the night."

I grin. "Activities you quite enjoyed."

She flushes.

"Are you here for more? I'm guessing your ass is a little sore, but if you want to go again, I can always use another hole."

She narrows her eyes, stands, and comes to me. "No, that's not why I'm here."

I grin. "There we are. Back to our corners. I wouldn't want you to think fucking would change the fundamentals of our relationship."

"We have no relationship."

"Oh, we do. It's a hate-hate one." She spins to walk away, but I catch her arm and tug her toward me. "I enjoyed fucking you, Dandelion. I enjoyed having you on your knees before me. And I really enjoyed taking your ass and watching you submit to me, to your own pleasure. Tell me something, do you still feel me?"

"Get away from me."

"Feel my cock stretching that tight little ass of yours?"

"Let go."

I lean in close because I want to drive this nail home. "Is my come still inside you," I ask in a low whisper and lick the length of her neck. "I'm hard all over again thinking about it. About how you looked. How you opened for me. How you sounded when your ass squeezed my dick when you came. Fuck, Dandelion. You know what I'd like to do now?"

She looks up at me.

"I'd love to fuck that pretty little face of yours. Stuff your mouth full and come down your throat."

"Let me go, you asshole."

"Do one thing for me first."

She tugs, but I hold tight. "What?"

"Slip your hand into your panties and show me if you're as turned on as I am."

She raises her free arm to slap me, but I catch her wrist and spin her so her back is pressed to my front, her arms trapped, folded across her chest.

"What happened doesn't change anything between us, Dandelion. You and me will always be enemies. No matter how many times we fuck. It's our destiny. Now get your ass out of my sight before I'm tempted to have you again. I'm not sure you could take me twice in one night. Do you hear me?"

"I hear you loud and clear, Bastian. Now hear me." She turns her head, so we look at each other. "I will destroy you. I will take everything from you and bring you to your knees. Because I'm with you. You and I are enemies. We will always remain enemies. But as far as destinies go, mine is to destroy you. To wipe the Del Campo name from the face of the earth."

"What's going on?" Amadeo asks from the doorway. He's showered and ready for the day. I see from the window behind him the sun is breaking the horizon.

I release Vittoria, who takes two steps away but keeps her glaring eyes on me.

"Your wife and I were having a heart-to-heart, weren't we?"

She sets her jaw and folds her arms across her chest.

"She was just telling me how she would wipe our name from the earth."

Amadeo grins, approaching his wife. He takes her chin in one hand. She looks up at him.

"I like a fighter. You, brother?"

I nod, not taking my eyes off her.

"Don't worry, Dandelion. I'd expect no less from you. You leave for Naples in a few hours, then we're off to New York. Go get some sleep." Her jaw tightens, and I know she doesn't like the idea of leaving her sister. My brother knows too because he continues. "Emma will be safe."

She sighs, then walks out of the room with one hate-filled glare at me. Amadeo looks at me once she's gone. He looks exhausted.

"Did you sleep at all?" I ask him.

"No, not really." He checks the time. "We have another meeting with Bruno before we leave."

"Why?" I ask. "I thought we had everything we needed."

"Something has come up," Amadeo says, expression grave.

"What?"

He sighs. "Lucien has submitted paperwork to take guardianship of Emma."

The thought of Lucien Russo having that little girl under his control burns. I don't know why but it does. "Does Vittoria know?"

Amadeo shakes his head.

"What are you thinking?" I ask.

"Vittoria will also file."

It makes sense. I know it does. But it bothers me. "So we're going out of our way to help her?"

"It's not exactly out of our way. The kid—"

"You heard what she said. What she wants."

"I also know you cornered her. If you trap a wild animal, it will fight. And she is as wild as they come."

"As long as you and I are aligned, brother."

He wraps an arm around my shoulders. "Always, brother."

31

AMADEO

Soldiers take Vittoria to Naples a few hours later after she's reassured a very anxious Emma that she'll be back. I've also reassured her that I'll check on Emma once more before heading to the Naples house. My brother and I meet with Bruno in Amalfi. I'm not taking a chance on any spies in my house.

The meeting takes more of the day than I like. Bastian and I fly by helicopter to the Ravello house as soon as it's over to make sure Mom is all right and let her know we'll be gone. She gets anxious when she doesn't see us every few days unless she knows in advance. But when we have an aerial view of the house as we approach to land, I'm surprised to find three large black SUVs lined up along the drive.

"Who the fuck is that?" Bastian asks.

I dig my phone out of my pocket to check for

texts I may have missed telling me someone was here, but I don't see anything. The chopper lands, and we climb out, keeping low until we clear the blades and dialing the number Jarno gave me for the soldier he was leaving in charge. I can't remember his name. I trust Jarno. Have since day one. Since bringing our mother here, I've left him to manage security until we get a team in place. Finding trustworthy soldiers has proven harder than it should. We are a family divided, maybe not openly or at least not completely so. But my uncle has quite some support. People who believe he should be head of the family, not me.

"Mr. Caballero," comes the voice on the other end.

"Who is at the house?" I ask as we approach the back entrance. The chopper's blades are loud as it takes off behind me.

"No fucking way," Bastian says, reaching for the pistol in his shoulder holster. I see him at the same time as the soldier answers.

"Sonny Caballero sir. Your uncle."

"I know who he is." I disconnect and set a hand over my brother's arm.

"Put it away."

"What the fuck is he doing here?"

"Bastian. He's with our mother," I say, tucking the phone into my pocket as Sonny stands up from his place on the terrace where he was seated beside my mother. Francesca is standing off by the door, looking displeased. I'm guessing she didn't send a message to let us know Sonny was here because she couldn't. Because this house is a secret location. No one knows about it apart from the handful of soldiers, Jarno, and Bruno.

"Well, well, both of my nephews. Isn't this my lucky day," Sonny says, beaming. "I was hoping to run into you as I visited with Nora."

"Uncle," I say. He stands about two inches taller than usual and looks very pleased with himself.

Bastian goes immediately to my mother's side and draws her away.

"I must admit, it's a secluded, out-of-the-way place, isn't it?" Sonny asks.

"What are you doing here?" Bastian asks and I can hear the effort it's taking him to keep his voice calm for mom's sake.

"I'm so glad you're both here," my mother says, coming to take my hand and look me over, nodding in approval while still holding Bastian's hand. "Are you boys hungry?"

"No, Mom, thanks." I try to smile at her, to keep from upsetting her.

"How about you, Bastian? You're a bottomless pit."

"Not now, Mom."

I turn to my uncle, but before I can say anything, my mother speaks.

"Isn't it a nice surprise to see Sonny?"

"It is nice," I say because Bastian won't. "I didn't realize you knew Mom was in Italy."

"Imagine my surprise to hear my sister was just a few hours' drive from me. I couldn't not come. I hope no one minds that I turned up unannounced."

"Of course not, Sonny. Don't be silly. We're all family." Mom says and looks at me, then beyond me into the distance. "I hope Hannah and your father get back soon. The weather looks like it's changing."

I glance at the sky. Darker clouds have rolled in. Rain is expected.

Sonny watches me as I smile at mom. "Francesca, why don't you and mom get us something to eat. I could do with a bite after all."

She nods, and the look in her eyes is trying to convey a message. I'll talk to her later. Find out exactly what happened. I notice Emma and the nanny are nowhere to be seen. I wonder if they're upstairs. It would be better if they remained hidden from view.

"It's a very nice property, Amadeo. Off the beaten path. Secure. But could leave you backed into a corner."

"How did you get the address?" Bastian asks.

He shrugs, sits back down, and picks up his whiskey. He casually crosses his ankle over the opposite knee.

"Was it a secret?"

"Our mother's safety is a priority. Given her mental state, I'm sure you understand the importance of that."

"I'm her brother. Your uncle. I should be included within the circle."

"Let's not bullshit, shall we, Uncle?" Bastian asks. "The family is divided. And you are the cause of that division."

"United we stand, divided we fall, blah, blah, blah. You were always the dramatic one, weren't you, Bastian?" He doesn't hide his distaste for my brother.

"Who told you the address?" I prod.

He shrugs a shoulder. "I can't recall, honestly."

"I'm not sure there's an honest bone in your body," I say.

"Nor yours. We are the same, Amadeo. Don't forget that." He glances behind me. "Where is your lovely fiancée? Or I guess it's wife now. I heard the happy news."

I pour myself a whiskey and sit down. I don't bother to answer him as I study him now that I know what I know.

Bastian remains standing, watching, and I wonder how close he is to pulling his gun out of its holster and putting a bullet between Sonny's eyes. Just getting it done.

"I'm confused, though? Is she with you?" Sonny starts, pointing at me, then turns his finger to Bastian. "Or you? Or both?" He grins like the cat who ate the fucking canary. "I bet between the two of you, it was a long night for her," Sonny says, eyeing us both. "Tell me, how does it feel to fuck the enemy's daughter? Because that's what she is, correct? Didn't her father give you two that nasty reminder of Russo power?" He gestures to our faces.

Bastian takes a menacing step Sonny. Two soldiers who are loyal to my uncle step forward.

"Bastian." I shake my head.

He stops grudgingly. I have no doubt he'd risk his life to take our uncle out. That's how deep his hate for Sonny goes.

I sip my drink and count to ten. I want to kill him as much as Bastian, but one of us needs to remain levelheaded.

"Since you're here, you save me a trip, Uncle," I say.

"Or aren't you enemies any longer?" Sonny continues. "Now that you've taken a Russo for a wife?" he asks, carrying on like I haven't spoken. "And what about you, Bastian. Does it bother you that he marries the whore? Not you?"

"You're a fucking bastard, you know that?" Bastian asks.

Sonny looks at me again. "Although I can guess the ulterior motive."

"My motivations aren't your concern. What is my concern is your loyalty to the family."

"Well, actually, two things." Sonny holds up two

fingers as if I haven't spoken, and I imagine how he would scream if I bent them backward, breaking them slowly. "One, your motivations are my concern as they impact me in every aspect. And two, my loyalties have always and will always lie with the Caballero family. *My* family. If Angelo had lived—"

"Yes, if Angelo had lived, he'd be the one you'd be answering to now. Why is that? Why did Grandfather set you aside, Uncle?"

At this, he bristles, his mouth turning down at its customary angle. This is the true face of my uncle. I don't miss the fact that it's not loss or sadness at the fact that his son is dead that he's expressing. It's hate.

"What's the matter, Uncle? Don't you miss your son?" Bastian asks.

Sonny looks like he'll lunge at Bastian.

Bastian smiles wide, liking getting under Sonny's skin. I can't help my smile, either.

"I had an interesting conversation with a man named Bob Miller the other night." I watch Sonny as I say it.

He looks genuinely confused now. "Bob Miller?"

"You may know him in our circles as The Reaper."

Hardness sets back in as he closes off his expression. "The Reaper? I can't say I do."

"No?" Bastian asks.

"Well, that's interesting because, according to

recently deceased Bob, you and he had struck a deal," I remind him.

He shifts in his seat and checks his watch.

"Tell me something, what would our cousins do if they knew you had a hand in events that irrevocably changed the future of the family? That put us at great risk and weakened us?"

"Us," he says with distaste, swallowing the last of his drink and standing. "You..." He gestures to us both. "You and I aren't *us*. You two are usurpers. Pretenders to the throne."

Bastian laughs outright at that. "Dramatic much?"

"A throne that does not want you." I study him as he calls for a soldier just as I hear my mother and Francesca come out of the kitchen. "And things are changing," he adds ominously.

"We made drinks and sandwiches. I hope you're all hungry," my mother says, oblivious to the tension among us.

"Uncle Sonny has to go, Mom," Bastian says, picking up a sandwich and biting into it. He is always hungry. "Maybe you can pack one up for him to take on his drive home. It is such a long way."

"You have to go?" Mom looks crestfallen. "You'll miss Hannah and Roland. I'm sure they'll be back soon."

Sonny looks at her then at me. He grins before turning to her again. "I'm sorry, Nora. Something came up. I'll see you soon, though. Remember," he says, wrapping a hand around her arm in a way I don't like and leaning in to kiss her cheek. "You owe me a visit at my house. I'll send a car and surprise you."

When he backs away, she looks at him in a strange way, like for a moment, she's herself and remembers the past. How Sonny turned his back on her just like her father did. But then it's gone, and she nods.

"I love surprises," she says, although a little more sadly.

As I stand, I make a note to tell her she's not to go anywhere without my permission. "I'll walk you out." I accompany my uncle to the front doors, where about half a dozen of his men stand around with my own. I see the one Jarno left in charge. When he sees me, he drops his cigarette to the ground, stubs it out, and stands at attention.

"Always a pleasure, nephew," my uncle says. I assume he's feeling his spine stronger for the soldiers he's surrounded with and their camaraderie with my own.

"Always." We don't shake hands as he climbs into his car, and they begin their procession toward the gate. But just before I turn to leave, the car my uncle is in stops, and he opens his window.

"I can leave soldiers, Amadeo, if you have need. You're a little light here, I noticed."

"We're fine." I'll be upping the count today.

"Are you sure? I'd hate for one of your houses to be attacked. You don't want rats."

His words rattle me, but I'm careful not to show it. "Goodbye, Uncle."

"Well, if you change your mind, let me know. I want to be sure my sister is well guarded, considering her mental state. Goodbye, boys."

32

VITTORIA

It takes me all of ten minutes to pack. I hate that I have to leave Emma now, but I know I must be present at the reading of the will. It's a requirement. At least I won't be gone long. I wonder about my strange conversation with Bastian. What he was suggesting about Emma.

I want to see Lucien, too. Talk to him. Find out why he didn't send more men after me when I was taken. Find out other things. About Dad. About what Amadeo and Bastian accused him of.

I watch clouds roll in over the sea, listening to the sound of rain falling softly at first, then more powerfully. It's so beautiful and strange, this change that comes over sea and sky. But there's something else too. Some sensation lingering. I feel it at my core, this ominous thing hovering like the dark clouds that hang over the sea, the storm wreaking its havoc.

I am served lunch and dinner in my room. I don't mind, although I expected the brothers back sooner. But no one tells me when Amadeo or Bastian will return.

It's a few hours after dinner when I hear a commotion outside of my room. The lock turns, and I'm on my feet, anxious to go, to get this done, and simply nervous. The storm has shaken me. Maybe it's the aloneness. I'm expecting Amadeo, but when the door opens, it's not Amadeo I see or the oaf tasked with guarding my door. It's another man, one who doesn't look at all familiar but gives off an energy of such malice that it takes all I have not to shrink away.

The man enters but doesn't close the door behind him as he stands, openly looking me over. I'm dressed in a simple navy mourning dress I'd brought with me. I would have worn it for the flight home. I will now. I fold my arms across my chest as much in an effort to shield myself as to appear stronger than I'm feeling.

"The princess in the tower," he says, and when he steps toward me, I get that creepy feeling I had when I first saw Sonny Caballero from across the room at the restaurant. That eerie sensation of something wicked, something wrong touching you.

"Who are you?" I ask.

"Nobody. Come."

"Where is Amadeo?"

"Downstairs. He sent me to get you."

"He's home then?"

He nods. "I was told to bring you. Let's go." He stalks across the room and takes my arm. I manage to slip out of his grasp.

"I'm coming. Don't touch me."

He snorts.

Why would Amadeo send this man to get me? His soldiers aren't friendly toward me, not even close, but this one, he's different. But it's a stupid question I'm asking. Why wouldn't Amadeo send him is the better one, the more apt one.

He wasn't terrible to me last night. Still, I have to remember he is making a point of choosing between his brother and me, and he's very clearly choosing Bastian as he should, really.

Maybe this is a show for Bastian. Or maybe it's to put me back in my place. To remind me and possibly himself that we aren't on the same side. He may not have beaten me, but he has kept me a prisoner. Blackmailed me into marriage. Bringing Emma just gives him one more bargaining chip. We're both collateral damage, not human beings, as far as he's concerned. He was very clear about that.

The soldier leads me down the hall and to the stairs. I notice how quiet the house is. How dark.

"Down," the soldier says when we reach the stairs.

I look back at him. Something isn't right. The house is too quiet. Where are the soldiers he usually has stationed around the house?

"Where is my husband?" I force myself to use the term to assert my position, but he just looks at me with flat, empty eyes.

"He's waiting for you and he doesn't like to be kept waiting. Move." He gives me a nudge, and I grip the banister so I don't go tumbling down the stairs. Once we're on the first-floor landing, I see the living and dining rooms are dark, too. But I feel a vibration beneath my feet. A beat. Music?

I turn back to the guard, who gestures down a dimly lit corridor.

"No. Tell Amadeo to come get me," I tell him, unsure why because he won't. But something tells me not to go with this man.

"That's not how this works, princess," he says with a sneer before taking my arm and forcing me down the hallway toward the door at the very end, where I can now hear music, but it's nothing I've heard Amadeo or Bastian listen to. I can see the light under the door, and I smell cigarette smoke as we near it.

"Let me go!" I struggle against the man who has me when we reach the door, and he opens it.

"Down, princess."

It's a basement and I can hear men, a lot of them, and music and the stench of liquor and cigarettes and sweat. And I know I don't want to go down there.

"Where's Amadeo?" I ask, panic making my voice higher. This isn't how Amadeo operates. Bastian? Is this Bastian's doing? Is it Bastian who has ordered me to be brought here? He hates me. Thinks I'm interfering in his relationship with Amadeo. Would he go around Amadeo to hurt me?

"Down there."

"Tell him to come up."

He shakes his head, mutters something, then shoves me forward. I cry out as I fall down half a dozen steps before catching myself, gripping the handrail hard to keep from falling down the entire flight.

The voices stop, someone's high-pitched, maniacal laughter the last to die out as they turn to look at me. I take in the scene, and full-blown panic sets in.

"I was told you needed humbling," the soldier above me says as he stalks down the stairs separating us. He takes my arm and hauls me to my feet to force me down the rest of the way. I'm reminded of the church. Of the guards my brother had arranged and how they'd disappeared. How alone I was with the brothers and their men. How at their mercy.

"Let me go!"

"Okay," he says with a chuckle and shoves me

down the last two steps so I land on my hands and knees on the concrete floor.

"What'd you bring us?" someone asks as I survey the scene. The large, mostly empty basement with too many dark corners to consider. The space at the center is lit by a naked bulb hanging from the ceiling. A large poker table on an old area rug is littered with cards, chips, and liquor bottles, and around it sits about a dozen men. Just beyond it is a table loaded with more booze and a cooler from which someone takes a beer, icy water dripping over his hand as he twists off the cap.

Nowhere do I see either Amadeo or Bastian. Only these men. Soldiers, some with guns in shoulder holsters, others with weapons laid on the table by stacks of chips. Music still blares from speakers, but apart from that, the men fall silent.

"Up," the man who dragged me here says, digging the toe of his boot into my side.

I look up at him and see the closed door beyond him. I'm the only woman in here with a dozen soldiers. Some stupid, naïve voice in my head reminds me that I have Amadeo's protection, but it offers no comfort. I know well how little that can mean when a woman is alone in a room full of men.

My vision falters, a blur of another room. Another time. I squeeze my eyes shut and shake my head. Cold sweat breaks out over every inch of skin.

It's dread. It's realizing just how powerless you are truly.

"What's this?" someone asks, standing to get a better look at me. I'm standing, I realize. I don't know when I got back on my feet, knees locked so I don't collapse.

"A gift for you." He turns to me. "Compliments of Amadeo and Bastian."

My heart thuds heavy against my chest. They wouldn't have. No. They wouldn't. Not even Bastian would do this. They aren't this cruel. This evil.

Balancing the scales. An eye for an eye. A rape for a rape?

No. They wouldn't.

"We need a girl to serve," someone says.

"Just serve?" another one asks, making a lewd gesture with his tongue and two fingers. The others laugh and look back at the hulking man standing between me and the stairs.

"Let me leave," I tell him in a voice I don't recognize. "Please."

"Oh, the princess can be sweet when she wants."

"Let me go."

"I don't think so. You heard the men. We need a bitch to serve." He points at a table stacked with bottles of liquor. "Get my friends some fresh drinks."

"And a lap dance," one of them calls out, which the others find hilarious.

"Where's Amadeo? I want to see him. He

wouldn't..." I trail off, though. What was I about to say? That he wouldn't have allowed this? Why wouldn't he? Why not give his men something to sink their teeth into. To make them grateful to him. There is unrest within the family. I know that. I saw it for myself. And I'm just collateral. The daughter of the man he hated enough to desecrate his corpse. The sister of the man who he believes raped his sister.

"Get moving, bitch." The man shoves me toward the liquor table, interrupting my thoughts, and I stumble forward, then pass the men, giving the table as wide a berth as possible.

I pick up a bottle of whiskey and step on something sticky as I make my way to the men around the poker table in my bare feet. I hadn't been wearing shoes when he came to get me, and it hadn't occurred to me to put any on. I glance at the stairs and see the one who brought me down lean against the far wall and light up a cigarette. He's huge. All of them are. He'll catch me if I try to run for it. And if he doesn't, one of the others will. So I begin to refresh drinks, which I end up sloshing on the first guy who tries to pull me down onto his lap.

"Now, that's no way to serve, is it?" he asks.

The men glance at each other, and the one closest to me takes the bottle from me as another one begins to tug the zipper of my dress down.

"No!" I try to get away, but he doesn't let go, and

the dress tears as I jump away only to stumble forward into another one's arms when he doesn't let go of my dress.

"That's already better," someone says as I'm turned around, jerked toward another man as more of my dress is ripped away. I'm spun this way and that until the dress is at my feet in tatters, my bra and panties on top of it. It's only then they let me go, and I turn to the soldier who brought me here, stumbling away from the table.

This can't happen. It can't.

He grins as he drags on his cigarette, makes a point of looking me over, and I do cover myself from him, from them.

That flash of a scene I don't understand slices through me again. It's like a lightning bolt, quick and electric, and it splits my brain in two. A place similar to this one. A basement. The smell is the same. Damp. Dank. A familiar face cuts into the picture, but it's gone as quickly as it came.

I stagger backward, set my hand against the cool wall to steady myself. Sweat pools under my arms and along my hairline. I'm going to be sick.

"Serve my friends," the man who brought me is saying.

I blink. Try to focus. This can't be happening. Please God, don't let this be happening.

"I want to go to my room."

"Serve, bitch."

Someone chuckles, the music is turned up louder, and between that and the blood pounding against my ears, I am deaf.

"I'm thirsty over here, sweetheart," someone calls out, holding up an empty bottle of beer.

I keep my eyes on the soldier who brought me down. Think. Think. Get away. Survive.

"Serve drinks, or you'll be serving something else."

No.

I pick up a new bottle of beer, walk over to the thirsty man and set it down, taking his empty one and holding it by the neck. I don't have to wait long for one of them to grab my ass, and the instant he does, I smash the bottle against the poker table and turn on him holding the bottle with its sharp edges between us.

But there are a dozen of them and one of me, and in an instant, I'm on my knees in the broken glass surrounded by them, pushed forward until I'm on all fours, glass digging into my hands and knees. I feel them all around me—their breath, their bodies, sweat, and liquor, and smoke. Someone pushes my face down on that filthy floor. I can't process this. Can't process that this is going to happen to me. I want to fight. I need to fight. I'd rather die than take this. I'd rather die. But it's no use. There are too many of them. And they're too strong.

THANK YOU

Thank you for reading *Ruined Kingdom*. I hope you love Vittoria, Amadeo and Bastian's story.

Their Story concludes in Broken Queen which is available in all stores now!

ALSO BY NATASHA KNIGHT

Ruined Kingdom Duet

Ruined Kingdom

Broken Queen

The Devil's Pawn Duet

Devil's Pawn

Devil's Redemption

To Have and To Hold

With This Ring

I Thee Take

Stolen: Dante's Vow

The Society Trilogy

Requiem of the Soul

Reparation of Sin

Resurrection of the Heart

The Rite Trilogy

His Rule

Her Rebellion

Their Reign

Dark Legacy Trilogy

Taken (Dark Legacy, Book 1)

Torn (Dark Legacy, Book 2)

Twisted (Dark Legacy, Book 3)

Unholy Union Duet

Unholy Union

Unholy Intent

Collateral Damage Duet

Collateral: an Arranged Marriage Mafia Romance

Damage: an Arranged Marriage Mafia Romance

Ties that Bind Duet

Mine

His

MacLeod Brothers

Devil's Bargain

Benedetti Mafia World

Salvatore: a Dark Mafia Romance

Dominic: a Dark Mafia Romance

Sergio: a Dark Mafia Romance

The Benedetti Brothers Box Set (Contains Salvatore, Dominic and Sergio)

Killian: a Dark Mafia Romance

Giovanni: a Dark Mafia Romance

The Amado Brothers

Dishonorable

Disgraced

Unhinged

Standalone Dark Romance

Descent

Deviant

Beautiful Liar

Retribution

Theirs To Take

Captive, Mine

Alpha

Given to the Savage

Taken by the Beast

Claimed by the Beast

Captive's Desire

Protective Custody

Amy's Strict Doctor

Taming Emma

Taming Megan

Taming Naia

Reclaiming Sophie

The Firefighter's Girl

Dangerous Defiance

Her Rogue Knight

Taught To Kneel

Tamed: the Roark Brothers Trilogy

ABOUT THE AUTHOR

Natasha Knight is the *USA Today* Bestselling author of Romantic Suspense and Dark Romance Novels. She has sold over a million books and is translated into six languages. She currently lives in The Netherlands with her husband and two daughters and when she's not writing, she's walking in the woods listening to a book, sitting in a corner reading or off exploring the world as often as she can get away.

Contact Natasha here: natasha@natasha-knight.com

NATASHA KNIGHT
sexy dark romance with heart

www.natasha-knight.com

Printed in Great Britain
by Amazon